Marc came face-to-face with Courtney

She stood in the living room, visible through the doorway as he emerged from the steamy bathroom.

Suddenly everything about her was a dare.

From the glossy black hair that would feel like silk to the touch to the clear eyes she raked down the length of him.

He stood wrapped in a towel.

Her gaze traveled the length of him again. There was surprise all over her face, her eyes widening, her lips parting.

But she didn't look away. She only stood there for a protracted moment, a deer stunned by headlights. And by the time she'd rallied, mumbling something unintelligible and turning away, it was too late.

Marc had seen everything.

This felt normal. A beautiful woman looking at him like he was a man. A woman looking at him with want in her eyes.

Yet she turned away....

Dear Reader,

Life is love. It's our chronic aspiration and the source of our greatest strength. Love inspires us to courage and moves us past selfishness to kindness and generosity.

Araceli would do anything to have love in her life.

Courtney fought hard to bring love to her foster kids' lives, but she kept love in the periphery of her own.

Marc had run far away from love and allowed it only an occasional visit. It wasn't until adversity forced him to stop running that he came face-to-face with how much of himself he had lost along the way.

When love brings these three together, they realize what was right before their eyes all along—with love, they can conquer anything.

Ordinary Women. Extraordinary romance.

That's what Harlequin Superromance is all about. I hope you enjoy Courtney and Marc's story. I love hearing from readers, so please visit me at www.jeanielegendre.com.

Peace and blessings,

Jeanie London

Love In Plain Sight

—

Jeanie London

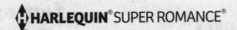
HARLEQUIN® SUPER ROMANCE®

Recycling programs
for this product may
not exist in your area.

ISBN-13: 978-0-373-71873-3

LOVE IN PLAIN SIGHT

Copyright © 2013 by Jeanie LeGendre

Printed in U.S.A.

ABOUT THE AUTHOR

Jeanie London writes romance because she believes in happily-ever-afters. Not the "love conquers all" kind, but the "we love each other, so we can conquer anything" kind. Jeanie is the winner of many prestigious writing awards, including multiple *RT Book Reviews* Reviewers' Choice and National Readers' Choice Awards. She lives in sunny Florida with her own romance-hero husband, their beautiful daughters and a menagerie of strays.

Books by Jeanie London

HARLEQUIN SUPERROMANCE

1616—FRANKIE'S BACK IN TOWN
1635—HER HUSBAND'S PARTNER
1699—THEN THERE WERE THREE
1716—THE HUSBAND LESSON
1739—NO GROOM LIKE HIM
1819—THE TIME OF HER LIFE
1843—RIGHT FROM THE START

HARLEQUIN BLAZE

153—HOT SHEETS*
157—RUN FOR COVERS*
161—PILLOW CHASE*
181—UNDER HIS SKIN
213—RED LETTER NIGHTS
    "Signed, Sealed, Seduced"
231—GOING ALL OUT
248—INTO TEMPTATION
271—IF YOU COULD READ MY MIND...

*Falling Inn Bed...

HARLEQUIN SIGNATURE SELECT SPOTLIGHT

IN THE COLD

Other titles by this author available in ebook format.

To my beloved Pup.
You are a joy! You make life endlessly fascinating with your inspired interests, your enormous heart and your delightful friends! <3 YOU <3

PROLOGUE

Before Hurricane Katrina

PAPA ALWAYS SAID love changed lives. I knew what he meant because love was all around me.

Every morning, Mama packed Papa's lunch. Always the same sandwich, container of leftovers from dinner, fruit and fresh-baked pastry. She stacked them in his lunch bag in the order he would eat them through the day.

A fruit for the morning to keep him healthy.

Leftovers for lunch with the sandwich, too, if he worked really hard. Sometimes he saved half for later.

He ate the pastry with his *con leche* in the afternoon when he needed a sweet for strength.

In between each layer would be a neatly folded napkin with a love note. One for every meal.

Hecho con amor para ti.

Gracias por nuestra hermosa vida juntos.

The love notes changed every day—all but one that read *Te quiero siempre.*

Mama did love him always.

She loved all of us. We were her family.

When I was old enough for school, I opened my lunch bag to find my own love notes. Mama would draw little hearts that would make me proud to be the beautiful daughter she loved so much. Or funny faces to make me laugh, because Mama did not have the family talent for drawing.

I never used my love-note napkins but always tucked them into my pocket, a secret reminder of how much I was loved no matter what happened through the rest of the day.

Paolo wasn't too little to notice. He didn't say anything because of his speech trouble, but I knew. He was quick-eyed for a little one. Mama counted on those eyes.

"Paolo, where did Mama set her keys?" she would ask. "Paolo, did you see where Mama lay her scissors?"

My baby brother would run right to where she had left whatever was missing.

Paolo wanted his own love notes. I knew because he would stick his chubby hand in my pocket and sneak mine. I told Mama one day, and the very next morning, my baby brother burst from our bedroom as I was readying for school with a love note he'd found under his pillow.

My life was filled with that kind of love. Every night after dinner, my family gathered in the living room. Some nights, I practiced stitches on scraps of fabric while Mama altered clothes to earn money.

Higher hems for the short ladies and expanded seams for the ladies grown too fat for their zippers....

Papa would sit at his easel, telling stories from his day and drawing whatever he thought might sell on weekends when he sat in Jackson Square making caricatures for the tourists.

Weekend after weekend, through the Mardi Gras parades and the steamy days of summer, I would sit beside Papa at my own easel, smelling the Mississippi River, an apprentice practicing my sketches and learning from my beloved Papa.

I loved those weekends.

"You must read your subject to know how to please them," Papa instructed. *"Do not choose a feature they might feel shame for. Choose one that helps them laugh at themselves. Laughter is a gift, and if you please them, they'll be gener-*

ous with you. Americans are very generous. They appreciate talent and will reward you for using yours."

I was eight when I drew my very first sketch.

My subject, an eccentric older lady who wore many big jewels, did laugh when she saw my finished product and gave me ten dollars. I felt such pride.

My second subject wasn't so pleased. I got a dollar in quarters and not even one tiny smile.

Papa hugged me. "Can't please everyone."

But I worried. "Maybe I didn't get the family talent."

He scoffed, making a big sound that filled the steamy heat of that perfect summer. "You are learning to use your talent. Do you think to be as good as your papa without much practice?"

I could only shrug, feeling too much shame for words.

Taking my hand that held the graphite pencil, he lifted it to his lips for a kiss, his whiskers tickling my skin. "There. Now you have even more family talent. I share mine, for I have much to spare."

That made me smile. A little.

"Love is the secret, Araceli. You must love this pencil," he said, very serious. "And you must love your subject. But most of all, you must love your talent, for that is the only way you will learn to use it. You must try new things and make your talent sing inside you and flow out onto the paper.

"Remember this." He smiled beneath his bushy mustache. "Love changes everything. It's everywhere. You just have to look. Sometimes it hides, so you have to look hard. But open your eyes really big." He shaped his fingers into circles and peered through them, looking silly. "It's always there somewhere. I promise."

CHAPTER ONE

Eight years after the hurricane

COURTNEY GERARD WENT on red alert when she glanced up to find her supervisor in the office doorway. She'd worked with Giselle since an internship in college. Courtney knew this look. *Not* good.

"What's wrong, Giselle?"

Working for the Department of Children and Family Services could be emotionally demanding on the best of days. Children in difficult circumstances troubled caring people, and all the social workers in the New Orleans DCFS cared deeply about the kids they managed. Giselle's expression promised this day wasn't even close to the best.

"Are you okay?" Courtney tried again.

Giselle lifted a disbelieving gaze and stood rooted to the spot. Courtney was on her feet instantly, the impulse to *do something* preferable over the powerlessness of *doing nothing.* She'd barely circled the desk when Giselle gave her head a slight shake as if mentally rebooting.

"Yeah, yeah. *I'm* okay." Sinking into a chair, she clutched a file folder as if her life depended on it. "We have a problem."

We could mean the social services department or just the two of them. Courtney didn't ask. Giselle was shaken, and struggling hard to maintain her professionalism right now. That much was obvious.

Leaning against the desk, Courtney braced herself. "Whatever it is we can deal with it. Right?"

Giselle didn't answer—another bad sign. She set the file between them, an innocuous folder with a case number and name in an upper corner that read Araceli Ruiz-Ortiz.

The case hadn't been Courtney's for long. Only since a drizzly, cold February morning earlier this year, when one of their social workers hadn't made it to work when expected. A multiple-car accident on Interstate 10 had robbed them of one of their team, a woman with a huge laugh and kind heart.

"Has something happened?" Courtney asked. "Is Araceli all right?"

Giselle opened the file, rooted through the documents and slid out a photo. "Who is this?"

The image was the most recent of the girl in question, which Courtney herself had taken on their first visit together. She'd snapped photos of all the kids in the cases she'd taken over, uploaded digital copies to the server and printed hard-copy files. Standard procedure. "That's Araceli."

"You've actually spoken with her?"

Adrenaline made the hairs along Courtney's arms stand on end. "What kind of question is that? Of course I've spoken with her. She's been my case since Nanette."

Since Nanette.

The euphemism for the tragedy that had impacted everyone in their close-knit department in so many ways beyond increased caseloads.

"Any red flags?" Giselle asked.

Courtney frowned. She interviewed all of her kids, checked in with each of them monthly. Giselle knew all social workers followed the same procedure, so unless she was implying that Courtney had stopped doing her job properly... "What sort of red flags? Abuse? Drugs? Gangs?"

"Maybe. I don't know. Did anything at all seem off to you? What were your impressions of the girl?"

Courtney scoured her memories, apprehension sabotaging her focus. "I have to work to engage her most of the time. She resents my intrusion in her life but has enough respect not to be overtly rebellious. She's sixteen. You know how those last few years till majority can be for some kids."

Giselle nodded. "When you get her talking, does she communicate well? How's her English?"

Courtney considered the girl she was scheduled to visit again in just another week. "Accented but okay. I noted my first impressions in my report. Her guardians can be problematic."

"How so?" Giselle latched on to that admission. "I need to know everything you can tell me."

"The mother communicates in English better than the father, but he's the one who likes to do the talking. He won't allow me to talk to his wife and let her translate. A cultural thing, I think." She shrugged, frustrated even thinking about how she could burn an entire afternoon going over every single thing once, twice, sometimes three times until satisfied she understood and had been understood.

"No hablo Español. Hablo muy poco de todos modos."

Señor Perea didn't seem to care that Courtney was the department go-to girl for all things French, including French-based Louisiana Creole and Cajun. Of course, there was a smattering of Spanish words in those dialects, so if he slowed down enough for her to catch the verbs, she could usually figure out the rest. "The situation was never optimal, Giselle. I'm not Nanette. She spoke Spanish fluently. You knew that when you assigned me this case."

Giselle inhaled deeply, acknowledging imperfect reality in that one gesture. "But I knew I could trust you to put forth the effort to make sure these kids were properly cared for until I could get someone fluent in Spanish to replace you."

What she didn't say was that there were other social workers in the department who might be good and caring but who would also let the language barrier deter them.

Courtney was detail-oriented and thorough. Always. She would take the time to be clear, even if it meant derailing her schedule. Even if it meant she didn't return to the office to start reports until after dark. Even if it meant she sacrificed a normal life to manage a caseload that had only grown in the years since the hurricane had leveled their entire agency.

They'd all been overworked before category-five winds had blown holes in the levees around Lake Pontchartrain, but since every record in every case they managed had been obliterated, they'd all been burdened additionally with rebuilding the system. A new system that wouldn't utterly and completely fail during a catastrophic natural disaster.

They'd all made sacrifices, were *still* making sacrifices, but some managed to juggle the additional workload better than others. Courtney didn't have a husband or kids awaiting her at home every day. "Will you tell me what has happened? You're flipping me out with this interrogation."

"You have to promise you won't panic." Giselle was the epitome of self-restraint, but everything about her begged Courtney to manage her reaction.

Giselle's need in that moment seemed impossible to meet. The best she could do was face her supervisor and close friend, and nod, hoping she could keep the promise.

Giselle held up the photo. "This is *not* Araceli."

It took Courtney a moment to wrap her brain around *that*. And in that one surreal instant, she took action again, reaching for the photo and inspecting it carefully, unable to absorb the overwhelming implications passively.

Same glossy dark hair. Same melting brown eyes. Same smooth caramel skin.

"I'm not sure what's going on, Giselle, but I promise you this is Araceli. I've met with her every month since Nanette."

Giselle pulled out another document with two photos stapled to the corner and set it on the desk between them. One eight-by-ten was a group shot of a classroom of young kids. Mr. LeGendre's third grade, according to the neat font imprinted along the bottom above the students' names. The other photo appeared to be the sort of proof used by photographic companies. There was a name and number beneath the face in that photo. The child was young like the ones in the group shot, maybe seven or eight, with a jagged smile where adult teeth were growing in.

Courtney scanned the group shot. She spotted Araceli's name but couldn't pick out the accompanying face from among the smiling kids. Reaching for the proof, she inspected the girl in that photo.

Gold skin. Glossy black hair. Melting dark eyes.

But a younger version of the uncommunicative girl Courtney met with every month?

A chill skittered through her, a physical sensation that made her breath catch hard. Grabbing the photo she'd taken herself, she placed them side by side, swung her gaze between them, made sense of the truth before her eyes.

There was something about the way the features came together that warned not even eight years could transform this child into the young woman who visibly reined in inconvenience each time they met.

Glancing up, Courtney saw her disbelief reflected in Giselle's expression. "Are you sure? This can't be possible."

"Apparently Araceli's file wound up on a compliance officer's desk. Turns out he used to be in the classroom before he went into staffing. He looked at the Araceli in the file and questioned whether she was his third-grade student. The classroom photo was his, but he still wasn't sure. He contacted the photography company on the off chance they had records since they're not based locally. You're looking at what he found."

A rare piece of evidence left after the hurricane. Courtney stared at the proof again and latched on to the first thing she could in the midst of her racing thoughts. The most irrelevant. The least horrifying.

"Why was a compliance officer reviewing Araceli's file? I should have been included."

"No meetings were scheduled because of this *situation*. Araceli, or the girl we thought was her, got into a fight with a weapon during summer classes."

The zero-tolerance policy changed the rules when a weapon was involved. "What weapon?"

Giselle scowled. "A chair. But given the way she used it… She has to be moved."

"Okay." Courtney rubbed her temples, willed her brain to reason. "Then where is Araceli, and who is this girl?"

"If we knew, we wouldn't have a problem."

That stopped Courtney cold. A powerful wave of vertigo rolled through her.

Two girls. One name.

A missing child.

Her heart pounded so hard each beat throbbed as reality narrowed down to the terrifying implications.

A missing child.

Details didn't matter. The situation simply didn't get any worse. Letting her eyes flutter shut, she blocked out Giselle's expression, the hard-won professionalism that wasn't concealing her panic.

Inhaling deeply, Courtney willed herself to think, to ask

the questions that were critically important now that *a child was missing.*

"Has anyone spoken to the Pereas yet?" She forced the words past the tightness in her chest. "What about this girl?"

"The FBI will conduct the investigation."

"Not the police?"

"We have nothing on Araceli but what's in this file," Giselle explained. "She crossed state lines during the hurricane evacuations. The investigation is out of police jurisdiction."

The hurricane.

Another euphemism. There had been hurricanes before and since, but Katrina was *the* hurricane. Giselle didn't have to say another word because again, her expression reflected the helplessness and horror of an event that had been far beyond the control of the people involved, an event that had challenged everything from their comfy worldview to standard business practice for this department.

All hard-copy documentation had been lost in the flooding. Out of the five thousand plus kids in foster care at the time, two thousand had been displaced by Hurricane Katrina, then many shuffled again a month later because of Hurricane Rita.

Kids had wound up spread over nineteen states in that mess, and social workers such as Courtney, Giselle and Nanette had tracked them all down again. The aftershocks were still being felt to this day, along with memories of the litany of priorities that had dictated their lives as they functioned from evacuation shelters because offices and homes had been flooded, cell towers had been down, and the city had been under martial law.

First, we keep you alive....
Then we get you safe....
Then we work on your health and medications....

Then we figure out where you belong....

Recalling that long road back to a functioning system brought another realization, one that hit with familiar category-five velocity.

The hurricane had been *eight years ago.*

"Tell me we have some other documentation, Giselle," she demanded. "Tell me we're not operating on what Nanette pieced together after the hurricane."

Giselle spread her hands in entreaty, motioned to the desk. She didn't have to say another word because they were both thinking the same thing.

The only person who might shed some light on this situation had died on the side of the road, surrounded by strangers on a drizzly February morning.

"Her work was stellar." Giselle assumed the crappy responsibility of verbalizing the doubt that would be cast on someone not able to defend herself. "I won't believe this situation is a result of negligence. That goes against everything I know about her."

"You're right. Absolutely right."

"The FBI will want conclusive proof, but we don't have any. Nanette looks culpable. This department looks culpable."

Which circled right back around to the *we.*

Giselle was responsible for this department and everything that took place within. Courtney was responsible for this case and everything that had taken place since Nanette.

A child was missing.

The only answer that mattered, the one that left her doing exactly what she'd been told not to do—*panicking*—was the very one she had no answer for.

What were their chances of finding Araceli alive?

"We had no way of tracking Araceli after the hurricane." Giselle riffled through documents one by one. "We can't prove Araceli's the child on one document in this folder. We can't prove we placed the real Araceli with the Perea family. We can't prove she's the Araceli in this Red Cross database."

Her voice escalated. "We can't prove she evacuated to the Superdome with her foster family, then got separated on the buses in Houston. We can't prove she went to Atlanta after being evacuated during Hurricane Rita. We can't prove she was the child we got an emergency injunction to remain out of state until the Pereas moved out of the FEMA trailer and back into their home. We have no idea who we've been shuffling around because the last known photo of Araceli is from third grade."

The papers were now all over Courtney's desk. Papers that proved nothing conclusively—except that Araceli Ruiz-Ortiz had gotten lost somewhere over the course of the past eight years.

Courtney walked to the window that provided no escape. She saw nothing but eight years stretching out like a lifetime, and all the horrifying things that could happen to a girl alone. The passage of time was marked only by the silence echoing as she mentally replayed every horror story she'd ever heard.

The young girl in Florida who'd been adopted by her longtime foster family and was tortured and starved to death instead of living happily ever after.

The twins who were kept in cages in the basement under the care of foster parents who'd been taking kids into their home for four decades.

The nearly three hundred *kids who'd been placed with a sexual predator over the sixteen years it took social workers to figure out that many of these kids were being molested.*

Negligence. Incompetence. Heartlessness.

Horror stories.

Most social workers weren't the careless or inept monsters showcased in the media. The majority were the ones the general public never heard about. Social workers who maneuvered deftly through the obstacle course among laws and legalities and court decisions for kids they were responsible for protecting.

Most social workers cared more for needy kids than they did their own paychecks, because no one got compensated for all the work. Most didn't mind the long hours, and usually found a way to squeeze in *just one more* kid when they were already burdened by a staggering caseload.

Given the crushing demands of the job, it wasn't hard to see how mistakes could happen even to the most caring and competent social workers. They managed needy kids' lives the way an air traffic controller oversaw airspace: the consequences of one oversight, one distraction, one error could result in the loss of human life.

The life of a child.

Courtney's thoughts slowed enough to finally see the street through the window. DCFS offices were located in a utilitarian building on Iberville Street north of all the French Quarter action. From her second-floor window, she overlooked the stone wall of the cemetery, discolored and stained like the mausoleums within, many overgrown with weeds protruding from odd places.

Interstate 10 ran the length of the cemetery and all the way to Florida. The green directional signs were the only splash of color in a scene that had never looked so bleak, washed in gray skies that promised rain. Somehow it fit that she couldn't look at the interstate without thinking of Nanette.

"What happens now?" she asked, her voice barely a whisper. "How do we find Araceli?"

Giselle could only spread her hands in entreaty. She had no clue, because how on earth did one go about tracking down a child who had potentially been missing for eight years?

How could they even hope to find her alive?

"DAMON'S COMING TO get me, right?" Marc DiLeo forced out the question through gritted teeth.

After all these months, he should have been used to *asking*. He wasn't. He resented the hell out of it.

Especially something as simple as a ride when he owned a Jeep and a Harley.

His older brother, Nic, glanced away from the road as they were driving down Canal Street in Nic's police cruiser. At least no one could see them through the heavily tinted glass.

Did anyone even care that he was being chauffeured to his therapy session because he couldn't drive himself?

No. It only felt that way.

"Damon's teaching a class," Nic said. "Anthony will pick you up, and if he can't get away, he'll send one of the guys."

Great. Now Marc's ability to burden everyone reached beyond family into the periphery, to the guys who worked in his younger brother Anthony's automotive garage.

This was his mother's fault. She'd bullied him into leaving Colorado Springs for rehab. Not that Marc had put up much of a fight. He'd been in a medically induced coma when many of the decisions about his care had been made. After the haze of anesthesia and painkillers from four surgeries had worn off, all the decisions had been made.

That had been the time to reassert control over his life. Only he hadn't had any fight in him.

So his mother had seized the opportunity to bring him home to New Orleans. And everyone paid the price because she was the only one of the bunch who didn't drive.

"Tell Anthony not to bother," Marc said. "I'll take a cab."

"Don't start with me. Everyone wants to help."

Help? This family would kill him with their help, which was why he had moved to Colorado Springs in the first place. "I'd forgotten what a pain in the ass an older brother could be. Good thing you're the only one I have. If I changed my name, I'll bet none of you could find me."

Nic gave a disgusted snort. But he glanced at the road. He scowled harder when some idiot in a showy Bimmer sliced out of one lane and cut into the other, forcing the Yukon in front of him to brake, and by default him.

"You know, you're a cop," Marc said. "You could pull that guy over and give him a ticket."

"You know, you're a jerk. You could try saying thanks for everyone's help and leave it there. No one has a problem getting you to and from your sessions."

"Wrong." *Marc* had a big problem.

Nic braked hard, and Marc instinctively grabbed the oh-shit handle to hang on as the cruiser swung toward the curb so fast the tires screeched. Marc's cane hit the door with a clatter. The cop lights flashed with an accompanying whoop of a siren, scaring the hell out of some pedestrians who broke formation on the sidewalk and scattered.

Nic didn't seem to notice. Or care. "Have all those pain-killers rotted your brain? Do I need to throw your sorry ass in detox?"

Sorry ass was right. Marc couldn't rebut that fact, but he wasn't listening to Nic rant, either. Guess this was his stop. He reached for his cane and the door handle. The handle moved, but the passenger door didn't open. Nic controlled the locks.

"Isn't there some law against double-parking?" Marc said. "You're a cop. You should set an example by observing the law."

"I'm not a cop," Nic growled. "I'm the chief of police,

which means I get to do whatever the hell I want. And right now I want you to listen to me."

Great. Marc's day was crashing and burning and he hadn't even gotten to physical therapy yet. Okay, to be fair he had practically begged for this confrontation. Nic's patience had been simmering for weeks. He was the oldest brother, and used to stepping in to clean up everyone's mess in this family. He'd been doing the job since their father had died, leaving their mother with a bunch of little kids who had needed caring for. The years since hadn't done much except shorten Nic's fuse.

Marc was usually exempt from the bullying because he was next in line to the throne, the only one who had been old enough to work and make a difference, which took some of the responsibility off Nic's shoulders.

Not today. Today, Marc had pushed too far.

"I want to know what the hell is wrong with you," Nic demanded. "I want to know why you're such a miserable pain in the ass to everyone who is going out of their way to help you."

"That answer should be obvious." It was stretched out awkwardly before him, braced at the knee and ankle for support. His busted and surgically pieced together right leg that impeded him from doing just about everything from walking to sleeping because of the never-ending pain.

"That's your leg, Marc. I'm talking about your shitty attitude."

Marc didn't bother replying. The shitty attitude and the answer would be the same. One minute he had been chasing a skip toward the Mexican border over rough terrain. The next he was ejected from his Jeep at ninety miles an hour.

At least the skip hadn't bolted. The border patrols had had to cut him out of an SUV.

Now, four months later, the skip sat in jail awaiting trial, and Marc was an out-of-work bounty hunter who could barely stand to take a piss let alone drive, living with his mother in this city he'd put behind him long ago.

"You're not usually so dense," Marc said. "I didn't realize becoming a father dulled the edges."

Nic clutched the steering wheel, knuckles white, visibly restraining himself. Probably wanted to throw a punch. When all else failed, restrain the idiot pissing him off. Made him a helluva cop. Probably would have thrown a punch, too, if all his high-tech computer cop gear hadn't blocked a decent shot.

"All right, Marc, you listen to me. And you listen good because I will not repeat myself. This is your one and only warning. Next time I will knock you down and keep you there while everyone you've been rude to takes a swing. You hear me?"

He expected an answer?

Nic exhaled hard, frustration radiating like heat off asphalt. "I get that it's taking you a long time to heal. I get that your leg hurts and the therapy is only making the pain worse. But you're alive, and you have a lot of people who care about you, even though you're pushing everyone away. The next time you want to open your mouth, just remember that if anything more than a thank-you comes out, my fist will be going in.

"You've got Mom worried sick. No one will drop by the house because you're so miserable to be around. You've even managed to piss off my daughter, who's in love with everyone and everything in this family. Really, man, you're making a hell of an impression on your niece. That make you proud?"

Pride would imply Marc cared. And Nic's daughter, Violet, was an impressionable teenager who needed a good dose of reality. She'd lived most of her life without knowing her father or this crazy family. She might have been better off living the rest of her life without knowing them.

"Do you hear me, Marc? I'm not playing. Knock it off with your pity party before you alienate everyone and wind up alone with your busted leg."

"What makes you think that's not what I want?"

A valid question. But Marc miscalculated the protection of the cruiser's computer gear because the next thing he knew, Nic's fingers were tightening around his collar until he swallowed hard against the pressure.

Damned painkillers were slowing his reactions.

"Get. Over. It." Nic spit out each word, the veins bulging in his temples.

Marc wouldn't give his brother the satisfaction of a reaction. He would sit here and asphyxiate. No sweat. A corpse in the front seat of the police chief's cruiser. Nic was the only one with a problem here.

He knew it, too. His gaze narrowed as he reined in his anger, emphasizing the point with another twist that nearly crushed Marc's windpipe.

Finally, Nic eased his grip. "You get what I want?"

Under normal circumstance, Marc wouldn't have taken this crap. But circumstances weren't normal. He couldn't throw off his brother. Couldn't even argue because Nic was right. Marc was a miserable asshole. He knew it.

The drugs were making his brain rot because he didn't care.

"Unlock this door before I put my fist through the window and you get blood all over your front seat." He forced the words out through his raw throat.

He wasn't playing, either. What was one more injury when he was a damned cripple already?

Nic must have recognized it, too, because he finally leaned back and warned, "Get a grip, Marc. Seriously. I get whatever the hell I want. I'm the chief of police in this town and your older brother. You're screwed either way."

That much was true.

CHAPTER TWO

Two weeks later

JUST DRIVING THROUGH New Orleans and parking in front of Mama DiLeo's house made Courtney feel better. As if she were somehow in control of her life. As if she somehow had a say. She didn't, but for one shining moment, she almost felt that way.

Late summer heat pounded at the windows even this early in the day, but she sat there, ensuring that her emotions wouldn't leak around the edges. Not usually a problem, but with life upside-down, the self-control she took for granted was giving her fits.

Courtney had been placed on administrative leave from work while the FBI conducted the investigation on Araceli Ruiz-Ortiz—a situation that had gotten worse when the girl they'd presumed was Araceli had also gone missing within days of the classroom fight that revealed this mess.

Life had come to a screeching halt for Courtney. Days that had passed at a frenetic pace and ended with still so much to be done were suddenly empty. Hour after hour, from the time she opened her eyes until they shut of their own accord—who could sleep anymore?—were minutes ticking by with no purpose.

No more caring for kids. No more stabilizing, learning and managing their lives. Her keys to the department had been confiscated. She had been temporarily evicted from her office and told to wait for others to sort out the situation of the mixed-up and missing girls. She had been told there was nothing she could do but catch up on things at home.

But all the jobs Courtney had once intended to squeeze into long weekends had been forgotten—the flower bed around her new shed, wallpapering the tiny interior of her niece's dollhouse, tiling the wall behind the sink in the kitchen. Somehow she had managed to be more productive during those weekends that passed in the blink of an eye than she did now with day after endless day free.

Two eternal weeks as the FBI launched an investigation with all the deliberation of a law enforcement agency that had no hope of finding Araceli alive. Courtney had been obedient, even patient, but as each day passed with a lot of wasted time and no discernible progress, she had grown frustrated and frightened.

After learning from Giselle that the FBI had been searching for the fake Araceli and hadn't yet begun a search for the real one, Courtney could no longer wait for others to *sort out the situation.*

So here she was at Mama DiLeo's house, two hours before Sunday dinner, armed with the beginnings of a plan.

Taking a deep, steadying breath, Courtney opened the car door, finally ready. She had to knock only once before a lilting voice called, "Coming."

The door swung wide, and Mama DiLeo was there, smiling as she recognized her guest. "Good to see you, honey. Come in."

Courtney couldn't quite manage a smile, but Mama smiled for both of them, a smile that made Courtney feel as if she mattered more than anyone in the world.

Mama DiLeo's unique gift.

She always dressed to the nines, and had rocked a pixie cut for as long as Courtney had known her. While she didn't stand much more than five feet two, including the heels, this widowed mother of six—five of whom were sons who reeked of testosterone—was a force to reckon with.

"Size doesn't matter when you have superhero strength," her oldest son, Nic, always said. *"Mama has it in spades."*

Courtney had seen this woman stop arguments with a glare. She could break up a physical tussle between her sons with one sharp command.

Those superpowers and the smile were already smoothing the edges of Courtney's mood.

"I'm really early," she said. "But I wanted to talk with you before the house fills up."

"Perfect. We have lots of catching up to do. I haven't seen you for weeks."

Since the bottom had fallen out of her world.

The house was unusually quiet today. During Sunday dinners, conversation swirled from the kitchen to the dining room to the family room down this hallway....

Everyone included. Everyone welcome.

The boundaries that constituted family were fluid with the DiLeos. There was always room for one more at the table. The front door was always open to anyone who needed a meal, a place to stay or some laughter. All that gracious hospitality was due to the enormous heart beating inside this one tiny woman. Mama DiLeo believed family was a function not defined by blood but by love.

Her heels tapped over the tile as she went to the stove and lifted the lid on a simmering pot, stirring the contents with a long-handled spoon. Steam rose, sending up a burst of garlic.

"Hope you're hungry." Mama set aside the spoon. "You're my angel today. I could use help cutting these vegetables. My assistants are running late."

"I should work since I forgot to bring anything. Not even flowers for your table." Which only served to emphasize her deteriorating mental state. She never came to Sunday dinner without swinging by the bakery, the florist or the wine shop.

"The only thing you ever need to bring is yourself, honey."

"That's all you're getting today, Mama. Good thing I know my way around a cutting board."

With a smile, Mama went to the sink and washed her hands. "We need to make a pit stop before we get started. Grab that basket from the baker's rack, will you please?"

Courtney did as requested and waited while Mama rooted through a drawer to locate a pair of clippers. Then Courtney followed her out the back door.

The scene from the porch was breathtaking. Mama was an inspired gardener, not in the traditional New Orleans sense of manicured lawns. She favored a more natural setting, with slate walkways lined with wildflowers, and benches beneath sprawling oak trees. Geraniums, hosta and butterfly bushes dotted the yard with splashes of color.

Courtney followed Mama to the herb garden, tried to absorb the peaceful setting to calm frayed nerves.

"So, what's on your mind that you don't want to discuss in front of everyone?" Mama asked as she knelt beside the garden to sort through a fragrant tangle of parsley and basil plants.

"I wanted to bounce something off you. I need some help, but I'm not sure I should ask for it. I trust you to advise me."

Mama snipped some leaves and motioned Courtney to bring the basket closer. "What's up?"

New Orleans might be the thirty-seventh-largest city in the nation, but Mama considered all the inhabitants related.

Family by blood. Family by love. Family by proximity. Family by work. Family by church. Family by krewe. A category for everyone she welcomed into her world. Courtney was one of the elite few with an official family connection. Sort of. Her brother Mac had married Mama's unofficial daughter, Harley, who had become attached to the family at a young age.

There was no possible way Mama didn't already know how life had blown up in Courtney's face.

"I'd like to talk with Marc about my work situation, Mama. He tracks down people, and I need his opinion."

Mama sank back on her haunches and glanced up. "That wasn't what I was expecting. Not Nic?"

"We both work for state agencies, and I would never put him in a position of conflict."

Mama frowned but conceded the point with a nod. "I already know why you don't want to ask Harley and your brother."

"All my family wants to help, of course, but everyone is so worried about Harley and Mac that I intentionally downplayed the situation so they wouldn't start worrying about me, too."

With Harley on bed rest for the remainder of her pregnancy, the whole family was in an uproar already. Mac was wrapping up their cases at their investigative agency and keeping up with their daughter's schedule, which was another full-time job. That had been the only positive to this situation—all the free time had allowed Courtney to help by chauffeuring her niece around.

"They won't be happy when they find out."

That was an understatement. "They're going to kill me. But I'll deal with them when I have to."

Mama pulled a face, and for a long moment, she just knelt there, clippers dangling from idle hands, clearly waiting. "Marc, hmm?"

"I would never dream of bothering him right now, but there's a lot riding on the outcome."

Children's lives.

Then there was Courtney's career. Giselle's reputation.

Nanette's legacy. Nanette above all provided a convenient scapegoat for the FBI. Her heartbroken family, still struggling with grief, faced a media storm that would trash a woman who couldn't defend herself. Courtney didn't know what had happened to Araceli, but she knew Nanette would not have been negligent.

Courtney would not stand by and watch people she cared for take the fall any more than she would take the fall herself. She would not stand by while the FBI took their sweet time covering their butts while there were children missing.

"That's what I want your opinion about. I know how difficult Marc's recovery has been. If you don't think it's a good idea to bring up work, I will not open my mouth."

For a moment, they considered each other. Then Mama's eyes fluttered shut, and she inhaled deeply. She remained that way so long that Courtney felt compelled to look away, as if she had distressed a woman who didn't need any more of a burden than to worry about the son she had almost lost.

Courtney would be left to accept that she was back to square one, all alone with the responsibility for a child's life, whether or not she was on administrative leave. *Where* Courtney was didn't matter.

Where Araceli was did.

But none of this was Mama's problem, and Courtney had no right to put this on her. While she trusted Mama to be honest with her opinion about Marc, Courtney also knew that saying no wasn't so simple for a nurturing woman who cared about people as much as she did. Mama was already worried about Marc. Now she'd start worrying about Courtney, too.

As the seconds ticked by, undisturbed except by the bees buzzing from flower to flower and squirrels scampering overhead, Courtney convinced herself that this was the stupidest, most selfish idea she'd ever come up with. She was being totally unfair.

Mama slowly rose to her feet.

Courtney offered a hand. "I am so sorry. I know you're worried about Marc, and the last thing I should do is give you something else to worry about. Please forget I said anything at all, and you have to promise me you won't start worrying about me."

Mama chuckled. Dropping sprigs of parsley into the basket, she lifted her gaze to Courtney's, eyes alight with laughter.

"Why are you apologizing, honey?" she asked. "You're an answer to a prayer."

MARC WINCED AS he put his weight on his leg, the pain that screamed through him literally stealing his breath. Why had he bothered getting out of bed?

Stupid question. If he stayed in bed too long his leg would stiffen and he wouldn't be able to walk all day.

Making his way down the stairs carefully, clumsily, he clung to the banister for support while trying not to drop his cane, his leg making each step dangerous. With his luck, he'd fall and land on his damned head, and Vince would finally convince their mother to turn the downstairs office into an invalid's bedroom complete with hospital bed. Of course, if Marc had any real luck, the fall might kill him. He would have been okay with that, too.

By the time he made his way to the last step, he was forced to stop and give his leg a break. The house was quiet, which was a good thing because another hour and everyone and their brother would show up for dinner. He needed caffeine before he could decide whether to contend with a shower and civilized company, or be uncivilized and hide in his room.

Either one meant tackling the stairs again.

From the hallway, he saw his mother in front of the sink.

She must have heard him because she turned. For a split second, her expression told him that watching him hurt. Even placing his body weight on one side didn't do a thing to minimize the pain of the leg he nearly dragged along. Throw in the fact that he was still half-drugged, and he must look like hell.

She quickly masked her reaction with a smile. "Good morning, sunshine." Grabbing a mug from the drain board, she headed toward the coffeepot. "We have company."

"There's a surprise," he shot back, deadpan.

Moving into the kitchen, he found their guest standing over the table chopping vegetables on a cutting board.

She met his gaze with gray eyes so clear they were almost startling. Or maybe it was the onions she was chopping that made her eyes seem so bright. He could smell them from here.

"*Hola,* Mac's sister."

"Hi, Marc," was all she said, her smile forced.

"You remember *Courtney,*" his mother prompted, narrowing her gaze so he knew she didn't like his rudeness.

Courtney Gerard was more than one of his mother's strays. Courtney had a family connection—not blood but close enough that he should have known her name.

He remembered a lot more than her name.

Courtney was Marc's Bathsheba. The exact type of woman who managed to catch his eye whether he was interested in her or not. Everything about her was long, from her willowy body and shapely legs to the glossy hair that flowed in an inky wave down her back. He remembered her all right, and it annoyed the hell out of him every time he saw her.

Which was every time he came home.

His mother pressed a mug of coffee into his hands, and he thanked her, leaning against the archway. He wouldn't give the ladies a show by sitting down. Not when he wasn't staying. The stairs were looking a helluva lot better than this kitchen right now. Half draining the mug in one swallow, he savored the heat that seared his throat.

His mother arched an eyebrow but didn't comment. She also didn't return the coffeepot.

He held the mug out. "You're an angel, love."

She topped him off, and he sipped again to make more room. He had to drink his fill now because he couldn't make it up the stairs with the mug.

"Would you like something to eat? Anthony brought doughnuts from Nicola's before church. There are still a few left."

"Doughnuts can't possibly touch whatever it is you're cooking over there. I'll wait until dinner."

That pleased her. All the sharp edges smoothed from her expression. All the disapproval gone as fast as it had shown up. Like a good Italian mama, feeding people always made her day.

She retrieved a colander hanging from the rack on the wall and brought it to the table, where Courtney cleared onions off the cutting board. "We've been chatting about Courtney's work," his mother said. "I'd like you to weigh in."

Marc could smell the setup from a mile away. He could sense it before Courtney even opened her mouth, a full mouth with dusky pink lips that made him think of kissing. And sex.

This woman needed to go home.

Or he needed to get back to Colorado.

"Wish I could, but I've really got to shower. I'm off to a late start if you want me for dinner."

His mother frowned, and in two quick steps, she was at the counter again, grabbing the coffeepot.

"Finish this up, so I can brew a fresh pot." She cut him off at the pass, wedging herself between him and the doorway.

"Won't take long, Marc. I promise." Courtney's voice was as crystal clear as her gaze, direct and to the point, yet still somehow smoky. Like sex. A voice that would sound good in the dark. "I'd like to get your input if you don't mind."

He did mind. She was suddenly twitchy, almost urgent. Then she opened that pretty mouth and launched into a sob story about missing kids and a federal investigation.

Marc wasn't sure what he'd expected, but if he had been guessing, this train wreck of a situation wouldn't have even made the list.

Marc was sure he'd once heard what she did for a living, because he remembered thinking she had the luxury of making herself feel good by trying to save the world. Great in theory, but he knew too many people who empowered themselves at the expense of others. He didn't respect the motivation.

Or maybe he just didn't like Courtney.

He damn sure didn't like her brother or the way he had used his money to steal Anthony's longtime girlfriend, Harley.

Or maybe Marc didn't like how he noticed Courtney. She looked like everything he wanted, but she wasn't anything he was interested in. He was honest enough to admit that to himself.

Whatever the reason, he had his own no-win situation to deal with right now.

"No matter how I spin it, the outlook is grim," he said, hoping to put a swift end to this interrogation. "If this kid hasn't surfaced in eight years, the chances of finding her alive are not good."

"But you do think it is possible to track her down, Marc, so at least we'd know what happened to her?"

God, he shouldn't feel anything, but that look on her face… She was desperate, and he couldn't offer much hope. "No one vanishes into thin air, but with kids, there is the unforeseeable luck factor. Freaks and traffickers prey on them. Or some random wacko may have taken a liking to her, and she wound up a nut job's thrill. The FBI will find your Jane Doe, just a matter of time, but no one may ever know what happened to your other girl."

To Courtney's credit, she took reality standing. No drama. No tears. No pleas for him to sugarcoat the truth. Just that lovely face growing brittle around the edges as she struggled to cling to a last bit of hope, no matter how unrealistic.

"Wish I had a better opinion. Good luck." He tried to make his escape.

But by the time he'd set down the cup and gotten halfway to the door, he heard Courtney say, "Even so, Marc, I have to look. Please tell me where to start."

The plea in her voice stopped him. "You start by figuring out when your real girl was last seen. Until you figure that out, you can't unravel where she might have gone."

"Okay." Her clear gaze clung to him, so eager, but the frown forming on her smooth brow convinced him that she didn't have any idea how to proceed.

He wasn't surprised. "I can tell you where to look, but I can't magically give you the instinct to know what to look for. I can't help you. You'll have to take my word."

This time, he was out the door before she could stop him with another question.

CHAPTER THREE

If Marc had not been starving, he would have stayed in his room until the house had emptied after dinner. Too many drugs, too many stairs and the effort of taking a shower had kicked his ass all over again.

He wasn't in the mood for people and wanted to sleep off the drug hangover. Unfortunately, between the smells of his mother's cooking and the noise level that told him how good the food was, he had no choice. He made a mental note to keep protein bars in his room for the duration of this visit so he could avoid family gatherings altogether.

Against his better judgment, he made his way downstairs again. The thumping of his cane must have announced his arrival because Damon said, "Guess who's gracing us with his presence."

Caffeine and a shower hadn't taken the edge off. If Marc had been thinking clearly, he would have used his phone and a twenty to bribe his niece Violet into bringing a plate upstairs.

"To what do we owe this honor?" Damon asked.

There were a few laughs from around the table, but Marc ignored his brother, which was easy to do since the kitchen looked like Bourbon Street on Fat Tuesday. He noticed Courtney immediately, seated beside his mother, quiet in the midst of all the noise, so beautiful. Sad, too, he decided. That was probably his fault. He should probably feel bad.

He didn't want to draw any more attention to himself

when he still had to get to the counter, and make it to the table with a plate and silverware while maneuvering through the obstacle course of people crowding the food. Then he'd have to get to his seat.

The table was full. His mother was all about first come, first served, and hers was the only reserved seat—the corner closest to the stove. This was her throne to hear her tell it, so she could easily replenish serving bowls. While Marc had been growing up, that seat had been at his father's right.

"My best girl and right-hand man," Marc could remember his father saying. *"My better half."*

Today, she was Marc's savior. After taking one look at him, she started directing traffic.

"Scoot the twins toward Anthony," she said. "Marc, sit next to Violet. She'll make room."

"Come here, Uncle Marc." Violet patted the space on the bench beside her, a strategic corner placement so Marc would be able to stretch his leg out of everyone's way.

By the time he dropped heavily onto the bench, food started making its way toward him. Marc turned his attention to filling his plate as the conversation resumed about the wedding. Nic was finally going to marry his high school sweetheart and the mother of his teenage daughter, Violet. This wedding was a long time in coming, and the family was thrilled.

Marc didn't want any reminders of the upcoming nuptials, though. When he had agreed to be Nic's best man, he had assumed accompanying his big brother to the altar wouldn't be a problem. Now the thought of being on display to a church filled with guests annoyed him. He'd already tried to beg off, citing an inability to accomplish his best man duties, but Nic had flatly refused to accept his resignation.

Marc made quick work of dinner, glad when the conversation turned from the wedding to the Saints' performance during preseason. Everyone had an opinion, and he listened, distracting himself from his awareness of Courtney, who ate next to nothing although she made a good show of pushing food around her plate.

He was probably responsible for her lack of appetite, too. His troublemaking mother must have thought so, because when the talk about the Saints lagged, she solicited opinions about whether or not he should help Courtney with her problem.

Marc should have seen it coming. He would have bet money Courtney hadn't. Her expression froze along with the fork she held over the plate.

"Wait a second." Anthony swallowed hard around a bite. "Am I hearing this right? Are you telling me Boba Fett DiLeo can't track down a missing kid? Who is this kid—the Golden Child?"

Courtney blinked a few times, still surprised her shitty situation had become the entrée of table conversation.

Violet pulled a face. "I know Boba Fett, but who's the Golden Child?"

"Vintage Eddie Murphy, niece girl," Damon said. "Before you were a twinkle in your daddy's eye."

Nic scowled. Some things never changed, and he did not like reminders that he hadn't been privy to the existence of his daughter until two years ago.

"I didn't say *can't* track down," his mother explained matter-of-factly. "I said *won't*."

Marc should have known nothing with this family could ever be simple. Setting down his water glass, he settled back to watch the show. He would not prepare a defense. He refused to play this game.

"I don't understand." Anthony feigned confusion. "Why won't you help out Courtney?"

Every gaze at the table was suddenly on Marc. As brother

in the middle, Anthony was slick. He had learned long ago to maneuver between family factions. The top shelf contained the power brokers—his mother, Nic, Marc himself. More often than not, Anthony preferred to swing with them, but there were times he played devil's advocate or peacemaker. He wielded humor and stupidity with equal skill, and usually managed to emerge from family disputes unscathed. Marc did not have the patience for his brother today. Any of them.

"I have helped. The lady asked for an opinion. I gave one."

The lady still looked like a deer caught in headlights, but she recovered quickly, suddenly becoming very interested in the food she'd been pushing around on her plate.

"Courtney, you better hope your missing kid didn't run away like this one—across continents." Damon patted the top of Violet's head, and she beamed at the mention of the antics that had led her to find the father she'd grown up without knowing.

Now she was the oldest grandchild and resident superstar, her status as shiny and new to the family made her special, and she was old enough not only to revel in her position but milk it for all it was worth.

"I'd have given Uncle Marc a run for his money," she said saucily. "Can you say South America to Louisiana? There are lots of countries in between."

Nic directed his scowl her way this time. "That's because you don't respect normal boundaries."

"I don't do continents," Marc said.

"Really?" Violet wanted to know. "Why not?"

"I can't legally bring anyone over the border," Marc explained. "That's half the fun of my work—luring criminals into the country, so I can catch him. Or her. There are lots of *hers*. None as pretty as you."

That earned him a high-beam smile, and for a moment,

Marc thought he might have redirected the conversation. No such luck.

"Then what's up with this missing kid?" Anthony persisted. "Not in any real danger, I hope?"

All gazes swung Courtney's way. She was caught and had no choice but to be sucked into this nonsense.

"It doesn't look good," she said simply. Then she made the mistake of pausing to draw breath.

His mother stepped into that breach and interjected her two cents about Marc's refusal to help. By the time she was done, everyone was making noise about how he shouldn't be able to live with himself if he didn't help track down a missing kid.

The only thing Marc could say for Courtney was that she clearly wasn't in collusion with his family. And the frown on her pretty face suggested she didn't much like being used as a reason to bully him. But she didn't *not* like it enough to open her mouth and tell everyone to shut up. He found that disconnect between self-interest and outrage, a struggle so evident on her face, interesting for the woman who had involved his mother in the first place. Then again, Courtney had arrived early to speak with him privately. She hadn't intended for him to be put on the spot. He gave her credit for that.

Which begged the question about why she was so solicitous. Did she feel sorry for him?

Marc shouldn't care one way or the other. But there was something about the way she sat there, scowling at his mother, slanting horrified glances at him whenever she thought he wasn't looking. Each time someone opened his mouth, she sank lower into her chair. She felt bad. That much Marc knew. And he didn't want to be the object of anyone's pity, not even for the time it took to finish dinner. So he did exactly what he had refused to do—defend himself.

"Listen," he said. "I'm with you. I don't want to think about anything bad happening to this kid."

"Then why won't you help Aunt Courtney?" Violet asked.

"Because the situation isn't so simple or else your father would be helping *Aunt* Courtney." What was wrong with his family? A few dinner invitations made someone an honorary member?

Damon snorted with laughter. "I thought you were the dude who never met a skip you couldn't track."

"I track people who want to vanish. That's a big difference from a little kid who all of a sudden went missing one day."

"What if she didn't just go missing? What if someone took her?" Anthony went the confused route this time. "Sounds like she disappeared a long time ago. How old was she, Courtney?"

"I can't discuss details," she said in an obvious attempt to redirect. "All I can say is the last accurate documentation we have on her was before the hurricane evacuations."

Just mention of the hurricane brought a collective gasp and a reverent silence that lasted all of thirty seconds until Damon opened that mouth of his again.

"Can you imagine a kid in that mess?" he asked. "You know what this place was like during the hurricane."

"No, I don't," Marc said. "I was based in Southern California, luring a corporate CEO from Beijing." Trying to work in between watching news of the hurricane and attempting to contact anyone who could tell him whether or not his family had evacuated or if they'd been blown away by the storm, too.

"The place was a war zone," Nic said. "Take my word."

Obviously everyone did because there were a few murmurs of assent and some nodding heads.

"God, the thought of a kid unprotected in *that*..."

Anthony's words trailed off. Obviously becoming a parent had added newfound understanding.

"New Orleans, *cher*." Damon glanced knowingly at Courtney. "Crime capital ten years straight. Kid could have met up with gangs, perverts. Hell, kid could have been trafficked."

Courtney visibly paled until her black eyelashes stood out against skin that seemed cast in ivory.

"Sounds like *someone's* police department isn't doing their job." Marc deflected the attention. Let someone else get rolled under the bus for a change. He didn't even live here anymore.

"My police department is doing just fine," Nic shot back. "No thanks to people who refuse to help. Like *someone* who shall remain nameless."

"I'm not sure why you all are so determined to involve me in Courtney's business. I gave my opinion. If this kid was trafficked, she'll probably be dead by now." He was the voice of reason. "Kids don't last long under those conditions. Not when they're turned into junkie whores."

Anthony's wife, Tess, dropped her silverware onto the plate with a clatter. "Gentlemen, do you mind? This is not what I call dinner conversation." With one fluid move, she was on her feet scooping up a plate and helping her daughter from the bench. "Violet, would you give me a hand with Rocco?"

Violet popped up and grabbed plate, drink and kid before Marc's sister-in-law had cleared the room.

Damon watched them go with a frown. "You can't even help Courtney take a look, Marc? What else do you do all day?"

Once, Sensei Damon would have wound up on his ass for that question. That's why he held tenth dan grades in five disciplines. An inability to control what came out of his mouth chronically had him in trouble with one or more of his brothers. He'd be dead if not for learning how to defend himself.

Now all Marc could do was motion to the leg stretched out and make excuses. "See this leg, champ? Taking about everything I have in me to get it up and running again."

"We're not talking ten-hour workdays here," Anthony pointed out.

"How do you know how much work it takes to track anyone? They teach that in automotive repair school?"

That blow hit. He could see it all over Anthony's face, and Marc was sorry about that. He liked Anthony. He really did. Out of all his brothers, Anthony was the one good-natured enough not to get on Marc's nerves most of the time. But if Anthony, and everyone else for that matter, was determined to back him into a corner, they had better prepare for him to come out swinging.

"Can you say physical therapy?" Marc forced calm. "And when I'm not torturing my leg into submission or hobbling around with this cane, I'm supposed to be *healing.* Don't any of you listen to Vince?" Time to roll the family doctor under the bus. Helping should be his choice, and he resented otherwise.

But resentment didn't cloud his vision, and he clearly saw his mother elbow Courtney under the table. The move was merely a nudge, intentionally meant to go unnoticed. But Marc noticed everything. Attention to detail was his gift, exactly what made him such a good hunter.

He watched the play of emotions across Courtney's face, waited to see how she would respond. She met his gaze across the distance, tried to look calm and collected when her discomfort was leaking around the edges in a big way. "Is it possible to explain how I should proceed, Marc? Point me in the right direction, so I know what I'm looking for."

Is it possible?

Looked like Anthony wasn't the only diplomat at the table. Courtney gave Marc an out even though she walked a tightrope among loyalty to his mother, desperation to track down her missing kid and looking herself in the mirror. She handled the pressure fairly well, considering she had already asked him this question.

When he replied, he addressed the whole table. "Frankly, I'm disturbed by the way all of you are trying to muscle Courtney and me into doing what you want. I shouldn't have to defend my decision. I'm the one who would be doing the work, and since not a one of you knows what tracking someone involves, I don't think you're in any position to tell me what I should be doing. And you definitely shouldn't be manipulating Courtney."

His mother scowled, but Marc's rant had the desired effect—for all of ten seconds the entire kitchen went silent. Then, in that moment of breathless pause, the security alarmed beeped when the front door opened.

"Uncle Vince," Violet squealed from the living room.

There was a muffled reply and laughter before footsteps echoed down the hallway.

Everyone was still staring at Marc when Vince appeared in the doorway, looking like a younger male version of everyone else around the table, only dressed as if he'd come straight from making rounds at the hospital in his jacket and tie.

"Hey, everyone." He waved, oblivious to the scene he'd stepped into. "Hope you saved some food for me. I'm starving."

His mother was already on her feet, closing the distance and giving her youngest son a hug. "You'll never starve in your mama's kitchen, cutie."

Vince smiled dutifully when she pinched his cheek.

"Come on, let's get you a plate." She was already on her way to the counter. "Courtney, will you please make some room on the table? That's right. Scoot the salad bowl back. Vince will fit next to you now that Marc has run off Tess."

"Will do." Courtney looked grateful to get out from beneath the spotlight.

His mother piled a plate with everything from the counter, then headed back to the table. "Come on and eat, Vince. You'll need energy to talk some sense into your brother."

Vince shrugged off his jacket and wedged in between Courtney and Anthony. "Which brother?"

"Marc." There was a *"Who else?"* in there.

Marc could see where this was headed. He steadied himself on the table while maneuvering his leg.

His mother kicked off the debate as Marc tried to make his getaway. "Courtney needs help locating a missing child," she said. "But Marc won't help her because he says he should be healing, not working. As his doctor, what do you say?"

Vince technically wasn't Marc's doctor. Not that he hadn't been dispensing medical advice since the accident. He had overseen every course of action, handled the medical decisions when Marc hadn't been coherent enough to understand his choices and make decisions. Now Vince spooned grated cheese over his pasta and played Monkey in the Middle.

He could go either way on this. He was even-tempered and comfortable in his role as family baby. He wasn't a pain in the ass like Damon or a bully like Nic or a backstabber like Anthony. He was a mama's boy by default, and that would count. But it also counted that Marc had spent the past decade helping to finance that expensive medical education, keeping a roof above Vince's head, a car under his ass and making the loan payments that couldn't be deferred.

Vince must have been thinking the same thing. "Without you I would have never made it through school, so you'll get perks as long as you want them because I appreciate everything you've done. Helping Courtney is just what the doctor orders."

"Keep your perks to yourself, doc." Marc shoved up from the table, leaning heavily on the cane. He was done.

Vince frowned. Their mother hovered behind him, patting his shoulder consolingly. She cut Damon dead with a sharp, "You better think twice before you open that mouth."

Damon's mouth snapped shut before he uttered a word, taking their mother's advice for once.

This damned family. Marc was done with being at their mercy.

Levering his weight onto his cane, he stood. For one shining moment, he felt some semblance of control, empowered almost, as he stared down at everyone seated before him, waiting expectantly for his next move.

"Courtney," he said, and met her surprised gaze. "You'll provide a place to work and transportation."

Her eyes widened, but she nodded.

"And pay my premium?"

She didn't even blink. "Yes."

Marc wasn't surprised. She came from money. Otherwise she would wait for the FBI like most law-abiding citizens. He chased people like her—the ones with enough money to think rules didn't apply to them. They broke laws, and if they were stupid enough to get caught, they had the means to try to escape paying the price.

Those were the skips he brought to justice.

This case would be different, but given his present circumstances...

Marc motioned to the door. "Then you're on. Let's go."

He began his trek across the kitchen. He headed down the hallway and didn't stop until he got to the front door.

He didn't need anything. Not his wallet. Not money. Not a damned house key.

The spare was kept under the porch swing if he needed to get in when his mother wasn't home. Courtney could drive him if he did. His cell phone and painkillers were in his pocket.

All he needed was out of this house.

"Go, GO, GO!" Mama said urgently under her breath.

Courtney stood and reached for her plate, unsure. "That was coercion. You all were merciless."

"Just another day in the DiLeo house." Vince shrugged and dug his fork into the pasta.

"Better hurry or Gimpy might get away." Anthony gestured that she follow.

"Leave the plate," Mama commanded. "Go."

So Courtney could face the resentful man who'd been bullied into helping her? Why had this seemed like a good idea again?

Hurrying from the kitchen, she saw the door wide open and Marc making his way across the yard. From behind, he could have been any one of his brothers, any one of the broad-shouldered, tawny-haired Italian boys with the big laughs and bear-hug welcomes.

Except for the cane. And the attitude. And the fact that she actually liked all the other DiLeo brothers.

Marc must have heard her approach because he said, "Can you get to your car?"

"I'm parked on the street."

"The Mini Cooper, right?" His tone made it clear he wouldn't have expected anything else.

She quickly realized he would have trouble getting in and out of her small vehicle with a leg that didn't bend easily. Covering the distance between them, she set her hand on his arm to stop him.

They needed to clear things up here and now.

"Marc," she began, but when he glanced at her, the whiskey eyes all the DiLeo boys had inherited from their mother belonged to a stranger.

How had she not realized he was even taller than Anthony? She had misjudged the distance because suddenly she was too close, had to tip her head back to meet his stormy gaze.

The impulse to retreat a step hit hard, but Courtney stood her ground. "Listen, that didn't go the way I expected in there. You don't have to help me. Not unless you're willing."

"You don't want to pay me?" he asked in that dark voice, throaty yet somehow smooth like molasses.

"No, that's not it. It's not the money."

Something flickered deep in his gaze. She might not know this man well, but she knew his brothers. Every one quick-witted and a bit of a ballbreaker in his own way. Marc was making her uncomfortable and didn't mind.

What was it about this man, the one and only DiLeo she didn't absolutely adore?

"I don't understand why you need to be rude, Marc. I know your family coerced you. I was there, remember? And if you remember correctly, I wanted your opinion. I never asked you to *do* anything."

"I don't come cheap."

"It has nothing to do with your fee."

"Your call, then. Pay me for my time and provide chauffeur services to everywhere I need to go, or let me get back to my busy day."

The *everywhere I need to go* made red flags fly. Did he mean everywhere he needed to go to discover what had happened to Araceli or did he mean everywhere *everywhere* he needed to go?

Courtney didn't ask. Ironically, she probably had less to do with her days than he did. And the only thing she cared about was finding Araceli.

"Getting you where you need to go is no problem," she said. "I'll make arrangements for a different vehicle if we need to do a lot of running around."

"We'll need to do a lot of running around."

"No problem." He was only trying to provoke her. She knew it, but she didn't want him to think he could push her around. As she faced Marc's somber expression, she suddenly felt as if her very life depended on standing up to this man.

So she stood there, gaze unwavering, though the effort cost. Her chest grew tight, making her breaths come in shallow bursts, but she refused to look away, refused to blink, even though her neck felt as if it might snap from keeping her head tilted.

"We're good then." He was the first to break. "You've hired yourself a bounty hunter. For what that's worth nowadays."

That said a lot about why Marc had resisted.

"Thank you." She meant it.

He leaned heavily on his cane and repositioned himself in the springy grass, and Courtney suspected she hadn't won that little battle of wills at all. Marc had probably only needed to move his injured leg so he didn't topple over.

His physical limitations were all too evident as he made his way to the car and braced himself with a hand on the door frame to lower himself into the passenger seat. She held the door, watched the muscles bulge in his arm. His jaw tensed as if he fought the pain of bending his knee to wedge his big body into the compact compartment.

She opened her mouth to tell him to use the seat release, but he was already there. The seat jumped back with a metallic spring, and his expression eased.

She didn't know what to say, so she circled the car, leaving him to pull the door shut himself. She had only meant to consult with this man, to be advised about how to proceed. Now she had her very own bounty hunter, broken though he was, and she had no clue about what came next.

He sat so close, his elbow propped on her console, his hand draped casually on a knee. Somehow he managed to fill up her spacious-for-a-compact-car interior, and she wasn't sure what to say or do.

Drive...that much was a given.

Cranking the car, she slipped the shift into gear, feeling flustered and off-kilter. Driving away from the curb, Courtney was determined to find her center and regain control. "So what kind of place do you need to work? Let's start there."

"Standard office setup. Wi-Fi. Printer. Fax."

Okay, great. "One office coming up."

He didn't reply, just stared ahead, so she drove along in silence, remembering what Mama had said about being an answer to a prayer. What had Mama wished for this son?

Courtney didn't have a clue. Up until Marc's protracted visit after his accident, she had seen him only a handful of times through the years. He was quiet, intense, brooding almost, and suddenly seemed to suck up more than his share of air.

CHAPTER FOUR

"Here it is—Beatriz Ortero." The librarian used the name I had gone by for years now. "I've been waiting for you to come in. I wanted to ask about your tutor. She hasn't been in with you for a while."

"Her schedule is nuts." I didn't sound too sure, even though I had known this question would come up sometime.

Not that I expected some random librarian to notice Debbie was gone. One of the neighbors maybe. Definitely one of the ladies at church if I had ever seen one. But I hadn't run into any yet—thank God—and I hadn't been back to our church since Debbie had gotten too sick to make it to services.

"She has conflict with an after-school program, so she makes me work online." I sounded more certain this time, more casual. "She doesn't want me to lose the habit of making a time and place to study. She calls it practicing for college."

Had called it, anyway.

But the librarian was not interested, which made me wonder why she had noticed in the first place. Her gaze darted to the window as some kids passed the glass wall that separated this librarian from the others.

The queen on her throne.

No, that didn't fit. This librarian in her bland-colored pants with her disapproving expression wasn't regal as far as I was concerned. She was annoyed. That much I knew.

Probably because the security guard hadn't noticed the kids. He was too busy puffing up his chest at the pretty page who shelved books.

She finally turned back to me. "Will you please let your tutor know the paperwork needs to be renewed if you want to keep using the tutoring room?"

"Does she need to come in or do you want me to bring her the paperwork? She still has a few weeks left of the program."

The librarian didn't answer. Instead, she leaned over and searched through a desk drawer.

So I stood there and didn't say anything, even when she glanced up as that same group of kids got noisy, jockeying to get through the teen room door.

The security guard still didn't notice. When the librarian looked in his direction, her expression pinched, her angular features converging at an imaginary point in front of her face.

If I were to sketch her, I'd exaggerate her pointy features and add whiskers, turning her into the rat queen. Of course, she probably wouldn't find anything to laugh about. But I would. And I had not had much laughter in me lately, so one smile might be worth getting stiffed a tip.

The image in my head smoothed away some of the worry. I just hoped this unhappy woman wouldn't take out her unhappiness on me since I was around the same age as the noisy kids.

She withdrew the papers and handed them over. I smiled and said, "Thank you," very politely, hoping to prove myself different than everyone else my age.

If I lost this tutoring room, I couldn't get another. Not without an adult. I didn't need a quiet place to study—my whole life was quiet without Debbie—but I would have trouble when I needed to present for one of my online classes. I

needed some place to videotape, and I couldn't invite anyone home. That would be breaking our most important rule.

Never ever let anyone know where we live.

Debbie had made me swear before she died never to break
that rule. Not until I was eighteen. Not until I could make
my own decisions, so I didn't get caught in the legal system again.

Debbie trusted me to care for myself far more than she
did the government, and had done everything possible to set
up life so it would continue without her. She had bought four
boxes of checks and had signed every single one so I could
pay the rent and utility bill on time. She had set up auto-
deposit on her trust fund, so it would continue to deposit
monthly payments until someone figured out she had died.

"It's not a lot," she had said, *"but it will be enough to
cover the rent and that's something."*

As always, Debbie had delivered even the most dismal
news with a smile and jingly laughter. An angel. That's how
I always sketched her. With wings and a halo. *My* angel.

The memory made me ache. Even after all these months,
the pain was still so big it stole my breath.

Most days I pretended Debbie was out on a church er-
rand or running to the bank whenever her old uncle would
surprise her with a check. Or that she'd been tired from the
chemotherapy and had gone to bed before me. But little
things, like this paper that needed a signature, got me every
time. So I stood there waiting for the rat queen to find her
keys, with my chest so tight I ached.

"Here we are." She stood and led me from around her
glass castle with quick steps.

The security guard straightened up as she passed, puffing his chest some more so the shiny buttons on his uniform
glinted importantly, but the kids behind the windows of the
teen room didn't notice her. There was more laughter, still

too loud, but she didn't slow down until we reached the tutoring room.

After unlocking the door, she flipped on the light. I thanked her and unloaded my backpack. I only had the tutoring room for one hour and my presentation would take forty minutes. Every minute under, and I would be docked five points off my overall grade. My GPA was my most valuable asset, second only to my talent, so I wasn't about to screw it up without good reason. I would never get scholarships otherwise. And I would need lots of scholarships to pay for the Art Institute of Chicago.

Setting the dry-erase markers on the whiteboard, I checked the time.

4:06.

The paperwork and key search had chewed into my hour. Sometimes the librarians would let me run over time if the room wasn't booked. Not the rat queen. She would be waiting outside the door and counting the seconds until my hour was up.

Slipping out the door again, I walked around the back of the audiobook section to the quiet study room, hoping to avoid notice. This is where the smart kids were, the ones with more to do than check their social media. The only thing we all had in common was that we couldn't afford our own technology. I had a tutoring room, so the rat queen should have known what kind of person I was.

A person with a plan.

A plan that was in big trouble when I looked around the quiet study room.

"Where's Peter?" I hissed beneath my breath, careful not to disturb the adults who were seated at the various study carrels.

The last thing I needed was more trouble.

"Don't know," Faffi whispered from her seat nearest the printer. Beside her, Sylvia shrugged.

Faffi was another person with a plan. I called her the screaming liberal. She had political aspirations and already served as an intern on a local councilman's campaign. She would love my presentation about immigration policies today. I argued both sides, but personally leaned left.

"Was he at school today?" I asked.

"I didn't see him." Sylvia's plan wasn't as specific as mine or Faffi's, but it didn't have to be. She wanted to be a doctor, which meant she had to rock her International Baccalaureate program to get scholarships to a good university. She was another one who would need lots and lots of scholarships to pay for school. Good thing she was brilliant.

"Are you talking about that kid on the skateboard?" Rohan tugged an earbud from his ear.

"Yeah, the one with the hair like that gay guy from *American Idol*."

Rohan laughed, loud enough to make me glance around to see if we were annoying the room's other occupants. Adults in a library liked nothing better than to narc on kids who weren't obeying the quiet rule. Rohan didn't seem to care. Maybe he didn't have to because he had such a cool name. Who knew they watched *The Lord of the Rings* in Bangladesh? "I saw him on the public bus this morning, but he wasn't at first lunch."

"I didn't see him, either," Faffi told me.

I sighed. Nothing was ever going to be easy, was it? I had to record four people, so the virtual teacher knew I'd actually presented to an audience. Peter had agreed to sit in so long as I paid him in cigarettes.

Would the rat queen sit in if I offered her the three packs of Camels in my backpack? I'd bet money the security guard would. If I had any money to bet. I didn't because I'd already spent what I had on three packs of Camels. Not to mention the time I'd wasted finding a convenience store to sell them to me without identification because I was underage.

"Come on," I said. "I'll figure out something."

I glanced at the clock on the way out. Six whole minutes to come up with a plan. Great. I got everyone quietly inside the tutoring room. Then I saw *him*.

He walked past the window, looking as noticeable as he had the first time I'd noticed him. Which was sort of strange really, since there wasn't anything that noticeable about him.

Except for the guitar slung over his back, he might have been any student from the high school. A senior, definitely. I wasn't surprised to find him here since we were only a few blocks away from where I'd first seen him.

He had been playing on the street corner across from the Western wear store where I usually set up my pitch. The lady who owned the store liked me. I was quiet compared to all the street musicians who played in the District, and I always chalked a brilliant design on her sidewalk space that made tourists slow down long enough to notice her store.

Whenever tourists sat for a caricature, they stared at her window displays. I always threw a cowboy hat or some boots and fringe into my sketches to get folks in the country mood.

We were a match made in heaven.

Maybe this guitar guy went to school, maybe not. But I remembered him. And his music. Not the usual country that every musician in town played. He stuck out in the streets the way I did with my art.

No, this guy's music was more varied, some folksy, some rock, some alternative. Definitely original. He had a raspy voice that managed to be smooth and clear. I liked listening to him. Yeah, that was why I had noticed him.

I didn't have time to think, so I acted.

He sidestepped the opening door with a quick move and a steadying hand on his guitar.

"Excuse me." For some reason, I sounded breathless, as if I had run to catch him.

He turned and stared down at me with eyes as dark as his hair. There was something Hispanic in him. No question.

Those dark eyes got curious, and I realized he was waiting for me to say something.

"Do you have forty minutes I could borrow?" I blurted. "Like right now."

A grin appeared as he stared at me, visibly deciding what to make of my random proposition.

"I have to tape a presentation for my online class, and I need four in my audience. Had a no-show."

I hadn't realized how cute he was, but it was impossible to ignore up close. He had these crazy high cheekbones and caramel skin. He was buff, too. The muscles in his thighs stretched his jeans like he was one of those cross-country runners who trained around the neighborhood.

"I'll pay you ten bucks." Same thing I paid everyone else. Except Faffi, who extracted payment whenever she needed me to do something for her. A budding politician. I would vote for her. "Or three packs of Camels."

That grin turned into a full-out smile. He had a dimple. "I'll take the Camels."

CHAPTER FIVE

MARC HAD BEEN enjoying his escape for the first ten minutes of the ride. Courtney didn't know what to make of him, had no clue what she'd signed on for. But she put on a good show. He respected that. Maybe because he sensed how uncertain she was, bouncing back and forth between appreciating his presence in her car but being worried about the way he'd gotten here.

Even he couldn't blame her. He hadn't exactly been accommodating, and his guess was she considered him the family wild card. Anthony would never have given her a hard time.

But any enjoyment Marc felt about escaping the prison his life had become ended when Courtney steered her overpriced toy car out of his neighborhood and headed into hers. He shouldn't be surprised that manicured lawns stretched back from the streets or that chain-link and weather-battered wooden fences yielded to expensive brickwork and ornate iron gates.

By the time she wheeled off a side street and pulled into a driveway, Marc remembered why he hadn't thought much of this woman's family. The Garden District mansion in front of him, all pitched eaves and wraparound gallery, looked like a house kids might tour on school field-trip day.

"So this is home." Not a question, but a stupid comment he should have kept to himself. The irony of all the stairs must be wearing on his impulse control. Stairs leading to the front porch. Stairs inside leading to one, two, *three* floors. Unless that top floor was an attic? He could hope.

Courtney nodded, silky hair threading over her shoulders with the gesture, drawing his gaze once again to her slender neck and the delicate curve of her jaw. "Well, half of this is home anyway. House was split into two residences."

"So you rent?" Okay, he wasn't really interested, but his lack of impulse control had started this conversation. Couldn't blame her for that.

"No, I own my side. Like a co-op."

Mortgage on half a place this size must be a small fortune that she surely couldn't be swinging on her social worker's salary. He knew what real estate went for in New Orleans because Nic had been hunting for a place to move his family into after the wedding. Especially in this part of town. Cheaper to pay a mortgage in this economy, which was why Marc owned two properties himself.

"Who owns the other half?"

"Admiral Patton and his wife."

No response was necessary, which was good since Marc didn't have much to say. Not anything that would be considered a constructive start to their working relationship.

And he was here to work. Period.

He needed to remember that, because everything about Courtney distracted him, from the hair she wore loose to the feminine way she moved. The only thing that grounded him was her mouth. Every time she opened it, he remembered who she was.

He'd known the Gerard family had money. The name was attached to some heavy hitters, and he'd heard of them all while growing up in New Orleans, names belonging to the longtime district attorney, some politicians and other visible city power brokers. Civil service seemed to run in the family like a luxury most people couldn't afford.

Courtney eased up on the brake, coasting the short distance to the garage, where she came to another stop. Slipping out the driver's side, she stood watching him put on a show as he pulled himself out of the car. She made a few false starts, as if she wanted to offer help but had decided against it.

A good call on her part.

When the cane clattered to the driveway, she snatched it up and offered it to him, seemed relieved to do something to dodge the tense silence. His frustration and her guilt for subjecting him to her toy car weren't a pretty combination. He didn't feel inclined to reassure her by cracking a joke or making excuses for the pitiful display he made.

Once he was solidly on his feet, Marc met her frowning gaze, felt every inch as broken as he was.

"I have an idea," she said. "I'll be right back."

Then she presented a show of her own, only she stole his breath as she ran lightly across the grass and up the stairs, taking two steps at a time. She unlocked the door, and the beeping of a security alarm startled the afternoon quiet.

Marc stood, propped on his cane, willing his pulse to slow. His heart throbbed so hard he could hear it. Unless that was just a trick of the quiet. He guessed this part of town was usually pretty calm. Maybe not along Rue St. Charles, but a few blocks back, where this place was. Another world, sheltered from the shrieks of sirens that riddled other neighborhoods. Or the exhaust-filled traffic that marked the business district and the French Quarter at all hours.

The beeping stopped and Courtney reappeared, resuming her attractive display with her fast, graceful movements and breathless smile. She dangled a key ring as she approached. "Your office."

She surprised Marc by leading him along a flagstone path toward the rear of the property. He hadn't paid attention to the building partially concealed in the shelter of trees. Had thought it was another detached garage at first. But on closer inspection, he realized it was too small to be a kitchen or the old slave quarters. Only one floor and no stairs.

"A guesthouse?" he asked.

"A cottage." Courtney preceded him to the door. "It's small. And no one has used it since a friend needed a place to stay through a divorce. We'll need to air it out."

"Your place or the admiral's?"

"Mine." She fitted the key into the lock while he clambered onto the porch. Thrusting the door wide, she grimaced. "I need to remember to open this place up occasionally."

She stepped inside, then held the door for him.

"A house and a cottage? A lot of room around here for one person."

"Wasn't meant for just one." She gave a shrug that was probably meant to be casual but didn't manage the job.

Unless he missed his guess, there was a lot more to that statement. A relationship gone south? There was enough room around here for a few families. Did a woman who made a career of micromanaging other people's kids even want a family? He didn't have a clue about Courtney's personal life, but Marc knew one thing—she had a story. His family probably knew every detail.

Courtney obviously didn't want to discuss her personal life and sailed into the living room, saying, "Fortunately, the place never gets too hot because of all the shade."

She took off again, heading straight to the windows that cornered two walls, and thrust aside long white sheers to reveal paned glass that overlooked the well-tended foliage and the back wall of the property.

Marc followed her only far enough to survey the place. Leaning against the wall, he appreciated this unexpected good fortune. No stairs. Not one.

She was right about the size. There was a living room, eat-in kitchen and two doors that most likely led to a bedroom and a bathroom. Under a thousand square feet by his estimation, but the open floor plan and floor-to-ceiling windows gave it a bigger feel. The living room was large enough to accommodate a furniture grouping around a television and an area with a corner desk that served as an office.

"Wi-Fi?" he asked.

"Mmm-hmm." She struggled with a stubborn window.

He didn't offer to help. Once he might have saved a damsel in distress. Now all he could do was observe, appreciating the sight she presented, her efforts to budge a stubborn window drawing the blouse tight across her back. And he did enjoy the sight she made with her arms outstretched, the curve of her waist visible beneath the cascade of dark hair.

The drug hangover must have finally worn off because to Marc's utter amazement, he felt a familiar throb as if his body wanted to prove that the rest of him wasn't as damaged as his leg.

This particular urge hadn't made an appearance since before the accident. He'd be an idiot to put too much stock in anything right now, but the simple fact that his reactions were still there reassured him.

"Jeez," Courtney said as the window shot open, throwing her off balance in the process. The sheers fluttered and she righted herself with a steadying hand on the frame. "Needs oil or something. I'll add it to my to-do list."

Then she vanished into the bedroom.

Marc didn't follow, didn't want to risk connecting the sight of Courtney with a bed, so he hobbled over to the desk instead.

Modem. Laser printer. Fax-copier-scanner combo.

None of the equipment appeared to have seen much wear, but that didn't surprise him. Why wouldn't she outfit the of-

fice in a place she didn't even open up for air? There was
no computer, but that wasn't a problem. If he'd been thinking when he'd left his mother's, he would have brought his
laptop.

He hadn't been thinking about anything but getting the
hell out before he killed someone. Starting with his mother.

Courtney reappeared. "How will this place work for you?
I mean, after it airs out, of course."

She'd only brought him here because he had made such a
pathetic sight getting out of her car. But Marc wasn't going
to dwell on that. Nor would he look a gift horse in the mouth.
"This place is good. I work better without distractions."

"No distractions here. The admiral works around the
yard, but he doesn't usually come back here. I think he got
out of the habit after selling the cottage to Harley."

Just then a few pieces of a puzzle clicked into place. "This
was Harley's old house?"

"I didn't realize you didn't know."

"I knew about her house, just not that you'd bought it."

Harley was the connection between his family and Courtney's. His mother would have adopted Harley long ago if the
State of Louisiana would have allowed it. They hadn't, so
Harley had contented herself with being an honorary family member, solidifying her place during years as Anthony's girlfriend.

Until Mac Gerard had come on the scene with all his
money. Now Harley brought her husband's family home for
Sunday dinner, too. Anthony didn't seem to mind. Marc
couldn't begin to explain the situation, didn't care enough
to try.

But anyone who had known Harley had known when she
purchased this place—her first home. And from that moment
on, Marc's visits had been punctuated with stories about
whatever work she'd been doing. Any time he had asked,

"How have you been, Harley?" he never heard about college achievements or career successes, but her accomplishments around this house.

"I sanded the floors to the grain before refinishing them," she had told him proudly. *"They gleam like new.*

"I tackled plaster last month. Repaired the damage from some old broken pipe, and now I'm texturing the walls. By the time I'm through, no one will know there'd ever been a leak."

Marc glanced around the room, at the bright white, finely textured walls, at the planked floor with the rich pine finish beneath the gleam of polyurethane. Both jobs done with care and attention to detail.

If anyone had deserved a home, that anyone had been Harley. She had grown up on the wrong side of Courtney's business—foster care. But if Harley had owned this place, then Marc knew Courtney must have purchased her portion of the property from her brother after Harley had married him.

He supposed that shouldn't surprise him, either.

"Oh, I forgot," Courtney said. "Let me run up to my house. Be right back."

She didn't give him a chance to reply, just spun around and took off again, leaving the door open behind her. The sound of her footsteps on the flagstones faded, and Marc took the opportunity to scope out the rest of the place.

The kitchen chewed up a lot of square footage, but as he ran a hand long the smooth finish of the wooden cabinets with their scrolled pewter handles, he could remember Harley talking about the months of work it had taken her to dismantle the cabinetry and refinish the wood. She'd lived without hinges and handles until she'd had the money to purchase the hardware so everything would match.

Such attention to detail because she had cared so much.

There were three large windows in the kitchen overlooking what appeared to be another walled edge of the property. Hard to tell with all the foliage. There were a lot of windows for such a tiny place, and he didn't have any problem imagining why the Harley he had known had been so in love with her home. Secluded. Airy. Traditional. Right up her alley.

Of course Marc had known the Harley who had been Anthony's longtime girlfriend. Not the Harley who had left his brother to marry Courtney's brother. *That* Harley was a stranger.

Hurried footsteps through the open door brought Marc around in time to see Courtney reappear, the shallow breathing and high color in her cheeks as if she'd run the whole way.

Covering the distance to the kitchen, she set a thick file folder on the table. "Lots of reading here."

Marc edged closer and flipped open the cover to riffle through the contents.

Reports. Court documents. Profile pages. Correspondence.

"How did you get all this?" he asked.

"It's the case file from work."

Normal rules just didn't apply to any of the Gerard family. Marc should have seen that coming. Courtney wasn't playing games. She had already made that clear. But this confidential file shouldn't be anywhere but in her former office, particularly during an ongoing FBI investigation.

She seemed to think she could do whatever she wanted to get what she wanted. Marc knew the type. He wondered if Courtney had a clue that he didn't think much of the way she operated. Or her family. She probably wouldn't care. She'd tell him to keep his opinions to himself and write him a check.

"So how do you want to do this?" she asked. "I'll swap

my car before I need to take you home, so any idea when you're going to want to leave?"

Marc smiled then, a real smile he didn't have to force for someone else's benefit. No, this smile just happened, a memory from days when he'd actually had something to smile about.

He didn't want the complication of Courtney Gerard in his life right now, and he certainly didn't need the complication of his attraction to her. He didn't like who she was or what she stood for. But compliments of his nuisance family, she was his to deal with for the time being.

So he would make the situation work for him.

Folding his arms across his chest, he stared at her and said, "I won't be leaving until we track down your kid. So why don't you swing by my mother's place while you're out and grab my things?"

COURTNEY STARED AT MARC and blinked stupidly. He was waiting for her reaction. That much she knew.

But she didn't have one. Not yet, anyway.

In that moment, she couldn't decide what surprised her more —Marc's declaration to become her guest or the purely physical sensation that dropped the bottom out of her stomach.

Because she stood close to Marc DiLeo?

Courtney knew this feeling, though she hadn't experienced the sensation in a very, very long time.

But…Marc DiLeo?

She couldn't begin to explain why she was suddenly so aware of everything about him. *Everything.* From the way he propped strong hands on the handle of his cane to the defiance radiating off him like summer heat. No denying he was an attractive man. That in itself was a DiLeo thing. Despite the scowl.

Was Courtney suddenly so aware of him because they were alone? Now that she thought about it, she'd never actually been alone with him until he'd finagled his way into her car today.

"Okay…well, okay," she said.

If Marc wanted to stay, there was no reason he couldn't. She didn't use this place, and more of his attention would be given to finding Araceli if he was away from family distractions. That worked for her.

"I'll need my things." His expression was inscrutable, just intense eyes and that hint of defiance.

Did he really expect her to deny him?

"We can swing by your mom's."

"You go. Tell her to throw my stuff in my suitcase. There's only one. Bring that and my laptop case."

He should probably tell his own mother to pack his things, but his defiance was instigating hers. She needed his help. If he wanted to stay in her empty guest cottage and bum rides, then her guest cottage wouldn't be empty anymore. No problem.

But she wouldn't run interference for Mama, who had bullied Marc in the first place. Mama had pushed the issue, and she deserved what she got. If Marc decided to temporarily move out, then Courtney wasn't about to feel bad.

"Sounds like you travel light," she said. "I'll go now then. Will you look through the file while I'm gone? We can work out the details of our arrangement when I get back."

"Sounds like a plan."

She slipped the cottage key from her pocket and handed it to him. "Make yourself at home."

Then she headed to the door, so very aware of each step, the measured length of her strides, the whisper of her shoes on the floor, the way her hands dangled at her sides as if she was suddenly unsure what to do with them. As if his dark gaze followed her every step. When she finally pulled the door shut, she inhaled deeply, apparently her first real breath in a while because she felt light-headed.

What was wrong with her?

She had way more important things to deal with than physical awareness of a man who was an idiot. Taking another deep breath, she walked briskly to her car. Anxiety must be getting the better of her or else her emotions wouldn't be all over the place.

Marc DiLeo? *No way.*

But even Courtney's dismissal of her haywire reactions didn't stop her from obsessing.

She bypassed Mama's house. Instead, she drove onto the expressway and headed out of metro New Orleans for her brother's house. She needed some time to wrestle her racing thoughts under control so she could effectively deal with Mama the bully.

By the time the security guard logged her tag number at her brother's subdivision, Courtney was grateful for every mile she had put between her and the man she'd left in the cottage. Mac and Harley's place bordered a conservation lot, and winding through the subdivision felt like driving into another world. The streets were shaded with old cypresses and oaks. The homes were set far back from the street.

Pulling into the driveway, she parked and peeked inside the garage to see if her brother's car was there. It wasn't, so she used her key to let herself in, calling out, "Harley, it's me. *Do not* get up."

There was no reply, so Courtney took the stairs two at a time and found her sister-in-law scowling when she walked into the bedroom.

Harley was such a beautiful woman, exquisitely feminine with big blue eyes and a cloud of red hair. She sat propped up with pillows, fully dressed in a comfy-looking shorts ensemble and strappy sandals.

"You look like you're going somewhere."

"I am," Harley said. "Insane. Just a heads-up."

"No worries. I can take you." A first since Harley had been Damon's protégé at martial arts from the time they'd been kids. She must surely have a black belt or two by now.

Harley narrowed her gaze and folded her arms. "Just kick me when I'm down, why don't you?"

"I would never."

"Why are you here? I know you didn't come to visit, because Mac wouldn't have left had he known you were on the way."

"Where is everyone? It's Sunday. Am I missing some performance I wasn't made aware of?"

"Mac and Toni are with your parents," Harley said. "Your dad is taking everyone out for dinner. Except me."

"I'm sure they'd have gotten takeout and picnicked with you, though. They're just looking for things to do that get Grandpa out of the house."

"No picnics. Dinner out works for all of us. I can't cook, and they've been hovering, trying to cheer me up. I'm so grumpy even I feel bad."

"Humph." Courtney sank onto the bed, careful not to jar the pregnant lady and the new little niece or nephew. "Now I'm sorry I didn't go to dinner, too. I went to Mama's instead."

Of course Courtney had declined her parents' dinner invitation specifically because she didn't want to get into the details about why she was on leave.

"Mama mentioned that you'd been there today."

"That was fast." Not a surprise, as Mama and Harley were mother and daughter in so many ways. "Did you hear that Mama bullied Marc into helping me sort out my little work problem?"

Harley narrowed a no-nonsense gaze. "What I heard was that your work problem wasn't as little as you said it was. Mama was tripping over herself to tell me what was going on without actually telling me what was going on. That was my first clue I might not have all the information."

Courtney attempted nonchalance. "I wanted to pick Marc's brain. I wasn't sure if I should, given his convalescence, so I went to Mama first."

Involving Marc even in a peripheral way would get back to Harley, so Courtney had known to have an explanation ready. Of course, her explanation didn't fit so neatly now that the situation had taken an unexpected turn, and she was here for the explicit purpose of swapping cars to chauffeur Marc.

Harley arched a delicate eyebrow as if silently chiding, *Is that really the best you can do?*

This day was turning out to be a mixed bag in so many ways. Courtney's only defense would be an offense, so she launched into one, explaining what she'd told Mama earlier without as many details.

Harley was positively scowling by the time Courtney finished. "There are children missing, an FBI investigation and you're on administrative leave. Did I get that right?"

Courtney nodded.

"I get why you didn't involve Nic, but why wouldn't you be up-front with your brother and me? We have some experience with this sort of thing, you know. Just a little."

"Sarcasm doesn't become you." Which was a joke, since Harley could wield sarcasm without even opening her mouth. "From where I'm standing, you and my brother have your hands full. Mom and Dad have their hands full with Grandpa, too. I'm trying to help everyone, not give you all more to worry about. Why on earth would I burden you?"

"Because you care about me enough to give me something to do while I'm languishing in this bed going insane."

"You're not languishing. You're baking my new little niece or nephew, keeping the oven all nice and toasty so she or he rises like a perfect little biscuit."

Harley practically growled, which forced Courtney to bite back a smile. Smiling would have been a mistake right now.

"Harley, there's a reason my brother isn't giving you work." Courtney gave her mouth something less offensive to do than grin. "Or your boss. Or me. My brother is worrying about his family right now, which is exactly what he should be doing. If I had wanted to add more to his plate or yours, I would have told you. I didn't. I've got things under control, so enjoy your vacation. Once our newest Gerard gets here, you'll be wishing you rested. You're not as young as you were when you had Toni."

Harley rested her head against the pillows with a sigh and stared at the ceiling.

Okay, maybe she was languishing.

Courtney was about to concede the point when Harley said, "I could advise you to do the same thing. Why are you taking on the FBI? Go home, take up knitting and let them do their job. But I know you won't listen, so do one thing for me since wondering and worrying won't be good for me or the baby. Or your brother for that matter, since he's the one trying to do everything because I'm down."

"What?"

Harley sat up again, leveled that bright gaze Courtney's way. "Be honest with us from now on. I seriously can't sit here with the seconds ticking by like years and not worry if I think you're hiding things. I'll worry even more. So will Mac. We're in panic mode already."

"Trust me. I know the feeling." Courtney sighed. "No

worrying about me. I've got things under control. Compliments of Mama and the bullying brothers, I've got Marc."

"Bullying brothers. Well said."

Courtney stretched across the bed. "You probably would have seen it coming. I didn't."

"Really? Well, you don't know Marc that well," Harley conceded. "He is not in a good place."

"He's alive after an accident. That's a very good place."

"No argument. But he's another one who isn't being honest. You two have that in common."

"Cut me a break, will you?"

That got a hint of a smile. "You've come to the wrong house for breaks. I'm fresh out. No breaks for Marc, either. It was only a matter of time before Mama found some way to light a fire under his ass and get him moving. Sounds like you and your *little work problem* fits the bill."

An answer to a prayer. Isn't that what Mama had said?

Had the prayer been to give Marc something to distract him from his pain and slow recovery?

"I think Mama might get a bit more than she bargained for." Courtney certainly had. She explained how Marc had invited himself to move in.

"He's staying with you?"

"No. He has apparently taken a liking to your old place, because he wasn't there ten minutes before informing me he wouldn't be leaving. What was I going to say?"

"You'll nearly be roommates. Good luck with that."

"Speaking of, would you mind swapping cars with me? There's not enough legroom in mine. I'm providing car service, too."

Harley nudged Courtney's leg with her foot. "The keys are on the ring by the door, but listen to me. Whatever you do, do not let Marc give you a hard time. I'm serious. And do not, under any circumstances, let him into your bedroom."

Courtney opened her mouth to issue a quick reassurance on that score, but the phone on the bedside table rang out a rock tune.

Harley reached for it. "Do you mind? Mac will freak if I don't pick up." She glanced at the display. "Oh, it's not— To what do I owe this pleasure?"

Courtney rolled over, ready to provide privacy, but Harley shook her head and cradled the phone against her shoulder to broadcast half of the conversation.

"No, where?" she asked. There was a beat of silence while the caller replied. "My old place? Really?"

Marc was on the other end of the line, and Courtney's reaction came fast. A fluttering heartbeat. A shallow breath.

Harley was watching Courtney so closely that a flush prickled her cheeks and she missed the next exchange. Harley arched an eyebrow, and Courtney forced herself to look casual. She wished she had stepped out of the room.

"Tell you what, Marc," Harley said. "Why don't you come over here and stay with me? We can both lie in my bed and keep each other company while we work. I've got my big tummy and you've got your wrecked leg. We'll make a great team."

Even Courtney could hear the disgusted snort on the other end and admired the easy rapport between two people who had known each other forever.

"Play nice with Courtney or you'll be answering to me," Harley cautioned before saying, "Thanks. You take care of you, too. Call me if you need help. I'll be here. In bed. Staring at four walls. Not moving."

Disconnecting the call, she set the phone back on the table. "Well, you're right. He's settling in for the long haul."

"You warned him to be nice. How much trouble am I in?"

Harley considered her. "Can't say for sure. Marc's off his stride since the accident. Any other time I'd tell you to lock your bedroom door and throw away the key so you don't get your heart broken."

Right. No problem there. "But now?"

"Now…well, I don't know. He's one grumpy bastard. More miserable than I am. That much I can tell you. But he and I aren't the same as before. He hasn't forgiven me for marrying your brother."

"You're kidding."

She shook her head. "Marc hasn't lived here for a long time. He stays up on what's going on, but that's not the same as seeing for himself. He's really hardheaded."

"Like the rest of his brothers."

Harley's expression was thoughtful. "Except this one has a marshmallow center."

Which was about the last thing Courtney expected to hear.

CHAPTER SIX

MARC SAT ON the couch in his new living room, grimacing as he grabbed a pant leg to hoist up his leg. The couch was just long enough to stretch out, and almost instantly the ache eased so he could attempt to think clearly.

Sunlight streamed through the windows, illuminating dust particles. And silence. He couldn't remember the last time he had heard so much quiet. Not since he had come home, for sure.

He should close the windows. The need for fresh air was yielding to the need for cool air. Despite all the trees, this was summer in New Orleans. God, he hoped there was central air or he might be regretting his decision. He was already starting to sweat, but he didn't have enough energy left to get up and deal with the situation.

Instead, he opened the file on the coffee table to start piecing together the mystery. He needed to learn all he could about the missing kid.

Araceli Maria Ruiz-Ortiz had been born in New Orleans. Her parents had been from Colombia. She had one sibling, a brother who was four years younger. The father, Silvio Ruiz, had drowned on the wharves where he worked unloading cargo on the river. Araceli had been seven. The mother, Gracielle Ortiz, had been a seamstress and housewife before the husband's death, a full-time housekeeper after.

Both parents had been in the country illegally.

"Not good," Marc said to no one in particular. He could

guess the next part of the story before setting down the pro-
files and starting on the court documents. Sure enough…
the mother had been deported during an immigration crack-
down when Araceli was eight.

The son had been at work with the mother when she was
detained, but Araceli had been in school. For some undocu-
mented reason, she had wound up in the care of a neighbor
before being picked up by Family Services.

The mother could have petitioned the court to let Araceli
live with the neighbor permanently or she could have arranged for her daughter's return to Colombia, but the mother
hadn't appeared in court or hired an attorney to appear on
her behalf. From there the situation got muddy.

When Courtney had said they didn't have much substan-
tial evidence to work with, she hadn't been kidding. Marc
got a clear understanding of what had taken place before the
hurricane, but nothing could be substantiated after. There
were documents with Araceli's name, but whether they referred to the real Araceli or Jane Doe was anyone's guess.

Justifiably, the FBI was taking the conservative route
with their investigation. They would have been crazy not
to go after their strongest lead, and that was Jane Doe. But
Marc also understood Courtney's frustration. She wanted
Araceli found and wasn't about to let rules get in her way.

He leaned back his head and closed his eyes.

The whole situation made his brain throb in time with his
leg. The words on the page kept twisting in his head until he
was rereading paragraphs and retaining nothing. He needed
to take some pills, but that would mean getting up because
he'd left his pills in the bedroom with his phone. All his
worldly possessions until Courtney returned with his stuff.

The next thing he knew, the sound of knocking awoke
him. He stared into the unfamiliar room, and it took a minute to remember where he was. The open windows. The

heat. The silky-haired woman staring at him from the open doorway.

His head felt clearer. The aftereffects of last night's drugs seemed to have worn off. Of course now that his eyes were open, his leg ached.

The never-ending cycle of his messed-up life.

"Why are you knocking? This is your place."

"But you live here now," she said. "Good thing the door was unlocked, because I gave you my key."

Easing around, he pushed himself up, feeling weird about being caught sleeping. Because he was supposed to be working? Or did the sight of this woman throw him?

The heat and quiet combined to make the moment surreal, the room bathed in the gray of twilight. A drowsy moment that might have been from a dream since his life of late had been filled with hospital rooms and doctor's offices and busy physical therapy sessions and the constant traffic in his mother's house.

And pain. That, too.

But Courtney hadn't been a part of all that. She was an unfamiliar addition to the equation. Dragging a hand through his hair, he looked away, crushed the thought that not so long ago, he wouldn't have been surprised about awakening to find a beautiful woman. Beside him. Underneath him. Times had changed.

"My money is on the foster parents," he said, ending the silence that was leaving him too much time to think.

Courtney glanced at the coffee table. "You went through the file already?"

He nodded, but she didn't reply. Instead, she maneuvered his bags through the door, then wheeled them to the bedroom.

"I'd offer to help, but by the time I get up..."

"No worries." She disappeared through the door only a

few steps later, long before he would have even been able to get up.

"Bring my laptop out here, will you?" He didn't need it yet but he would eventually. She'd save him another trip.

"Here you go." Reappearing, she set the leather case beside the coffee table within reach.

To his surprise, she bypassed the room's chairs, flipped on a light and plunked down on the floor in front of the coffee table. So close he might have reached out to touch her. If he had wanted to touch her, which he did not.

"So where do we start?" She reassembled the shuffled paperwork into some semblance of order. "Do you have any questions about the file or would you like to work out our business arrangement first?"

There was nothing to work out. She would pay him or not. Simple. But he kept that to himself and went the professional route, since she was going out of her way to be so accommodating. "All expenses plus the roof and transportation. My premium is ten grand. Five K now. Five K on delivery."

She blinked. Silence stretched between them.

"There's no bounty on this kid," he finally said. "So I won't be making my usual twenty percent."

"You factored in the roof and car service?" She sounded surprised.

"I won't have power of attorney to bring in this kid, so we could be talking questionable legalities."

And he wasn't the only one who ran the risk of interfering in an active federal agency investigation. She was definitely walking a thin line, but her potential legal troubles were her problem, not his.

Marc leaned forward and clasped his hands. "Let me explain what I do for a living. First off, I'm a free agent. I'm the guy bondsmen and insurance companies call when a criminal defendant defaults on bail. Think of me as a fixer for businesses that are willing to pay a lot of money so they don't lose a hell of a lot more money. I don't get called for defendants who get sprung for a hundred grand. We're talking a minimum bail of six hundred grand and usually upward of two or three million. Bounty is twenty percent. You do the math."

He gave her a chance to calculate, then added, "You're getting the family discount. I was never your cheapest option, so if you want to reconsider, now would be a good time."

He was out of his mother's house already, so he'd get a lift to the airport and hire some nurses or something when he got back to Colorado. Maybe new doctors and therapists would help him get past this plateau he'd hit. Or wouldn't be so tightfisted with the pain medication like his brother the doctor.

Courtney looked like she might be reconsidering, and for one hopeful moment, Marc thought he might get off the hook.

"Are you worth the money?" she asked.

He wouldn't even dignify that question with a response.

She narrowed her gaze but didn't look in the least bit deterred. Her expression grew determined right before his eyes, a fierce combination of snapping gray eyes and pouty lips.

"Let me rephrase that, Marc. Do you think you can find out what happened to Araceli? You've seen the file. I don't want to waste time—mine or yours."

"That's good." Even with his busted leg, he was better than most bounty hunters. But what he found most telling was her question.

Find out what happened to Araceli?

From where he was sitting, she didn't sound as if she held much hope of finding this kid alive. He respected, albeit grudgingly, that her expectations were realistic. That was a plus. He also thought it was interesting she would still entertain spending a chunk of change to unearth what had happened to this kid.

"Clarify something for me, Courtney."

She nodded. "Of course."

"From what I read in that file, you were only assigned this case earlier this year. No one can seriously believe you're responsible for a kid who may have vanished any time in the past eight years. So why are you on administrative leave?"

Her sigh issued through the quiet, a sound that had the ability to bring that quiet to sudden life. Marc could practically feel *her* in that sigh, despair, frustration, fear. Only the two of them existed in the world right now. Him. Her. And the problem that had brought them together.

Bringing her legs up, she wrapped her arms around them until her body was neatly compacted. Resting her chin on her knees, she finally met his gaze.

"Administrative leave is standard procedure whenever there's an active investigation about a case worker. The protocol is in place to protect the department and me and minimize the amount of damage the media can do. It doesn't matter how long I've managed the case or whether the FBI will clear me of responsibility. They will because I haven't done anything negligent, and when they do, the investigation will end. I'll be reinstated and get back to work."

"So what's wrong with enjoying a paid vacation while they figure things out? I want to know why you're willing to drop a lot of money and take so much risk to do what the FBI is already doing."

From his perspective, two plus two wasn't adding up, and for some reason, understanding her reasoning was important. Not that he would necessarily believe her, but he wanted to know.

"I can't sit around waiting." She tucked her knees even

closer, drawing in on herself. "What if you're right and the foster parents are lying? What if they harmed Araceli? What if something happened to that child and people who were supposed to protect her just gave away her name as if she didn't matter?

"Marc." Her voice trembled when she said his name, a plea for understanding. "There were three other kids with that family. Now they've been moved and my caseload has been divvied up among my coworkers. Even my supervisor is in the field, and it isn't as if any one of us had a light caseload to start. How am I supposed to be okay with that?"

She swallowed hard, visibly wrestling her emotion under control, and sounded stronger when she said, "That child has been discovered missing on *my* watch. It doesn't matter that the case hasn't been mine long. It's mine now, and I have to be able to look at myself in the mirror. I can't if I don't do everything in my power to find out what happened. I'll pay your premium if you think you can help me."

Marc had been wrong. There was hope in her, enough to fork over good money and put up with his shit.

For her peace of mind? To clear her conscience? To assuage her guilt for inconveniencing her coworkers? He heard what she said but resisted believing her. Why?

Marc didn't know, but to his surprise, he no longer felt as inconvenienced by the idea of helping. Why? He didn't have an answer for that question, either. Not good. He wasn't invested in Courtney or her problems, but he reacted as if he was.

A sign of emotional instability?

That question had an answer—one he didn't like. He had to get himself back under control. Work was the place to start.

He extended his hand. "I'm worth the money."

Relief softened her heart-shaped face, smoothed away

the frayed edges of her expression. She went from zero to sixty before his eyes, and to his surprise, she didn't shake his hand but propelled forward to hug him.

Her arms slipped around his shoulders, and she gave an impulsive squeeze that exposed him to the full impact of her.

Cool silk hairs tickling his mouth.

Sleek, toned arms tightening around him, close enough so he could feel the soft swell of her breasts.

The feminine scent of her, something faintly floral that reminded him of flowers and river and heat, all New Orleans.

Then just as fast, Courtney sank back, looking as wide-eyed and surprised as he felt. Only she was far more forgiving.

With a sheepish laugh, she said, "Thank you so much, Marc. I completely appreciate your help."

Marc wasn't nearly as forgiving because every muscle in his body galvanized, and the sensation made it hard to catch a breath. He *knew* this feeling. He had also known being around this woman when his defenses were so low would be trouble.

"I need to wrap my head around this." He tapped the folder. "Come back in the morning."

For a moment she only knelt there, still smiling, and his abrupt dismissal only registered in degrees.

"Oh, okay." She hopped up.

He could tell by the way her smile faded she hadn't yet figured out what to make of this change of plans.

Not that they actually had plans. He was winging it. Still, something about her looked injured. Spinning on her heels, she headed toward the door.

And he was treated to the sight of her retreat.

"See you tomorrow," she said softly before pulling the door shut behind her.

Marc wasn't sure how long he sat there, just coming down

off the sight of her. But time passed before he no longer noticed his shallow breaths or his racing pulse. Eventually, his
awareness expanded to include how stiff he felt from sitting
for so long. And the throbbing. He hadn't noticed that for a
while, either, but now the pain was back with a vengeance.

Or had it been happening all along and he hadn't noticed?

Grabbing his cane, he forced himself upright, went to the
bedroom to retrieve his pills. He could start some preliminary research before they kicked in. Maybe he'd even get
some real work done if the pain subsided enough to allow
him to concentrate.

But he couldn't take his pills unless he ate something, or
else he'd feel even worse than he did right now.

"Shit." Slipping the pill bottle into his pocket, he headed
for the kitchen. What were the odds that Courtney kept food
around for unexpected guests? The way his luck had been
running lately… His first glance at the kitchen wasn't promising.

He hadn't noticed that the refrigerator door was ajar because it wasn't plugged in. He scoured the cabinets and didn't
find a damned thing but empty storage canisters, plates and
glassware. He found a drawer filled with silverware. There
was dishwashing soap and dish towels. Oven mitts, too, if he
wanted to cook. The place was a fully equipped hotel. Only
he hadn't thought to shop before checking in.

He flipped the faucet. There was water to go along with
the electricity. He supposed that was something.

Making his way to the bedroom, Marc tried to look at the
bright side. No more stairs and no more noise. He had a
phone. He could call for pizza delivery.

But after searching for the number and placing his order
for an extra-large thin crust with extra jalapenos, Marc
groaned when the retailer asked, "What's the address?"

A few blocks off Rue St. Charles in the Garden District wasn't going to get a pizza delivered any time soon.

"I'll have to call you back." He disconnected.

Waiting until the display cleared, he intended to call Courtney for the address.

Except he didn't have her number.

His phone GPS wouldn't yield a physical address and Courtney's name wasn't listed as public record. The admiral's would be, but Marc couldn't remember the last name.

"Okay," he said aloud then sat at the kitchen table.

Dragging another chair close, he propped up his leg and weighed his options. He could call Harley or his mother. Either of them would have Courtney's number. Or he could hoof it down the driveway to read the street sign and house numbers. Or he could save himself a few steps and knock on Courtney's door and ask her in person.

Marc decided he wasn't *that* hungry.

THE COTTAGE LIGHTS didn't shut off until the wee hours. Courtney knew because she hadn't slept until the wee hours herself. Not that she had slept much then. Those hours between late night and dawn would be better described as fitfully dozing in between dreamlike images of the man currently inhabiting her cottage and nightmare visuals of every horror story she'd ever heard of happening to a child.

So when the sun rose, ending the misery of her restless night, she stood in a hot shower for a long time, determined to sear away all remnants of the previous day and frazzled night to start the morning with a fresh outlook. The shower worked, because for the first time in weeks, she actually felt as if she had some small grip on the situation, some small hope that she might be moving toward getting answers.

Because of Marc.

She wondered if he had fared any better than she had last

night. Were late nights his thing, or had his leg been troubling him? Courtney had no clue, but she did know there was nothing by way of staples in the cottage. So she made a full pot of coffee instead of her usual four cups and rummaged through her fridge to find breakfast. Today was a new day, so they needed to establish a working relationship.

She whipped up an admirable omelet with some random artichokes and an onion, took a few bites, then arranged the rest with the thermos of coffee on a tray and scribbled a note for her neighbors.

A friend of mine is staying in the cottage for a bit. Just wanted to give you a heads-up so you don't worry if you see a strange man there. His name is Marc. I think you'll like him.

Courtney wasn't sure about the last part. Any other DiLeo and she wouldn't be lying. But the truth wouldn't work, either. *I had to provide board to a man in exchange for his help. He's a jerk, so just ignore him.*

The thought made her smile, which proved she was in much better spirits today.

After taping the note to the admiral's front door, where he'd find it when he went to get the newspaper, she retrieved the tray and headed out the back.

She tapped lightly on Marc's door, unsure whether he would be awake, but she could hear him moving around inside almost immediately. His cane rapped on the wooden floor, growing louder until the door opened. He stared down at her in all his morning glory. His hair was damp, curling slightly around his ears and nape, darker than she was used to seeing, making gold-brown eyes seem even darker. He hadn't bothered to shave, but his cheeks were pink from scrubbing above the stubbly line of his jaw.

"Good morning," she said, taking action against the intimacy of the moment. "I thought you might be hungry, so I brought breakfast. Do you like eggs?"

"Feathers would work right now." His voice was gravelly. He hadn't been up long, either. "And coffee, too. Man, you're an angel."

Everything inside Courtney reacted to his praise, a flutter that ran through her from her head to her toes. She'd thought she'd been awake before. She hadn't been. Suddenly, her senses came alive. She could hear the day dawning. An unseen bird singing in the leaves overhead. A pair of squirrels chattering as they raced up a tree by the garden. A car sailing down the street, tires chewing up the dewy asphalt. The scent of Mrs. Ellen's roses on the misty morning air.

And Marc, so masculine and noticeable in a way she didn't want to notice him.

Stepping aside, he allowed her to enter. Courtney steered toward the kitchen, remembering Harley's warning.

I'd tell you to lock your bedroom door and throw away the key so you don't get your heart broken.

At the moment Courtney could certainly see why Harley might worry. None of the DiLeo boys were exactly saints when it came to women. It was just the nature of the beast with really good-looking Italian men. Vince got around less than his brothers because he'd been in medical school, but he'd still brought home his fair share of women for Sunday dinner.

There was a legal pad beside a notebook computer. Judging by the chair arrangement, he'd been seated with his leg propped up.

She set down the tray with a full complement of silver and condiments, and poured coffee into a cup. "I brought sugar, but I didn't have milk. Not even powdered creamer packets. Hope that's okay."

"I drink it black, thanks. Are you eating?" he asked in that husky morning voice as he circled her then sat.

"All yours."

That seemed to please him, because he didn't even ask what was in the omelet even though the caramelized onion and artichoke weren't exactly identifiable. He took a heaping forkful, and his expression transformed.

"Oh, yeah. Thanks." He went for the next bite.

Courtney poured a half cup of coffee for herself. She didn't really need any more caffeine since she was already treading a fine line between excited and jittery, but she did need something to do so she didn't stand there watching him.

Marc didn't appear to want to be stared at, either, because he slid the notebook her way and said between bites, "I was working on today's schedule. Why don't you take a look?"

Gladly. She sat across from him, sipped from her cup and perused the itinerary scrawled on the legal pad.

Therapy.

Shopping.

Office.

No times were listed. She felt deflated, and that small sense of relief she'd had to be taking action vanished. She didn't see how any of the items on his list were going to produce results. "You have a therapy session today?"

He nodded. "That a problem for you?"

Nice of him to ask, since he'd mostly been making demands. "No. Just tell me when and where, and we'll get there."

"Great. We're going to start by establishing a timeline and looking for Judas. That means I'll be spending the morning staring at my computer screen and making phone calls."

"Who's Judas?" She didn't remember seeing the name in Araceli's file.

The way Marc patiently set down the fork made it clear he wasn't used to explaining. There was a bit of drama about the gesture, making it a physical sigh of exasperation. "Judas is any person who will give us information about our kid's situation and her foster parents. I don't know who this person is yet, but that's who we've got to find. If we're lucky, we'll come across someone who'll be happy to run their mouth so we can figure out where we need to start looking. *Judas.*"

"Got it," she said. The approach made sense even if it wasn't what she'd expected. "So we're not going to talk with the Pereas ourselves then?"

"The FBI already did. They claim Jane Doe is the same girl who came back from Atlanta. What's your take on that?"

"It is plausible, I suppose. Araceli had only been with them for two weeks before the evacuations. Then she was in Atlanta for two years, and that amount of time will make a difference on a child at that age. Especially if one isn't well acquainted."

"So you believe them then."

Courtney shook her head. "I don't know. I never had the feeling that anything was going on that shouldn't be, and I'm trained to notice that sort of thing. The kids were fine. Not perfect. These situations are never perfect, but nothing to make me question whether or not they were well cared for."

She shrugged. "The Pereas didn't seem to be anything other than what they claimed to be—longtime foster parents. But someone is hiding something, otherwise why would the girl I thought was Araceli run if she didn't have anything to hide?"

"She obviously knows she's not Araceli. Do you think the Pereas know why she ran? Do you think they lied to the FBI?"

"I'm not saying they're lying, but I think they could also know more than they're admitting."

He gave a snort, then went back to work on the plate. "How is knowing more than they're admitting *not* lying?"

Okay, so she shouldn't sugarcoat the truth with Marc. "Agreed. So what happens after we find Judas?"

"No clue yet. Won't know until I find him."

He wasn't inspiring much confidence that she would get her money's worth, but Courtney was determined not to lose faith. "But you're comfortable with your plan?"

He used his coffee cup to motion at the legal pad. "Got it written down. I'm good with the plan."

They'd already covered therapy, and shopping was self-explanatory, so she went for... "What happens in the office?"

"Research. I've got to figure out who the major players were around this kid, then how to get at them."

"Oh, like addresses and phone numbers. Depending on whom we want to contact, I may be able to get some of that information."

"Through your work contacts?"

She nodded.

"Listen, Courtney. We're going to need to keep that sort of fishing to a minimum. We can't be obvious about what we're doing. It will be counterproductive."

"Then how do we get information?"

"Subtly. We can't always knock on somebody's door and say, 'I'm here to ask you a few questions.' We're not the FBI, and unless I'm wrong, you don't want to be flashing your DCFS badge so the FBI knows you're investigating when you're supposed to be on administrative leave. Do I have that right?"

She nodded, feeling stupider by the moment. Why had she gone out of her way to cook this man breakfast again? For what he charged, he could have had groceries delivered and hired someone to cook. "What if someone offers information in conversation? Is it okay as long as I don't specifically ask?"

"As long as you're not obvious." Marc poured himself more coffee. "Want me to top you off?"

Another glimmer of a civilized man beneath the annoying exterior. There was still hope. "No thanks. I'm good."

He drained the thermos into his own cup. Evidently, he needed the caffeine more than she did. "See those numbers at the bottom of the page? That's my bank account number so you can transfer the money. A check will work, too, but then we'll need to drop by the bank while we're out."

"How about you do the dishes while I transfer your money? Otherwise I'm going to deduct a fee for breakfast."

That made him smile. Just one quick glimpse of a grin that made her realize she hadn't seen him smile much. Not on this visit. Not on the others. But she was struck by how one grin made him seem so much more like his loud, laughing brothers.

"You want them dried, too?"

He was a comedian like his brothers, too.

CHAPTER SEVEN

HIS NAME WAS Kyle Perez. He was almost eighteen and had only been in Nashville for a month. He had come here from New York, where he had been staying with family. Not parents. I found that significant but didn't get too nosy.

After I had given him the Camels for helping me out at the library, he had hung around and asked me how long I'd been drawing on the streets.

Drawing? Papa surely rolled his eyes up in heaven.

But Faffi had given me a thumbs-up behind Kyle's back and shot me a *Go for it!* look.

So Kyle had noticed me in the District, too.

I asked him if that had been why he had helped me out. He told me that had been the *only* reason. And he'd said it with a smile that made a pencil-point dimple in his cheek.

If I'd have been *drawing* him, I'd have emphasized the dimple big-time. And the dark eyes. Eyes so, so dark they were midnight ink, or the velvet-black of the river at night. Eyes that dark might look flat or one-dimensional, but not his. They were reflective, so much so that I knew he was teasing when he'd said, "The Camels were a bonus."

I'd had a good feeling about him that day, so when he showed up across the street from the bike path this afternoon, I wasn't really surprised.

Maybe I should have been. I hadn't been able to move cities since Debbie had gotten sick, so I had moved around *this* city until I had chosen my favorite places to work. Only two—the riverfront park and on Broadway in front of the Western wear store. But I liked to switch it up. Got a little more exposure that way and avoided drawing too much attention from the beat cops during the weekdays when they always assumed I should be in school with the rest of the people my age.

Had Kyle come across me by chance today? A happy chance? Because I was happy to see him, I wasn't going to lie.

Peering over the easel where I had placed my sketchbook, I watched him set his guitar case on the sidewalk and kneel down to unhook the fasteners. I liked how he handled his guitar. With the same sort of respect that I handled my equipment.

The way Papa had taught me.

"You must love this empty paper for its inspiration and endless possibilities...."

Kyle loved his guitar that way. Maybe he thought of the strings as endless possibilities, too. I didn't know, but I was kind of surprised by my curiosity.

I was very curious. He never looked my way, but I sensed that he knew I was here. Maybe I was being fanciful, too alone in my head lately.

But Kyle inspired me today. I stopped working on a street scene—bikers riding on the path along the river with the stadium in the distance. I had been working on atmospheric perspective lately, teaching myself to create interesting effects that didn't jar the eye. I flipped my sketchbook to an empty page, and as the sounds of Kyle's guitar drifted across the busy street to reach my ears, I reached for my best pencil.

I closed my eyes. I had to listen hard to hear his music over the noise of the street—the cars whizzing by with a rush of wind and the grinding of tires, the blast of a horn from down the block, someone's bass making the ground reverberate like an unsteady heartbeat. But beyond all that, the honeyed sounds of Kyle and those strings making music.

When I opened my eyes again, I had my inspiration. I pressed the pencil to paper. He made a handsome subject, standing with his foot braced against the wall behind him, dark head bent low as he coaxed music from those strings.

But I was drawn to his hands, so I sketched the way he cradled that guitar as if it were a part of him. And I sketched for real today. My art. Not my living.

Even from this distance, I could make out his fingers, strong, squared, a little rough around the edges. I didn't know anything at all about guitars, but this one seemed to be a nice one. Not new, I didn't think, but one that fit him comfortably. He seemed to bow around it, the sleek curves of the guitar fitting neatly into the hollows of his body.

I tried to shadow his fingers enough to catch the caramel color of his skin. Perez was obviously Hispanic, but there was something more in his features. His cheekbones were sharp, his jawline cut. His hair was black silk. It looked as if it would be soft to the touch. Whatever it was made me think he was a little different, special even.

I hoped he'd come back another day because I wanted to do a few more sketches of him and work them into my portfolio.

He had a much better afternoon than I did. People passed by his corner, slowing their steps to enjoy the music. Not many stopped, but quite a few tossed money into his open guitar case.

I didn't make out nearly so well. All the long hours of the day, and I'd only sketched two paying customers. Some days were just that way. And I wasn't sorry for the time I had spent sketching my music man across the street.

And I did have twenty bucks to show for my efforts.

I was considering when to start breaking down my pitch

when Kyle finally stopped playing. He collected the money from inside his case and tucked his guitar away carefully. He still hadn't looked my way. I hadn't caught him at it, if he had. But he slung his case over his shoulder. Then he lit a cigarette, took a deep drag and crossed the street.

He was coming to see me. I knew it the instant he hit the crosswalk, sensed it in the way my nerve endings sparked to life. If he had kept walking, I would have felt disappointed. Maybe even stupid.

But he looked all casual, as if he had only just noticed me sitting here, and I quickly flipped a page on my sketchbook, so he wouldn't see what had inspired me all afternoon.

He stopped short at the edge of my pitch—my gallery. I had chalked on the sidewalk a whimsical underwater scene complete with sea life. Fish, sea horses and dolphins. There was also a mermaid gliding through coral, and very cartoon-like anemones in yellows, oranges and pinks that contrasted wildly with the turquoise and green background.

My nod to the river.

"Wow," was all he said, the toes of his scrubby gray Converse sneakers edging the whitecaps I'd drawn as a border. He flicked the ash from his cigarette in the direction opposite my sidewalk art.

Respect. I liked that.

"Looked like you had a profitable afternoon." I smiled. No sense pretending I hadn't noticed him when I'd spent hours glancing his way.

"You do this everywhere you work?"

"Wherever I set up my pitch," I explained. "Marks my turf."

"Does it draw them in?"

I knew who *them* was. Anyone and everyone who would appreciate my art enough to be generous. "It does—the ones who want to be drawn in, anyway. Not everyone does."

He pulled a face like one I might sketch in a caricature. "You get decent business over here. Everyone's riding a bike."

"Not quite everyone." I laughed a little. I'm not sure why, but I was surprised at the way I sounded, somehow more alive. Like when I sketched with a pencil with the exact perfect edge. Not freshly sharpened, but after a bit of use, when I coaxed the graphite to perfection. Of course, a perfect edge only lasted for a few strokes before the point was dull and the whole process started over. Such was life.

"Business is a little slower over here compared to Broadway," I admitted.

"Then why do you come here?"

I shrugged. "So people see my work. Some people walk Broadway so fast they don't see anything when they look down."

"Not the tourists, though, right?"

"No, not the tourists." I gave him that point. "But I don't want to become a fixture."

He considered me for a moment while dragging off his cigarette. A Camel. One of mine, probably.

"I need free Wi-Fi. Can't go over my data plan." He held up his phone. One with a touch screen that appeared to have been dropped a few times, if the cracked display was any indication. "Do you like coffee? There's a place over on Fourth."

For one crazy moment, I stared—it took me that long to figure out whether he had just asked me out.

I didn't want to seem too eager. But I also wasn't stupid. I didn't know Kyle Perez. He could be a trafficker for all I knew, and I had no interest in drugs or sex or getting into any sort of situation that might get out of my control. I have a very good head on my shoulders, Debbie always said.

Still, I didn't feel a threat. I usually trusted my insides, but I couldn't let new people into my life so easily. Not even for coffee.

"What about Mike's?" I offered a compromise. "It's around the corner, and they have free Wi-Fi."

If he was disappointed, he didn't let me see. He flicked the cigarette butt into the street and nodded at my gear. "Sure. Want some help packing up?"

I nodded. And while I folded up my easel, I knew my next sketch of Kyle would be capturing his look of thoughtful approval as he slid my sketches into my portfolio case.

CHAPTER EIGHT

"SEE YOU MONDAY," the physical therapist said.

Marc grunted at the guy, who made a few notations in a chart before taking off.

Fridays were always the worst. Marc tried to work harder to make up for the two-day weekend, even though the therapists claimed the effort was wasted. He kept up with the exercises at home, but they didn't pack the same punch. And none of this effort was moving him closer to regaining control of his life. He had to fight every step of the way. And keep fighting.

Working his way around the table, Marc shifted his leg in increments, unwilling to sacrifice a few pain-free seconds after the massage. As soon as he placed his two-hundred-pound self on this leg, the pain would be back.

He hadn't yet gotten off the table when he saw her. Just a glimpse in his periphery, but he couldn't have missed that heart-shaped face even from a distance.

Her gaze widened in surprise. She had been busted watching him and knew it. To her credit she didn't hide, but stepped into the doorway and approached.

He'd told her from the first that she needed to entertain herself during his therapy sessions. He didn't care what she did, didn't even mind waiting for her to pick him up, but she sure as hell wasn't welcome here. Not when he spent two hours torturing his muscles until the rest of him was trembling and sweating. Not pretty.

Marc wasn't sure why he didn't want Courtney to see him like this. Why did he care what she thought?

"I'm sorry to intrude." She eyed him as if he didn't look much better than he felt.

"What?"

She stood her ground. "My boss called, and we've got some new information. The FBI has a lead on our missing girl. Her foster parents suspected one of the boys she had been seeing was involved with a gang, so they forbade her to see him. They thought she had complied, but now it seems she has been sneaking around behind their backs."

Just what did Courtney consider groundbreaking about this news that couldn't have waited until he got in the car?

"Your boss volunteered all that?" He sounded more doubtful than he intended, but he couldn't seem to let her off the hook. Not when he was still sweaty from exertion, still resentful that she was here before he'd pulled himself together.

"That's why she called."

Marc swung his legs around a lot faster than he should have. Reprieve over. Pain shot up half his body with the effort, and he exhaled hard against the sensation, telling himself he didn't care about Courtney. He dangled his legs over the side of the table, stopping before he lowered to his feet. That show of bravado would have been stupidity.

"A gang," he said. "Am I supposed to be surprised?"

"Guess not." She sounded hurt.

"Shouldn't take Agent Weston too long to track down this kid." He reached for his cane and slid off the table.

This time he braced himself against the pain. And avoided looking at Courtney.

"Listen, Marc," she said. "My boss has had the Pereas in her office a few times. They're trying to get information about the investigation, too. They really seem to care about what happens to this girl. My boss thinks they might be telling the truth—that they may not have known the girl wasn't Araceli."

What was he supposed to do with her boss's opinion?

"I've got to shower." He didn't look back as he worked his way through the obstacle course of the physical therapy center.

The shower didn't do much but clean him up. Every fiber of his being wanted to head home for a nap. He'd been weaning himself off the painkillers so he could think clearly. As a result, he hadn't been sleeping well. But by the time he got to the car, he couldn't bring himself to admit he needed a nap.

Courtney was the variable. Big difference from his brothers running errands or making cracks about how he fell asleep sitting upright. Throw a beautiful woman with dark hair and creamy skin into the equation...

He met her gaze. "Let's go try to catch up with the kids who stayed with the Pereas and Araceli."

"Rosario or Tayshaun?"

"Girls talk more."

Courtney obviously thought better of trying to engage him in conversation as she maneuvered through Friday traffic toward the community center, where a girl who'd once lived with the Pereas assisted in an after-school program as part of her high school work experience classes.

The silence left Marc plenty of time to notice Courtney. The way she studiously avoided looking at him. The way she tried to act comfortable.

He knew better. There was something about sitting together in the quiet that made being alone more intimate.

He noticed everything about her, and could admit to some relief that the physical need for sex was returning. Need signaled healing. But while his body might want sex, his body also made logistics a real problem. And Courtney underfoot reminded him of this double-edged sword.

And he wondered why he was in a crappy mood.

They arrived at the community center to find the playground packed with kids. On swings. Basketball courts. Around picnic tables. Crawling through play yards. Marc reached inside his laptop case for a notebook and press pass that contained his head shot and name of a fake media group.

"I talk," he instructed Courtney as they made their way inside the facility. More slowly than usual, which was saying something. "You smile and look trustworthy."

She rolled her eyes.

They were greeted at the reception desk by a community center supervisor.

"Where can we find Rosario Mantanzas?" Marc asked. "She's an assistant with Brooker Elementary's after-school program."

The guy wasn't thirty, Marc estimated. Dressed in standard camp counselor gear—cargo pants and T-shirt—he wore a lanyard with a whistle and badge around his neck. After frowning at Marc, he slid his gaze toward Courtney, who flashed a gracious smile. Sure enough...*instant credibility*.

"I know Rosario," the supervisor offered. "She has third-graders on the basketball court. Head through the center and out the back doors. Can't miss her."

"Thanks." With Courtney beside him, Marc made his way through the auditorium, where kids sat at long tables. There was a fragile quiet, the kind where all it would take was one good shake before the cork blew. Kids looked up as they passed, earning scowls from the adults who patrolled the perimeter.

"Eyes on homework, please," someone said.

They emerged through the doors and were blasted by noise. Kids talked, laughed, shrieked. In addition to the kids on the basketball court, playing some sort of ball game that didn't remotely resemble basketball, there was a woman who appeared to be in her early twenties and a teenager wearing tight jeans who was most likely their target.

"Find out if she's our girl," Marc said.

Courtney went straight up to the girl in the tight jeans with her hand outstretched. "Hi, we're looking for Rosario."

"I'm Rosario." The girl hesitated before shifting a puzzled gaze between them. "Who are you?"

Marc flashed his press pass. "We're journalists doing an exposé for Hurricane Katrina's anniversary. We've been talking to kids who got separated from parents and guardians during the evacuations. Your name was listed on the Red Cross registry. Mind if we ask a few questions?"

"I didn't get separated," she said quickly. A pretty girl who dressed trendy, she obviously wasn't comfortable talking about the past with strangers.

"According to the records, one of your family did."

"They weren't my *family*." She stepped away to grab a kid who was straying past the confines of the court area.

Okay, he'd hit a tender spot. That was not what he'd been going for.

"No wandering off, Nathanial," Rosario said automatically. "Stay here with us until it's your turn again." Then she glanced back at Marc. "I'm on the clock. I can't take my eyes off these kids. There's only two of us out here and a lot of them."

"We won't be too distracting. Scout's honor."

The girl wasn't buying it. He'd pissed her off with the family comment and made a mental note to come up with another label. Was *foster* family PC?

"We'd really appreciate your help, Rosario." Courtney sat on the bench, seemed to be settling in. "We're writing articles to remind our readers that we need to keep putting safeguards in place, so if we ever have another hurricane, or any natural disaster, kids need to be handled better. We don't want what happened the last time to happen again, if we can help it. Too many kids were separated from their parents and guardians and siblings. Took forever to get everyone back together again, and a lot of people were scared for their loved ones."

Rosario considered her. "Haven't they done something already? You'd think they'd have learned after that big mess."

"I know." Courtney extended her hands in entreaty. "That's why we're writing our articles. Don't get me wrong. A lot of good improvements have been made, but there's still a lot of work to be done. We don't want anyone getting lazy, and you know how easy it is to forget. Time goes by and it's like the hurricane never even happened."

"I don't know anything," Rosario said. "I stayed with everyone I was supposed to. We took a bus to Houston then we took another one to Shreveport. What do you want to know?"

Marc liked how Courtney engaged the girl by asking for help, implying she could make a difference. Well done. So he kept his mouth shut and let Courtney do the talking.

"Just had a question about the kids you were with during the evacuations. The database reported that one of them didn't get on the same bus with you. A girl named Araceli. By any chance do you remember her or what happened?"

Rosario frowned, then was distracted when the ball headed their way, and the kids around her squabbled to get into the action. Marc leaned on his cane, debating whether or not sitting would be worth the effort. He didn't want to get knocked on his ass, which was where he'd land if those kids tripped him.

But the ball headed in another direction, and everyone settled down to watch the game and await their turns.

"Yeah, I remember Araceli," Rosario finally said. "She didn't come with us. Never saw her after that."

"Do you remember why she didn't make the trip? Like who she might have gone with, or anything at all that might help us figure out why so many kids got separated?"

"We had to wait forever for the buses, and everyone was freaking out. We were like the last ones to get on the bus." She cocked her head, silver earrings dangling with the motion. "I don't think there were enough seats, and the bus driver said everyone had to have a seat. Araceli was the last in line, so she had to go with Señor Perea's friends."

Courtney leaned back and hitched an arm over the bench. "So she didn't get a seat because she was in the back of the line."

Rosario frowned. "She didn't stay close to us. Señora Perea was always telling her to keep up or else she would get lost."

"Did your guardians want Araceli to go with their friend?"

"God, no." Rosario shook her head vehemently. "Señora Perea pitched a fit. She wanted us all together. She said Araceli could sit on her lap, but the bus driver said no. *Señor* Perea said we'd all have to get off then, but the people who were getting us on the buses said they didn't have time for us to wait until we found a bus with the right number of seats. They said the other bus was going to the same place."

"But it didn't."

Rosario shrugged. "I don't know what happened. Señora Perea told us Araceli wouldn't come back to live with us until all the repairs were finished on the house. She said they didn't want to move Araceli around too much because she was having trouble settling in. Whatever that meant."

Rosario herself was seventeen now, which meant she was close in age to Araceli.

"How was she having trouble?" Marc asked. "Do you remember anything specific?"

"She didn't talk a lot. That was for sure. Cried at night. I used to hear her because we shared a room."

"Did you like her?" Courtney asked softly.

"At first I was excited another girl was living with us, but she wasn't any fun. She never wanted to do anything. All she did was draw pictures in her notebook and cry at night. I felt kind of bad for her."

"Because she was quiet and shy?"

"Because she couldn't stand up for herself with the boys. They picked on her and made her cry more, if that was even possible."

"Sounds like boys," Courtney agreed. "What did they do?"

"Araceli had this notebook she drew in. But it had other pictures in it, too. Not ones she drew but really good ones. Pictures someone drew of her family I think. Tayshaun got a hold of it one day and ruined some of those drawings with magic markers. He drew mustaches and weird hair. Stuff like that." Rosario inhaled deeply as if the memory still carried weight.

Marc would bet money this kid was sharing the whole reason she still remembered Araceli, a girl who hadn't lived with her a full two weeks so long ago.

"Araceli lost it," Rosario admitted. "I thought she was going to choke to death because she couldn't catch her breath she was crying so hard. I felt so bad. Señora Perea finally had to carry her into the bedroom. Didn't stop the boys from being so horrible, but Señora Perea paid closer attention. I was glad Araceli didn't come back to live in the trailer with us. It wasn't nearly as big as the house. I was glad when I finally got to go live with my grandmother."

"Is that who you live with now?" Courtney asked.

Rosario nodded.

"That's wonderful," Courtney said conspiratorially. "Do

you know that's one of the best parts of my job—meeting lovely young women like you and getting to hear your happy endings."

That got the first hint of a smile. "I'm going to college next year. The community college, but I've got scholarships."

"Congratulations." Courtney clapped for good measure, and Rosario's smile brightened. "Any idea what you want to study?"

"Maybe I'll be a nurse. Then I can always get a job."

"That's really smart. I heard that the health field was the number one field to go into now."

"I know," Rosario agreed. "And I'm really good in science and math. I'm taking trig this semester."

"Good for you. No wonder they're offering you scholarships. Sounds like you have a great plan. Smart girl."

Marc shifted the notebook, and Courtney got the hint. She extended her hand again to Rosario, who took it eagerly. "I wish you all the best, Rosario. You've been really helpful. Thanks so much. Hopefully, we'll raise some awareness."

"I hope so."

Then the ball swept in again, and the kids pounced on it. Marc beat a fast retreat to get out of the way. As fast as he got nowadays.

But Courtney was right on his heels, and they headed back toward the building. "Didn't you want to ask anything else?"

"What's left to ask? God, I love kids. Even the older mouthy ones. No filters. Love it. And you're a natural interrogator. You can do the talking."

Courtney didn't reply as they headed back through the auditorium. But when they emerged into the parking lot, she said, "You must have gotten more from that conversation than I did. All I heard was that we corroborated what the Pereas told the FBI and what's in the Red Cross registry. And that Araceli was unhappy."

Marc nodded. "We've established constancy with the Pereas' behavior. And your friend's opinion by the way. Rosario would rather live with her grandmother, so she didn't strike me as overly loyal to Señor and Señora Perea. I gauge that as an unbiased opinion. They tried to keep their foster kids together and didn't give up Araceli easily."

They arrived at the car, but Marc didn't open the door even though Courtney had already unlocked it. "We know that Araceli was not only having trouble settling into her first foster home, but she might have even had a reason to not want to be there."

Courtney inclined her head, considering. "Got it. Because the boys were harassing her. Most of my kids don't want to be in foster care. They'd rather be at home with their families without all the problems and grief."

"It's another piece of the puzzle. We also learned that someone Araceli cared a great deal about liked to draw."

"Wow, Marc." She gave a small laugh.

"Good job," he said quickly. He didn't want to give her any reasons to smile. Not when her smiles sped up his pulse enough to remind him he couldn't act on the impulse.

But Courtney smiled anyway, and his pulse ramped up.

No surprises here.

CHAPTER NINE

"Do you know you are one hard person to find, Beatriz?"

I recognized Kyle's voice, and glanced over my shoulder to find him standing just outside my pitch—today a brilliant purple-and-gold creation I'd stolen straight from the Disney movie *Tangled*. Perfect to attract kids during the Labor Day festival, where I was painting faces.

Not the most interesting of my commissions, but painting ornate masks made of stars, rainbows and tiger faces on fidgety little kids could be more challenging than anyone might expect. The kids themselves were always so excited.

I waved one last time to little Eri, who now had colorful music notes and a piano keyboard mask from chin to forehead, and thanked her parents for five bucks they'd stuffed in my tip jar. Then I turned my full attention to Kyle.

"Am I?" I asked innocently, but I was intentionally hard to find, even when I didn't want to be.

"I've been looking for you since last night." He was peeved. He didn't come out and say it, but annoyance was all over him. No dimple.

I was not sure what to make of him. We weren't friends, just sort of getting to know each other over common interests. We were street performers. I wasn't sure what to say, so I didn't say anything.

He dropped onto the park bench with a huff and didn't seem to care that I was trying to work. "How is someone supposed to get a hold of you when they want to share good news?"

Okay, the weirdness passed. I got where he was coming from. "You found me. What's up?"

He almost blinded me with his smile. "I got a gig."

For a second, his announcement hung between us, and it was just him and me and his news. The other gazillion people along the riverfront on this sunny Labor Day had vanished.

"A gig? Like a real one?" Dropping my paintbrush into the water cup, I gave him my full attention.

He nodded, trying to look casual when excitement dripped off him like all these little kids getting their faces painted.

"Where?"

"That venue I was telling you about, where I wanted to grab coffee. I've been playing open mic night since I got to town. This week, I premiered my new songs, and management called and asked me if I wanted to open next week's event."

"OMG. That is awesome." I didn't have any hesitation about showing my excitement, so I hopped off my stool and gave him a big hug. "When is it?"

He didn't seem to mind. In fact, his chuckle made me think he liked my hug a lot. "Friday night. I want you to come."

"Tell me when and where."

There would be an admission cost, but I wouldn't miss his first real gig. I'd make out good today. Face painting was always profitable. And he wasn't playing the Grand Ole Opry.

I sat back on my stool again and told him, "I'm not surprised, Kyle. Your music is really great."

He liked that, too. Stretching out his legs, he folded his arms over his chest and tried not to look too proud. "Great, huh? You think so?"

I nodded, not shy about sharing my praise. Generosity was important among artists. Papa believed that with all his heart.

"Creativity is a tough business," he had told me so long ago. *"You have to believe in yourself always. No matter what others say. Take what helps you and throw away the rest. And always be generous with your praise, so it comes back to you."*

"I do." I liked how my words made his smile wider. "You don't play the same sound over and over again in your songs. You would be surprised how many street musicians do. I know because I hear them all day long. But your songs have poetry and feeling and variety. You've got folk with your sound and some rock and some bluegrass. Then there's that one that sounds gospel."

I might be an artist and not a musician, but I had lived in Nashville for a long while. No one could live here and not learn about music. By the time I finished my opinion, he had visibly puffed up. If I was sketching him then, I would have worked with the lines of his brow to coax out that proud expression. Not conceit, just satisfied. As if somewhere deep inside, he'd needed to hear what I said.

That's when I realized something about Kyle. He was new to Nashville. He had his friend he stayed with, a guy he had worked with on some songs while he had been in New York. All the other people he hung out with belonged to his friend. Maybe I was the first person he had chosen since coming here. He was excited and he wanted to share with someone who was his.

We were alike that way. Only I'd been here long enough to have people. I had library friends. My Western-wear-owner friend. I was even on a first-name basis with a few municipal police who walked the downtown beat. No one knew anything about me, and it might not be much of a life, but it was my life. And it was more than Kyle had right now.

He got distracted when a group of teens stopped to admire my sidewalk mural. "This place is hopping."

"Labor Day downtown festival." No surprise there.

"I should have brought my guitar."

I shook my head. "It's a park festival."

"And?"

"No street performing in city parks," I explained because I didn't want to see him get run off. His music moved me, like any good art should. I wasn't just being nice. His music was great.

"What are you doing?"

"I'm a street vendor." I pointed to the seller permit attached to my easel. I had covered it with clear plastic wrap so it wouldn't get wet.

He got off the bench and inspected the permit. "Do I need one of these?"

"I don't think so. I do because I sell my art. It's the only reason I can work in the park."

"Expensive?"

I rolled my eyes. "Like two hundred bucks, but I couldn't be here without one. There are big fines if you get caught." And then the police would want to talk with my legal guardian, which would be a big, *big* problem."

Kyle let the permit fall back into place. "Had no clue. Thought I just needed to pick a place and start playing. It's Nashville, country music capital of the world."

I laughed, guessing he hadn't been a street performer in New York. "We are allowed free expression, but there are rules. If you ever go back to New York, you can play your acoustic guitar but you can't play an electric with an amp. And you have to set up twenty-five feet away from a token booth and not block the escalator or stairs. Those sorts of things."

He was interested. I grew in his opinion just then, and I felt knowledgeable, like I had something useful to share.

"You've been to New York." Not a question.

I nodded. "More places to work in the summer. Not so great in the winter."

"Is that why you came to Nashville?"

I couldn't get too personal with anyone, but I could share my dreams. Those were mine, and I hadn't had anyone to share them with since Debbie. "I'm working my way toward Chicago. I want to go to the Art Institute when I turn eighteen."

He considered that, sat on the bench. "Why don't you just go there now?"

"I've got a steady gig with the Western wear store." Debbie had set up everything before she died, so I could renew my permit and keep working until my eighteenth birthday.

Until I was safe.

"I can't apply until I'm ready to graduate high school, anyway," I added.

"Yeah, I hear that. My grandmother didn't want me to take any time off after graduation. I'm going to college. But right now my music is more important."

I didn't understand that. "You can't do both?"

School was everything. The whole reason Papa had brought Mama here when they found out they would have me. Things hadn't been so easy in Colombia. I would have thought Kyle understood.

He told me he had been born in Puerto Rico and come to the States by way of Greece, where his grandparents lived, then New York where he had some cousins. And Florida, but I didn't know who lived there. He hadn't told me about his parents.

Maybe school was important to me because I had important plans. But Kyle sounded like he had some pretty big plans, too.

"Right now I just want to write songs," he said. "And make money. I'm looking for a real job."

"You making money when you perform? I have no clue what street musicians average, but I can earn anything. Some days I sell nothing. Other days I make a hundred bucks. It's crazy."

"Drawing a bunch of cartoons?"

"They're called *caricatures*."

The dimple made an appearance, which told me he was teasing. "Okay, so you're in Nashville for a while."

"That's the plan. Still have a bunch of classes before I can graduate." I could have been done, but I'd chosen to take advanced placement classes, which were a lot more work.

Debbie had told me to take them because they counted for college credit and were free. She was the queen of free—*had been* the queen of free. I wanted to harden against that pain when I thought of her, but I felt soft inside. Like wet chalk.

"So are you going to come to my gig?"

"Wouldn't miss it," I said. "But you're going to have to tell me where this place is."

"I can show you. What time will you finish working today? They have a coffeehouse at the venue. And a skate park, too, if you're into that."

"A skate park? Is that the church place over on Fourth?"

He looked a little uncomfortable. "Yeah, but it's not too church-y. I've been doing open mic night since I got here. They've got some people who start things off by preaching, but all you have to do is say 'Amen.' No big deal. Since I'm not old enough to get into a bar yet, my options are limited."

"Amen."

He smiled. "You won't have to do anything church-y. I promise."

"I can handle it," I said. "I've been to church before."

"Cool." He stared at me and smiled as if I had given him a present and he wanted to give me one back. "So, you want to go for coffee after work? Then you can tell me how to get a hold of you since you haven't given me your phone number yet."

Emphasis on the *yet.* And even though I'd had tons of practice dodging this kind of personal question, I found myself stupidly unprepared when I admitted, "I don't have a phone."

"Really?"

I shrugged lamely.

"I thought you wouldn't give me your number because you didn't know me."

Even though he thought I was blowing him off, he'd kept coming to find me. I liked that. A lot. And I knew right then that if I'd had a phone number, I would have given it to him.

CHAPTER TEN

COURTNEY FINALLY TRACKED down Araceli's old neighbor. No phone number, but a physical address that was the most recent she could find. She glanced at the time displayed in the lower corner of the notebook computer screen.

11:11 a.m.

"Make a wish," she could hear her mom say her in memory.

They would always stop whatever they were doing, close their eyes and hold their breath. They would wish as hard as they could—and still did if they were together—during this magical time when, for a tiny span of breathless seconds, the world seemed filled with endless possibilities.

Courtney closed her eyes. She held her breath and wished with every ounce of hope from a lifetime of wish-making that two missing young girls would be found alive and not too much worse for wear.

Please, please, please...

Her wish was undeniably a tall order, but when she opened her eyes, the display read 11:12 a.m. The moment had passed. The magic was gone. But her hope rekindled for a while longer.

She glanced over her shoulder at Marc, still seated at the kitchen table poring through printouts from the National Center for Missing & Exploited Children, which had been so instrumental in helping to reunite kids with their families after the hurricane.

Maybe her wish should have been that she wouldn't go all soft inside every time she looked at the man.

Another tall order.

She had hoped that all this time they'd been spending together would make her feel more comfortable around him. She wouldn't have been interested in Marc DiLeo even if her entire world hadn't come crashing down. By all accounts, the man was a player. When he wasn't convalescing, he traveled nonstop with his work. He obviously didn't value family. By *her* account, Marc was a miserable bastard and unnecessarily rude. Demanding, too.

Courtney had learned that firsthand as they worked together day after day from morning until night, researching everyone who had been involved in Araceli's life. There was absolutely no reason why she hadn't already become immune to this man.

If anything, she was *more* aware of him. He couldn't shift around in the chair, take a drink or make a phone call without her pulse speeding up and her gaze riveting to him.

She was desperate. True. She needed Marc to tell her where to look to find the answers she needed about Araceli. Also true. But there was something inexplicably reassuring about his presence that defied every rational explanation.

"I have the most recent address for the neighbor who took in Araceli after her mother was deported." She dragged her gaze to the clock on the wall beyond his head, a distraction from the sight of him. Marc leaned back in the chair and ran a hand through his hair, showcasing his chiseled profile and luring her gaze right back to him. Personality aside, the man was a visual treat. No denying that, whether she liked it or not.

"I thought the utility company didn't have a record of her after the building was condemned."

"They didn't. I tried a few other places."

"Good work." He sounded pleased, but he was hurting, too.

She'd learned to identify the signs. The constant shifting of position. The way he ran his hand through his hair, and the tiny frown lines between his brow deepened. Add the bruised circles around his eyes that suggested he hadn't slept well, and Courtney knew the long hours of searching were taking a toll.

She felt bad, would have felt worse if not for her own struggle not to notice everything about him. "Just another day on the job."

"How's that? You work with foster kids. Shouldn't foster homes be stable environments?"

"They should be, but kids don't usually go into foster care unless they come from *un*stable environments. And even though custodial guardianship may change, kids don't automatically lose contact with their families or loved ones. Except in situations that involve abuse, we try to keep up communication with people who are important. Those families can often lack resources."

A mild understatement. All too many didn't have landlines or even cell phones. Since Courtney was responsible for overseeing communication between her kids and their loved ones, she had no choice but to be creative to keep records as accurate as possible. She generally managed, evidenced by the fact she was on a first-name basis with so many of her kids' schools. She was the go-to girl when administration needed contact information; since addresses and phone numbers changed so fast, families often didn't bother updating emergency cards.

"You're a gold mine for dealing with kids. I'll give you that," Marc admitted. "The National Center for Missing & Exploited Children is turning up solid information."

Everything inside bloomed beneath his praise, at the approval in his voice. A thrill of pleasure, for heaven's sake. A *thrill*.

Courtney should not care what Marc thought. Not about her abilities. Not about her. They were working on a common goal. Of course she would help in whatever way she could.

"Their database and media presence were invaluable after the hurricane." Propping her feet up on the arm of a nearby chair, she forced herself to sound matter-of-fact, unaffected. "I can't tell you how many families they helped reunite. If it wasn't for the NCMEC, I'd still be looking for one of my kids. Jamal wasn't with his foster family during the evacuations. He made it to the convention center in Austin, but Red Cross lost track of him there. NCMEC put his information up, and he contacted me through them."

"Where was he?"

"San Diego. He'd caught up with some acquaintances from the neighborhood and wound up living with them in a donated apartment. I'd have never found him."

Even after all these years, the memories were vivid. Fear hadn't been the worst part, because everyone had known the hurricane would eventually pass. But the powerlessness to control the devastation of peoples' lives had been far worse than the physical effects. Levees and houses could be rebuilt, but peoples' lives weren't always so easy to fix.

Marc embodied that realization. He sat there, uncomfortable from sitting in a way he probably had never noticed before. One incident and his life changed so dramatically. A simple reality with far-reaching consequences.

Was that the conflict she saw in him?

She recognized people who were struggling. "My job can be challenging on a normal day," she admitted. "You have no idea how many kids live with parents and siblings who don't have the same last names. Sometimes parents were never married. Sometimes they divorced and remarried. Sometimes they have kids with different fathers."

People struggling. Many fighting for something better, or just to find some balance, to get back to normal.

Was that what Marc struggled to do? And why, oh, why did she care so much? No matter how much she told herself not to. She shouldn't be interested, shouldn't analyze every tight-lipped revelation, trying to understand him.

Trying to make excuses for his rudeness. Because that's exactly what she was doing, Courtney realized. She was trying to rationalize the man's behavior and find the loving and funny DiLeo center that must be inside him. Why? To make herself feel better about responding to him?

"I deal with people who can afford to hide their paper trail," he said, "so I know what to look for. This… Well, this is different." He scanned the table and the documents spread out there. "We'll go see the old neighbor. I want to hear what she has to say before we tackle Atlanta."

Something in his voice made *tackle* sound physical. Courtney wondered if he was thinking about travel. As far as she knew, he hadn't ventured much past Mama's house since the accident. Now, because of her, he'd not only left his home, but hadn't been back since.

An answer to a prayer? Or had she complicated his life and forced him to struggle harder? She had complicated her own life with her preoccupation with him. That much she knew. But there was more. An urgency to know whether she was helping or hurting Marc with this search, whether she was an answer to a prayer or just one more complication in his struggle.

Why? The question nagged at her. Because she wanted to believe that deep down inside this man's alleged marshmallow center was a part that wanted someone to care about him.

Even though every single thing Courtney had heard about him—had seen with her own eyes—indicated otherwise?

God, she really was lame.

"I think we should go see the neighbor now." Marc stacked printouts and moved them to the edge of the table, completely unaware of her inner turmoil. "Probably stand a good time of catching her since it's the weekend."

"Do you think we have time before dinner?"

Leaning his head back, Marc shot her a sidelong glance that made the turmoil evaporate beneath a physical wave of awareness that had her heart pounding fast. Ugh. *So* lame.

"What dinner?" he asked.

"It's Sunday, Marc. Your mother expects us."

"I didn't commit to dinner."

"It's Sunday, Marc. Your mother expects us," Courtney repeated.

He just stared.

Stubborn? Harley hadn't been kidding. So what broken part of Courtney responded to this ridiculous behavior? *Something* had to be wrong with her. "You haven't seen anyone but Nic all week." And that was only because he'd dropped by under the pretense of discussing the tux fitting to make sure Marc was still alive. "Your mother was nice enough to call with an official invitation."

"She called you. Not me."

"She called you, too, but you haven't picked up her calls. She told me."

"That's because I'm on vacation from family." He gazed at her with those melting eyes, as if he might will her to co-operate. "I don't live around here and haven't for a long time. I'm used to peace and quiet. A week hasn't been enough time to recover from three months of being held hostage."

"Marc." She exhaled his name on a long breath, determined to get a grip on herself. "A vacation, really? I can't imagine what more you could want in a family."

"Quiet would work for starters. I vibrate after ten minutes in that house."

Dragging her feet off the chair arm, she stood and pulled out the paper tray on the printer, buying time, dodging that look on his face that was demanding she understand and promising he wouldn't back down until she did. This man was so used to getting his way. No wonder she was defenseless against him.

"You've got one of the best families," she reminded him. "Not everyone is so lucky."

"Which reminds me..." He let his words trail off until Courtney turned around again. "I haven't seen much of your family. Anything deep and dark you want to confess? I'm curious about why you spend so much time with mine and not your own."

"Deep and dark?" She rolled her eyes. "Um, no. My family happens to be as wonderful as yours. Just a lot quieter."

"Then why don't we go there for dinner?"

Reaching for a ream of paper, she could feel his gaze on her. All the way down to *her* deep, dark places. "I'm dodging my family. Well, most of them. My brother and Harley are onto me."

"You're dodging your family, but you're taking me to task for dodging mine. Do I have that right?"

"Not even close."

His gaze glinted. "How's that?"

"Honestly, Marc." She couldn't hold back an exasperated sigh. Could the man really be this obtuse? And shouldn't that discourage her reactions to him? Nowhere in her life plan did she ever consider becoming involved with a stubborn, rude, obtuse man. "I live here. I'm not just in town for a visit. I've earned the right to dodge them because I'm involved with them all the time."

"How does that make any sense?" He sounded surprised, and Courtney liked that she got a reaction. He was so unmoved most of the time, so distant. Let him see what it felt like to engage for once, since he was so busy sucking her in against her will.

"It makes all the sense in the world. I don't want them worrying about me. Not right now. Everyone has their hands full. Mac and Harley are worried about the baby. My parents are worried about the baby and my grandfather."

"What's wrong with your grandfather?"

"He's old." She set paper into the tray, so grateful for a distraction. "My parents and the housekeeper make sure someone is with him all the time, but he needs more help than they can provide. He doesn't agree, unfortunately, and refuses to let them hire a caregiver."

"Can't blame him. Who wants a babysitter?"

There was so much in such a simple statement. When she faced Marc again, she found his expression inscrutable, as if he'd already shut down and distanced himself from any emotion. Asking for help didn't come easily for many people, especially strong, independent men like her grandfather and Marc DiLeo. She could understand that.

He dismissed her by sitting up and grabbing a notebook. "Tell my mother we're busy and can't make it."

"I'm not lying to your mother. If you don't want to go to dinner, then tell her."

"It's not a lie. We're busy."

"My brother and niece will be there. I'm going. I want to get there early enough to help your mother get dinner on the table. And I've still got to swing by a store to pick up something to bring. I can come back and pick you up after dinner if you want to visit Araceli's old neighbor then."

He didn't reply, but he was no longer so impressed with her, which was fine by Courtney. Any distance between them would be greatly appreciated. She couldn't imagine why he worked so hard to keep his distance from his family, but the problem was all his. That much she knew. What that problem might actually be...well, she didn't have a clue.

And didn't want one. She shouldn't be expending this much energy conflicted and concerned with this man.

After printing out the address and map, she shut down her laptop. If he got in the car, fine. If he didn't get in the car, fine. In fact, she hoped he didn't. She would enjoy a break after spending most of their waking moments together all week.

Courtney liked the idea of a break so much that she ran to her house to freshen up without even saying goodbye. Blessed, quiet moments without the man's gaze on her, without his selfish nonsense, without her thoughts racing as she reacted to every word out of his mouth.

But her break was short-lived. When she reemerged from the house, she found him standing beside the car.

Why wasn't she surprised?

Without a word, she got in the car. So did Marc. He didn't say a word, either. Each second ticked by as if a dare. The ride became a silent power struggle as she drove to the fresh foods market.

Courtney wheeled into a parking space in the busy parking lot and battled the urge to speak. She didn't invite him in, either. He had two legs if he wanted to join her—they worked well enough to make it into the market.

Marc broke first. As she was about to slam shut the car door, he asked, "Will you pick up some flowers and a bag of licorice? The black kind."

She nodded. She'd buy him anything as long as he stayed in the car. He did, and she took her time inside, deliberating on what kind of licorice to buy—prepackaged or bulk kind, which was more expensive. She mentally calculated how many bottles of wine to bring, then debated whether to buy a mix of reds and whites. She settled on five bottles of her favorite red table wine.

Then she headed to the flowers, where she inhaled hot-house roses, and ultimately decided on an autumn bouquet with orange mums, yellow roses and bright purple statice.

And only when she couldn't stall any longer or risk missing dinner, she returned to the car.

Marc had tilted the seat back and rested his head against the door. If not for the way he'd tried to awkwardly stretch out in the confined space, he might look as if he'd be content to wait there all afternoon.

He wanted to miss dinner, of course, and the thought annoyed her, as if she had played right along with his master plan. She continued the silent treatment while situating the bags in the backseat.

"Here, I'll hold the flowers," he said.

She passed him the bouquet, and he glanced at the wrapper. "What'd everything cost?"

That question required a verbal response. No way around it. "Receipt is in one of those bags."

Marc tracked down the receipt and surprised her by stuffing cash in the car console. She'd gotten used to footing the bills lately and wondered why he was suddenly shelling out cash for hostess gifts for the family he didn't want to visit.

Courtney pulled into traffic and ignored him some more, bullying her attention on the neighborhood as she drove past.

New construction coexisted with old all over the city. Lots still sat vacant and overgrown even after all these years since the hurricane. But the terrain didn't hold a candle to the man beside her, staring out the window as if the world passing by had nothing to do with him.

It should have everything to do with him.

What was it about him that made him such an enigma? He was clearly selfish and ungrateful. Any man with a family that cared as much as his did should be thankful. Even her own close family was nothing compared to the DiLeos, who shared life in such big ways, cheering one another on.

They looked out for one another, too. When Anthony built the location for his automotive repair business, he'd shared the wealth by incorporating extra square footage for Damon's martial arts studio and Mama's hair salon.

They'd all rallied around Marc after the accident. Mama and Vince had hopped on a plane. They'd brought him home to ensure he was well cared for. But Marc fought against all that caring as if it was the very last thing in the world he wanted.

What was wrong with this man?

Was he so self-absorbed he didn't realize how many people in the world yearned for a smidgen of the love he took for granted? And how had Mama, probably the most generous person Courtney had ever met, spawned this unappreciative son?

That was a total mystery.

But Mama had apparently missed him during this past week, judging by the way she cornered Marc in the hallway.

"What beautiful flowers." She maneuvered around the bouquet to hug him. "How have you been—oh, Marc, is that what I think it is?"

Courtney hung back and pulled the door shut quietly.

When Mama stepped back, she held the bag of licorice. "I am hiding this bag so I don't have to share."

"No one wants it, Mom," Marc said. "You're the only one who eats the black kind."

"I know you say that, but it always vanishes."

"That's because you eat it by the handful."

Courtney watched them, all her frustration with Marc draining away in the face of the adorable display he and Mama made. These two people cared so much about each other. There was simply no missing it. Mama stretched up on tiptoe to pinch Marc's cheek, and he skillfully deflected all that love at each turn.

"You're my favorite," Mama told him. "But you knew that already, didn't you?"

"Yeah, yeah, yeah." He pulled a face. "Today."

She dragged him down to plant a kiss on his cheek, then winked at Courtney. "Hello, honey. Come on in. Thanks for bringing this one with you."

"Happy to share the wealth."

"More than happy, I'd bet." Mama chuckled. "Dinner won't be long. Hope you're hungry." Motioning Courtney to step around Marc, they preceded him into the kitchen.

"You holding up?" Mama asked.

What did Courtney even say to that? She wondered if Mama referred to the search. But she knew her high-maintenance son better than anyone, surely guessing that he had been running Courtney ragged. "Work's going well."

"Glad to hear that." As soon as they were out of earshot, she whispered, "Hope he's being helpful."

"Wouldn't stand a chance without him."

Mama smiled, obviously pleased. "I'm glad you're here."

Courtney emerged in the kitchen, which was filled to overflowing as usual, and she had no sooner said hello than her niece slid off a bench and broke away from the table, sparkly heels clacking over the floor.

"Toni beans, my little peanut. How are you?" Courtney asked as she was caught in a full bear hug.

"I've been waiting for you. You have to help me and Dad make a plan for the wedding in case Mom can't go."

This beloved child, with a head full of wild red hair like

her mother's, looked so worried that Courtney gave another reassuring squeeze.

"You're right. We need to come up with a plan, so Mom can share in the fun."

"Come on and sit with me and Dad. We've got to plan." Toni caught Courtney by the hand and pulled her toward the table.

She caught sight of Marc watching her from the doorway as she squeezed onto the bench beside her baby brother, another man with sleepless smudges beneath his eyes.

Mac planted a kiss on the top of her head and whispered, "You've been keeping secrets."

"Your wife has too much time on her hands."

"Speaking of," Mama said, coming up behind them, running interference to save Courtney from her brother's scolding, "how is Harley holding up?"

Mac knew exactly what Mama was doing. He narrowed his gaze at Courtney, a promise that they would continue this conversation at another time, then he launched into an update about Harley's condition. There were questions, well wishes and promises for prayers from all around the table.

And above all, so much love. Everyone in the room spread their affection around as if caring transmitted on their smiles, their laughter, their hugs. They could afford to be generous. They were all living their lives filled with…well, *life*.

They were planning weddings and having babies, nurturing loved ones and stretching young wings. They were reveling in the highs and being consoled through lows. Even those who might not want to be consoled were dragged along anyway. Like Marc. Cared about against his will. They were giving and taking and laughing and loving and *living*.

Not Courtney.

As she watched Mama direct traffic to make room for Marc to sit at the end of the table, Courtney was struck by just how much she hadn't been living her life. She had hidden the truth from her brother, and had only reached out to Mama in desperation, a step she'd felt so guilty for taking. She'd been shocked by the way life had come to a crashing halt because she had nothing to fill her days. Because she had been sitting on the sidelines of life, watching the action.

Like the man now seated at the end of the table, the leg stretched out before him only the latest in a long line of excuses to keep everyone at a distance. A man she found herself drawn to against her will.

Was it any wonder?

She wouldn't have believed until this very moment how alike they were.

CHAPTER ELEVEN

"ARE YOU TELLING me you're *not* here to ask about Araceli like those FBI people?"

One look at Blanca Calderone's wizened face, the arched eyebrow over features creased with age, and Marc knew this woman shouldn't be taken lightly.

She might be half his size—four feet nine, maybe ten if she stood up straight. He could have probably exhaled hard and blown her over. He knew she wasn't *that* old, but she hunched as if her frail bones weren't doing the job of holding her up.

But she was sharp.

So Marc had to choose between sticking with his cover story—immigration article—or shooting straight with the lady.

"We're not the FBI," he said. "But we're probably here for the same reason—to find out about the Ruiz-Ortiz family."

She eyed him narrowly. "Why is everyone all of a sudden interested? Those official people wouldn't tell me anything. I mean, something is up. Why else would anyone be asking after all this time? If they wanted me to be straight with them, you'd think they would return the favor."

Marc wondered how forthcoming Mrs. Calderone had been. But however the FBI chose to run its investigation was its business. Courtney should at least be pleased the agent in charge seemed to have finally gotten around to asking about Araceli.

Courtney stood a step behind him in the narrow hallway, her smile—hopefully—lending him credibility so they
weren't lumped in the same category as tight-lipped government agencies. "We're here because Araceli is missing.
We're looking for her."

"I knew something was wrong. Knew it right here." Mrs.
Calderone stretched big-knuckled fingers over her heart.
"I'm sure sorry to hear that. The girl wasn't in any trouble,
was she? Running with a bad boy or into drugs?"

"That's what we're trying to find out."

Courtney leaned in closer and said, "We won't stop looking until we find her, but we really need your help."

Then she sidled up against him until they were side by
side, and her arm pressed against his, a closeness that felt a
lot bigger than an accidental touch. His body came alive, so
starved for attention that he noticed this woman, even when
he shouldn't, impacted against his will. His well-honed self-
control gone. Another unexpected side effect of his new circumstances.

The woman sized up Courtney for a long moment. "Tragedy what happened to that family. Such nice people, raising
their kids right. They should have let that child stay with me.
I told them. She was miserable."

"Who'd you tell?" Marc asked. "And when?"

"Protective Services. When they came to get her. After
her mama was hauled off by Immigration."

"But they didn't listen. They just packed Araceli up and
took her with them, didn't they?" Courtney asked quietly,
apparently familiar with the drill.

The woman nodded, features sharpening in the well-worn
creases of her expression.

"Was that the last time you saw her?" he asked.

Mrs. Calderone shook her head and surprised them by
saying, "Ran into her during the hurricane evacuations."

He could feel Courtney's excitement. Her muscles tensed, and that slight contact between them conveyed so much when she asked, "The Superdome, or another shelter?"

"Superdome. Before the craziness. That poor child begged me to keep her with me. She just wanted to be with familiar people. That's not a crime."

"No, of course it's not," Courtney whispered.

Marc steered these two back to the pertinent again. "Did you let her stay?"

Mrs. Calderone eyed him slyly, as if he was trying to trick her into admitting something that might have repercussions.

"All this happened a very long time ago, so don't worry about consequences," he said.

"We're not the police or the FBI or Immigration," Courtney said in that voice that commiserated. "But we need information to figure out where Araceli might be. She's sixteen, and too many horrible things can happen to a girl that age."

Marc had to give Courtney credit—she didn't miss a beat. She imparted just the right amount of information without tipping her hand. She understood people, read them easily, an ability that made her handy to have beside him.

"You're right about that," Mrs. Calderone finally said, clearly reassured. "Which is why that girl should have gone with her mama. Or I would have gladly kept her with me, and if I thought it would have been in her best interest, I would have hung on to her during all that craziness."

Courtney's expression softened as she watched the older woman. "You didn't think that was best for her?"

"Protective Services already told me there was no way Araceli could stay unless her mama went before the judge and gave permission. I knew Gracielle wouldn't come back. If she had money for that trip, she would have sent a plane ticket for Araceli. That little girl was everything to her. But Immigration just whisked her off. It's a crime what they do, arresting people when they walk out their doors, tearing families apart."

She spread those gnarled hands in entreaty. "Protective Services would just come back and collect her as many times as she turned up. Araceli was going to have to make peace with her new home whether she wanted to or not, so I brought her back. I didn't want her to get lost. People were crazy during that storm. No one was safe. Especially not a little girl. I knew I was doing the right thing, but it broke my heart."

Mrs. Calderone stared up at them, worry clouding those small, bright eyes. "Did I make a mistake? Her family was so good to me. I couldn't live with myself if I didn't make the right choice for that child."

Courtney opened her mouth to reassure the woman, but Marc cut her off at the pass. The doubt was unexpected.

"What makes you think you might have made a mistake?" he asked.

"The FBI people were asking all sorts of questions about whether Araceli looked abused. Would I have brought that child back to people who were abusing her? Honestly. The girl wanted to be with people who loved her. What child wouldn't? But with the way things were during the hurricane…you could feel trouble brewing with so many people crowded together, all worried and scared. I had a hard enough time hanging on to my daughter's children. Not a place for a child alone."

"You didn't make a mistake." Courtney couldn't resist. "You did what was best in that terrible situation and got Araceli to safety."

Which may or may not have been true, according to Rosario and her stories of tears and bullying.

"Did Araceli tell you why she was so unhappy?" he asked.

"She missed her mama and baby brother. She was scared

she would never see them again, and they would forget her. I told her that would never happen. She said that's what her foster people said, too. They really seemed like decent people, and nothing that child told me made me think otherwise."

"What happened when you brought Araceli back to them?"

"They were relieved. They didn't yell at her for running off. I would never have left Araceli if I thought she would be hurt. Protective Services shouldn't have, either."

"They should have protected her." Courtney exhaled raggedly, a sound that filtered through him in the thick air. She visibly withered, seemed to feel the reprimand as if she alone was responsible for this missing kid. She wasn't. But what she knew and what she felt were clearly two different things.

"What can you tell us about Araceli's real family?" Marc wanted more information, wanted to give Courtney something to hang on to right now, something that would erase the tight edges of fear from her face. "We know her father worked on the docks and died in an accident about six months before her mother was reported for working illegally, but we don't know much beyond that. Anything you can tell us might be helpful."

"They were a nice family. Gracielle would help me with my grandchildren. She would bring food or get them to school when I visited the doctor. Silvio took the children out for Halloween every year. I always knew they would be safe with him. He was a good provider. He worked every day to care for his family, and so he could send money home to Colombia."

"He was able to do that on what he made working at the docks?" Marc asked, surprised. Two-plus-two were not adding up.

"He worked the weekends in Jackson Square."

"What did he do there?"

"Drew tourists."

Courtney frowned up at him, and in the split second he saw understanding dawn on her beautiful face. "Mrs. Calderone, do you mean draw, like sketches or caricatures?"

"Caricatures? *Dibujos*." She visibly searched for the word, her creased face twisting with concentration. "Drawings."

"Araceli's father was an artist." The revelation dropped a piece of the puzzle in place. The good sketches in Araceli's sketchbook could have only been her father's. No doubt the kid would have been devastated if they'd been willfully ruined by a bully with a magic marker.

For the first time, Mrs. Calderone smiled, her creased face stretching to reveal smooth-edged teeth. "Wait here."

Backing away from the door on shuffling steps, she vanished into the bowels of the dark apartment. He glanced down to find Courtney staring up at him with those clear eyes. He didn't have a clue what she was thinking, only what he was feeling.

Proximity was getting the better of him, the way the top of her head reached his nose, as if the cool scent of her hair might overtake the mildew in this hallway.

He stared down into her face, the perfection of her features, the expression shadowing those wide eyes, her mouth parted around a breath. They were so close, he could have bent his head, and his mouth would have been on hers.

His body vibrated with that realization.

"Araceli has been gone for years." Courtney's words were a frail whisper that didn't penetrate the dark, dank hallway.

But they penetrated *him*. How long had it been since he'd been with a woman? Too long. And right now, with his insides alive for the first time in so long, the only thing that stopped him from capturing that mouth with his was her distress.

And the realization that a kiss was about all he had in him. Nothing more would happen. He could kiss her. He could cop a feel. He could plow through all the sassy remarks and the demands to play nice with his family. But how could he make love with this busted leg in his way?

Sex?

The idea was a joke. A joke as bad as the rank smell in this hallway.

But Courtney was oblivious to his turmoil, was trapped with some unsettling realizations of her own.

He was such a jerk. She was all torn up about this missing kid, and he was worried about himself.

"Marc, if the Pereas and Mrs. Calderone are telling the truth, and we've got the Red Cross registries to prove Araceli made it to Atlanta, then that means Jane Doe must have been the one to return to New Orleans."

He'd already realized that, but understood why Courtney hadn't. The fact that Araceli may have been missing for years had always been a possibility, the most likely scenario even, but narrowing the time frame of her disappearance didn't leave room for much hope.

Courtney couldn't afford to lose her grip.

And in that moment, Marc understood, as if they were the only two people who knew what it felt like to be robbed of hope. He found himself unable to resist touching her. He slipped an arm around her shoulders and steadied her, gave her a shoulder to rest against, offering all he had to give right now, but taking as much as he gave.

"Don't jump to worst-case scenario," he whispered against her hair, soft against his skin. "All we know is that Araceli made it to Atlanta with the Pereas' friends. We've heard nothing to indicate she was harmed. All we know is we had one unhappy little girl who didn't want to be in foster care."

"You think she may have purposely taken off the way she did to find Mrs. Calderone in the Superdome?"

"I'm saying it's something to consider."

"She was eight years old, Marc. A little girl." Her tortured voice tugged at him. "She could not fend for herself at that age. There's no possible way."

He searched for something to reassure her, *anything* to help her hang on to hope. She felt responsible for this child. Rationality had nothing to do with why. She cared. How had he ever thought she didn't genuinely care for these kids?

"Remember what I said about the unforeseeable luck factor? We have no clue what may have happened in Atlanta."

She trembled against him, a silent shudder that ran the full length of her.

"Luck comes in both the good and bad varieties."

"There's more of the good kind than bad." He needed to believe that, too. For the sake of a child, and far more selfishly, so he had something to hang on to. "We hear about the bad more often because the media's so damned irresponsible. Look at that girl who got nabbed on her way to the bus stop. Everyone thought she was dead for what—sixteen, eighteen years? She turned up alive because she ran into some good people."

Courtney jerked back so fast that he caught himself against the doorjamb unsteadily.

"*Not* the best example," he said quickly. "Sorry. But at least that girl is alive. *That* part's good."

She looked haunted. He was. He was an idiot. So caught up in the feel of her pressed against him that he didn't know what was coming out of his mouth. All he could think about was how right she would feel in his arms. *So right.* "Come on. You're the one who deals with kids. You know better than I do what a kid that age is capable of. They're resilient."

"I know Araceli wasn't thinking about potential consequences. Like what might happen to her in the middle of a hurricane without adults to protect her. She probably was just thinking about how she didn't want to deal with any more bullies who destroyed all her mementos from home."

No argument there. "Then we'll operate on the assumption that whatever happened in Atlanta had the good luck factor."

That there was still hope.

He knew how easily his words could turn out to be a lie.

Then the sound of Mrs. Calderone's slippers shuffling over linoleum, and they looked to this old woman to give them something, some reason to not lose all hope.

The woman reappeared, holding several folded and yellowed pieces of paper that she kept stored in an airtight plastic bag. "So many things were destroyed in the hurricane. Not these scraps of paper. I always thought they must be some kind of sign I would see Gracielle again, so I kept them safe."

Courtney took the squares of paper, neatly folded, a stack of one, two, three, four sheets. She carefully unfolded the first to reveal a pencil sketch of a face.

The striking image was the face of a man who wasn't old. Early thirties, maybe. He had crinkly hair of an indeterminate color, big eyes, a mustache and a stubbled jaw.

"Who is this?" Courtney asked.

"Silvio. Araceli's papa. A good man and a very great artist."

"A self-portrait?" Marc scanned the depicted face. It was more than the effective shading or the balance of the features. Much more than the confident use of lines that came together to bring the image to life.

The true skill was the way all the elements created emotion on the face. Though the man's expression was pensive, something about his eyes made Marc think this was the face of a man who laughed often. A man content with his life.

Marc agreed with Mrs. Calderone. The man who had sketched himself did indeed have talent.

"Silvio drew many pictures, of himself, of Gracielle and their family, of me and my grandbabies, of the dog that hid in our building always waiting for food. Always drawing. He would sit on the front step at night with his drawing book and a pencil while the children played in the street."

Courtney unfolded the next sketch to see a beautiful woman with dark hair and eyes that smiled on the page. Another depicted two young children seated close together on a couch with a book spread across their laps. Araceli and her brother?

"Amazing," Courtney whispered. "How did you get them?"

"I stole a whole folder when the super emptied Gracielle's apartment after she was taken away," Mrs. Calderone said proudly. "I knew only these would matter to her. She wouldn't care about clothes or furniture. Silvio's drawings were all she had left of him. I wanted to give them to Araceli once she was settled, but the hurricane came. The flood destroyed the folder, even my drawings. You find Araceli and tell her I have something that belongs to her, but she must come claim it herself."

Courtney unfolded the final drawing. Not a sketch like the others but a caricature. The cartoon image was of a girl with a ponytail seated in front of an easel with a marker in one hand and a wad of cash in the other. The scenes bordering the girl were easily recognizable—three spires of a church, a statue of a man seated on a horse, an artist's pitch along a gate. Chartres Street or St. Ann or St. Peter...

Jackson Square.

"He was teaching Araceli to draw?" Marc asked.

Mrs. Calderone smiled that toothy smile. "He was an artist. He came from generations of artists in his country. He was very proud. He was teaching his daughter. If Silvio had lived, he would have taught Paolo one day, too. He wanted his children to have an education. That is why he came to America."

Mrs. Calderone smiled fondly. "But Silvio did not want them to lose touch with their roots. When Araceli wanted to play with her friends on Saturdays, she was told her job was to carry on the family tradition. Silvio always said one day she would thank him for teaching her to work hard because she would never starve if she could draw to make people happy."

Courtney glanced up at Marc, disbelief all over her lovely face. But there was hope, too.

He rallied first. "Mrs. Calderone, I can't tell you how helpful you've been."

"Do you think you will find Araceli?"

"We're going to do everything in our power to find her." To Marc's surprise he meant what he said. This search had become about more than proving himself. Sometime since he had started working on this case, when he wasn't paying attention, he had begun to care about what had happened to a little girl whom no one had noticed missing for too long.

And for the woman who cared so much.

COURTNEY WAS GRATEFUL for Marc right now. He rested his head back against the car seat with his eyes closed. He hadn't once spoken since they'd left Mrs. Calderone's neighborhood, but she found his presence reassuring. Alone would have been so much more than she could handle.

He had directed the search, was responsible for every piece of the puzzle they put in place. Sure, she was paying him, but there was a personal cost for him, as well.

She had witnessed the cost earlier. Mrs. Calderone's building had three flights of stairs, and Marc had been forced to climb every single one because the antiquated elevator had been out of service. Mama and Vince might be convinced work was what Marc needed, but Courtney saw the struggle up close and felt guilty.

She hadn't counted on any of the emotional elements of involving Marc in this search. How could she have anticipated being physically attracted to this man? She hadn't even known she was so needy that all Marc had to do was sit there and breathe to make her feel better.

Which begged the question: When had her life dwindled down to days strung together running from one responsibility to the next, busyness masquerading as life? Why hadn't she noticed?

Courtney had lots of answers—none of them good.

Her disengagement from life had been gradual, a series of quick choices that had ultimately led to the monumental place she was now—alone and surprised by how she had let her life slip away. An unexpected end to her engagement. The derailment of her plans for a future that had involved more than work. The hurricane and the aftermath. The rebuilding of systems within the department, which had taken *years* to complete.

The list went on.

And here she was, attracted to a man just as disengaged as she was. An emotionally unavailable man.

"If we go back to your place, I'll sit down and pass out," Marc said without opening his eyes. "I need to clear my head and think. How about a Starbucks?"

"You got it." Would caffeine help clear her head, too?

Courtney headed west, cutting through town and heading to the location on the corner of Magazine and Washington, where there was outdoor seating so he could stretch out his leg.

Fresh air would do them both good, she decided. The heat of the day was winding down, and she needed to get a grip on herself. Her emotions were all over the place. But reining in the way she felt wasn't going to change the reality of six, possibly eight, long years when a beautiful child should have been growing into a young woman. Wasn't going to change the reality of all the time she had wasted in her own life.

But Courtney was responsible for her life choices. Not so for Araceli.

If Jane Doe had returned to New Orleans instead of Araceli, would there have been any reason for Nanette, or the Pereas, to suspect the girl wasn't who she claimed to be? Jane Doe did fit Araceli's description. But had the child who'd returned been a budding artist?

Would anyone have known if she was or wasn't?

Not Protective Services, whose job was to protect, not acquaint themselves with a child's talents.

Not the Pereas, who had welcomed Araceli into their home only briefly before the hurricane forced them all out.

Not Nanette, whose job was to acquaint herself with the child's talents, and protect her and manage her needs—but Nanette hadn't had any time to get to know Araceli, either.

The unforeseen luck factor, as Marc would say. But for Araceli, it had been bad all the way around.

So many variables came into play in this situation. Two weeks in a home wasn't nearly long enough to settle in, let alone establish routines and memories that might ultimately arouse suspicion that Jane Doe wasn't exactly who she said she was.

So the girl they knew only as Jane Doe just stepped into Araceli's situation and took over her life. Jane Doe was complicit—that much seemed obvious.

And she had not managed this switch alone.

The Pereas had entrusted another foster family with Araceli during the evacuations. The only possible explanation Courtney could see involved that interim family keeping up documentation, remaining in contact with Nanette and the Pereas, collecting funds to care for Araceli, then sending Jane Doe back.

Why? Why? Why?

A thousand possible explanations raced through her head, from the unlikely to the horrific.

By the time she crossed Canal Street, she could no longer contain the frenzy inside her.

"Everything comes back to the foster family in Atlanta, doesn't it?" she asked. "You thought the foster parents were responsible from the minute you read Araceli's file, and you were right. Only not the Pereas, but the foster family in Atlanta, the Aguilars."

"That's the most likely explanation, but we don't know that yet. We don't have facts, and until we do, we're speculating." He finally opened his eyes, his molten gaze somber. "You'll only make yourself nuts running through too many possibilities. Emotions fuel your imagination, and that's a dangerous combination when you're worried. The facts will tell the story. Most of the time it's just best to let them."

There was compassion in that advice, hidden beneath a matter-of-factness so easily mistaken for indifference. But that compassion could only be had from understanding. "You have to do this in your work, don't you? Stick with the facts, I mean."

"This case is different from what I do. I track down people who don't think the law applies to them. Most are criminals, or they wouldn't jump bail in the first place. I'm usually killing myself to find them so the trail doesn't get cold."

Then how was he well-versed on the way caring fueled anxiety, and how to counter the effects?

"This case is exactly the opposite," he explained. "We're tracking down people and events from a long time ago, like we're working a cold case. When I'm tracking a skip, my information is usually current, and I'm only interested in my premium."

Was Marc saying he cared about what had happened to Araceli? This man who kept everyone at a distance? Courtney knew little about his life beyond the family he avoided. She knew only bits pieced together through the years, stories heard during family dinners, news shared that kept Marc a part of the family even though he was almost never at Mama's kitchen table.

And Harley had warned that Marc was a charmer. But Courtney had never heard about any long-term relationships. To her knowledge, he had never brought a girlfriend home. From her vantage, he appeared a man of few commitments.

And content that way.

But as Courtney pulled to a stop at an intersection, she remembered the licorice from earlier today, and Mama's response.

A marshmallow center? That's what Harley had said.

"I agree with Mrs. Calderone," Marc said. "What happened to Araceli's family is a tragedy. I can't believe Immigration."

"No easy answers for the situation," she agreed, appreciating a reprieve from her thoughts.

"I don't think the answer is deporting parents. Araceli and her brother are U.S. citizens. All Immigration did was split up a family and give you another kid to deal with."

"Sometimes they're able to send kids back with their parents, but you might be surprised by how many parents don't want that. They'll sign away custodial rights so kids can stay in this country."

"In foster care?"

She nodded, glancing in the side mirror as she merged with traffic on Magazine Street. "If parents can't be sure they'll be able to feed or protect their kids, then foster care seems like a better option. Not all kids wind up in our system, though. Deportation is always a possibility for people here illegally, so some families make arrangements for the kids in case they don't make it home. Friends. Neighbors. I even knew of a situation where parents left their kids in the care of a teacher. If Araceli's mother had made written arrangements, she could have legally left Araceli with Mrs. Calderone."

"Mrs. Calderone didn't sound as if she thought Araceli's mother would have left her."

"Unfortunately, that's the risk she took."

Marc scowled. "I haven't seen this side of you. I thought you were all sunshine and daisies and save the whales."

"What side?"

"The chilly side. Brrr."

"Oh, please." She scoffed, prickled by his opinion. "Dealing with the facts, Marc. Just as you advised."

"Still one pretty piss-poor way to live. Look at Araceli. Leaving kids here seems like a big risk."

"People who come here illegally are gamblers. If they weren't, they would have applied to get into the country legally. They roll the dice because life here is better than what they've leaving behind. They can usually find work and make enough to live and send money home to relatives. Their kids get free educations and health care and whatever special services they may need. What we provide is attractive."

Marc stared out the window as they passed a pristinely

landscaped bed-and-breakfast set back from the street. "I'm surprised. I took you for a crusading liberal who wanted liberty and justice for all."

She wondered why he had formed this impression, chided herself for caring what he thought. *Save the whales. Liberty and justice for all.*

The man was a jerk. Why couldn't she seem to remember that? "I don't think the immigration situation is so simple. I see the reality in my work, and the government can't throw enough money at the problem to fix anything. But they try, which is why we're in the mess we are economically."

His eyes widened in feigned surprise. "A political rant? I shouldn't be surprised with all the district attorneys and council members in your family."

For a man who couldn't remember her name when she had come to see him at Mama's not that long ago, he seemed to know an awful lot about her family. "I am not ranting, thank you very much. The more the government takes on, the more quality of service suffers. And not only in my field, either. But for social workers they cut back funding to the point that doing our jobs properly is nearly impossible. Without sacrificing our entire lives, anyway." Her words ended with a jarring ring that resounded through the confines of the car.

Okay, a rant.

"Guess that answers the question about why you're not married and making babies like everyone else around here," he said. "I wondered why all you do is work."

So, he'd noticed.

"Yeah, that's my life." Stupid flyaway emotions had her heart pounding because he had noticed enough to wonder. Had he seen what she had been avoiding? This man who seemed so skilled at reading people, at understanding their motivations and projecting their action. Courtney shouldn't be surprised, but she was. Surprised he would notice *her* when he had made his reasons for helping with this search crystal clear. Autonomy. Escape. Money.

Or was there more? There was so much about this man she didn't understand. Courtney told herself she didn't want to, either. She had let her life dwindle to next to nothing, but now was not the time to look for quick fixes to the problem. Not with missing kids and FBI investigations and while she was at the mercy of an emotionally unavailable man with some obvious issues of his own.

Thankfully, she was saved from further obsessing when she pulled into the parking lot at Starbucks.

But Marc obviously wasn't through yet. He just sat there after she put the car in Park and shut off the engine. She could feel his gaze on her, intense, and she avoided him by reaching for her purse in the backseat. No doubt she'd be paying for their drinks.

"You work so much because you really care for your kids," he said, a simple statement.

But there was something else in that observation—she wasn't sure what. Pulling her purse into the front seat, she turned to find him watching her. Their gazes met, and she wondered why her caring about kids should surprise him.

But it had. She didn't know why, but she could tell by the way he considered her, as if revising his opinion and not afraid to let her know that she'd risen in his estimation. The stern lines of his mouth softened somehow, and Courtney knew right then that she couldn't afford to glimpse the man behind the surliness and sarcasm, to see another side of Marc. Not when she already was so drawn to him.

So Courtney was extremely grateful when the jangling ringtone of her phone startled the moment. She grabbed it from the console and scrolled through the display to find a text message from Giselle. Four simple words that changed everything.

They found Jane Doe.

CHAPTER TWELVE

"Oh. My. God." I clung to Kyle's belt loop as he led me through the crowded hallway. The Venue was nuts. People crammed wall to wall, rocking out as the last band worked its set.

He blocked for me, like a football player barreling through the crowd, and I hop-skipped behind him, laughing and breathless, protected by his broad shoulders and the guitar case slung across his back.

We burst through the door into the night, and he came to a sharp stop as we cleared the swinging door. It slammed shut with a bang, and the sudden silence was deafening.

"Oh. My. God," I whispered this time, reverent, like when I was in church.

Kyle had crushed his performance. He was a performer, and I hadn't known. He worked the crowd so naturally that people shouted to keep him on stage. But he was cool. He didn't cut into the next band's time. After playing an encore piece, he packed his equipment and cleared the stage. The guys who ran the place were impressed. They caught up with him before the next set was over and invited him back.

Kyle was thrilled. He didn't even bother trying to play it cool, and he laughed, and we danced, and he introduced me to his roommate and their friends.

My ears still rang from the hours of pounding music. We had danced to every set since Kyle's, and dragged our excitement outside to make the night crackle. The air felt cutting and sharp as I caught my breath. Even the stars shimmering against the sky made the dark gleam.

"Man, I don't think I could have asked for tonight to go any better."

"You were awesome," I agreed.

That got a lopsided smile, but Kyle was so happy he hugged me, a full-out hug that crushed what little breath I had left.

I went all fluttery inside, a feeling that seemed to go along with the excitement. Then he laughed again, rocking on his Converse and shoving his hair from his sweaty face until the glossy waves stood on end.

"You know what the best part of tonight was?" he asked in a voice rough from making so much music.

I could think of many best parts. From his success to dancing close to him for the rest of the night. But the excited replies faded as quickly as they'd come to mind. Somehow joking didn't fit the moment, so I only shook my head.

"That you were with me."

We were standing so close that I could feel the heat radiating off him, mingling with my own. I felt flushed and aware of everything in a way I hadn't ever before. It was the night, and I knew it, but when I gazed up into his eyes, the world seemed to vanish, and I could see only him.

He meant what he said. No jokes came to mind this time, because he had put words to how I felt.

"That's your gift," I said softly. "You put feelings into words. That's what makes your music so special."

And him. He was special, too. I might not know him very well, but I *knew*. I had a gift, too.

He lowered his face, and my heart stopped. I thought he might kiss me. But he only rested his forehead against mine and breathed in a broken breath. As if it took lots of strength to *not* kiss me.

Such a sweet gesture.

Mama and Debbie would approve.

I touched his cheek. Rested my fingers against his warm skin, felt the texture of his stubbly cheek.

We didn't need words just then. Being close was enough. His breaths brushing my breaths. Our skin gently touching. I could have stood there forever.

But I knew nothing lasted forever.

The Venue door swung wide. We weren't close enough to be hit, but the appearance of a group broke our moment. Kyle stepped back first, protective as he slid his arm around my waist and led me away.

Another fluttering inside.

We stepped off the curb, and I looked around at the street. "Where are we going?"

"Do you have to head home yet?"

It was late. I could feel it in the air, could sense it in the quiet street. "No."

"Good. I'm so keyed up I'll never sleep. Do you like tea?"

I couldn't honestly say I was a fan, but I didn't want to disappoint him. "I definitely don't need coffee."

That made him laugh. "There's a place down the block. It's open pretty late. I'll get my gear tomorrow. Edwin locked it in the director's office. I'd need his help lugging it home anyway. Unless you can carry an amp or two."

I only smiled, but I could have carried his equipment. I was used to lugging my own junk around. Artists had tools, too, and I noticed he didn't leave his acoustic guitar. I understood.

We walked side by side, talking about the night. The tea place wasn't far, and it had all kinds of weird drinks that I'd never heard of. I let Kyle choose for me. I didn't care. The warm tea felt good on my throat after singing and shouting all night. And I was with Kyle. Nothing could be better.

"So where did you learn how to write music?" I asked when we bypassed a table to sit on a big couch. "You had way more original stuff than I knew, and that's saying a lot since I've heard you play tons of times."

"I took guitar lessons when I lived in Florida. And I belonged to guitar club in school."

"You're very talented with the training you had."

"You know all about that," he said with a grin. "You're an entrepreneur. The youngest one I ever met. The most talented."

"Thank you. That's a big compliment."

"All that stuff on display in the coffee shop was by a local artist. Your stuff is way better."

"Really? Wow." I didn't want to admit that I hadn't paid much attention because all my attention had been on him.

Then he told me about his grandparents in Greece, and how beautiful it was there. A place filled with inspiration. He'd also lived there when he was younger, and had gone back to see his grandparents for a few months after graduation.

But no mention of parents. I found that strange, but didn't question him. Not when it meant I would probably have to answer questions about my own.

"Why'd you come back to the States if it's so great there?"

"The money wasn't working out for me. I was working so much at stupid jobs that I didn't have time for my music. Made sense to come back over to really give my music a go."

"Is that your plan?"

"That's my plan." He was so earnest. "I know I should be practical. I don't like always worrying about money, but if I don't give it a real shot I'll never know if I can do anything with it. I have to at least try."

"I know about dreams." I couldn't tell him about my family or my angel Debbie, but I could tell him about my plans.

"I've been working on my portfolio for two years. As soon as I get a few more semesters completed, I'm applying for a scholarship to the Art Institute in Chicago."

Then I would have a career and earn enough money to find Mama and Paolo and bring them back to the United States.

"I think you're doing that already. You must have had some training."

"I learned from the best artist I ever met when I was young." I had to stop and swallow hard as an image of my laughing papa filled my brain. Images. My gift. "Now I take classes online."

"They have art classes online?"

I nodded. "You would be amazed at how much stuff there is free, online and at community centers, too. Artists want to share what they know. I take classes and workshops all the time." I didn't have any other life. Not since Debbie had died. "And I always learn something. Even if it's what not to do."

He laughed at that. Wrapping his hands around the cup, he shook his head. "I can't believe you don't have a phone or a computer."

"I have what I need. I work my magic with my sketchbooks and pencils."

"And you make money. Face painting. Cartoons—"

"Caricatures."

"You're a registered seller. That's impressive. I have a lot to learn."

"You'll learn." Of that I had no doubt.

The tea place finally closed at one. Weekend hours, I guessed. But when we got back outside, I knew the excitement of the night had finally faded into the mist rolling off the river.

Time to head home.

"So where to?" he asked.

OFFICIAL OPINION POLL

Dear Reader,

Since you are a book enthusiast, we would like to know what you think.

Inside you will find a short Opinion Poll. Please participate in our Poll by sharing your opinion on 3 subjects that are very important to all of us.

To thank you for your participation, we would like to send you **2 FREE BOOKS** and **2 FREE GIFTS**!

Please enjoy them with our compliments.

Sincerely,

Pam Powers

YOUR OPINION POLL
THANK-YOU FREE GIFTS INCLUDE:

▶ **2 HARLEQUIN® SUPERROMANCE® BOOKS**
▶ **2 LOVELY SURPRISE GIFTS**

OFFICIAL OPINION POLL

YOUR OPINION COUNTS!
Please check TRUE or FALSE below to express your opinion about the following statements:

Q1 Do you believe in "true love"?

"TRUE LOVE HAPPENS ONLY ONCE IN A LIFETIME."
○ TRUE
○ FALSE

Q2 Do you think marriage has any value in today's world?

"YOU CAN BE TOTALLY COMMITTED TO SOMEONE WITHOUT BEING MARRIED."
○ TRUE
○ FALSE

Q3 What kind of books do you enjoy?

"A GREAT NOVEL MUST HAVE A HAPPY ENDING."
○ TRUE
○ FALSE

YES! I have placed my sticker in the space provided below. Please send me the **2 FREE** books and **2 FREE** gifts for which I qualify. I understand that I am under no obligation to purchase anything further, as explained on the back of this card.

❑ I prefer the regular-print edition
135/336 HDL F5JY

❑ I prefer the larger-print edition
139/339 HDL F5JY

FIRST NAME

LAST NAME

ADDRESS

APT.#

CITY

STATE/PROV.

ZIP/POSTAL CODE

"To the bus stop on Church Street."

"All right. Let's go." Then we headed to the bus stop, our conversation winding down, just content to be together.

Until we arrived at the bus stop. Kyle started rooting through his wallet for bus money, and my heart stopped.

"You take this bus home, too?" That was a pretty big co-incidence.

"Beatriz," he said patiently. "I'll see you home."

"I appreciate that, but you don't have to. I'm good. Really. I'm only a block away from my stop at the other end."

Of course, just as I said that, some guy shuffled out of a nearby alley. A vagrant.

Kyle rocked back on his heels and folded his arms over his chest, stubborn all over him. "You don't even have a phone to text me and let me know if you make it. I don't mind the ride."

Well, this was new for me. I was usually a master at dodging out of places so I never had to let anyone know where I lived. Not that there were many people interested in knowing.

Maybe that was the problem—I wanted Kyle to know. I wanted to be a normal person on a date. Not someone who always had to hide in the shadows, avoid getting too friendly. Someone who couldn't really live my life. I had become lonely since Debbie.

"You don't want me to know where you live, do you?"

The question hung in the quiet dark for a moment, as if it had a life all its own. More of a life than I had. "It's not that I don't want you to know. I can't."

I wasn't sure if that was the best thing to say, because that explanation invited more questions, but I knew he was really disappointed, maybe confused by all my secrets.

"That doesn't make sense. Why can't you tell me? I'm not letting you hop on a bus at one in the morning. That's crazy."

No, I was crazy. My feelings were wild. One minute I was on top of the world, and the next I felt as if I might burst into tears. The night had been perfect, and I didn't want to see it end. Not like this.

"I'm not like you, Kyle." My voice trembled. "I'm not out of school and on my own. That's all I can say. I really like seeing you, but there are certain things I can't share. If that's not good enough, I understand."

But I didn't. My life was my life and I couldn't risk it for anything. Especially not a boy I'd only just met.

He visibly reined in his emotion, the sharp edges of his expression smoothing out by slow degrees, reminding me, oddly enough, of Papa when Mama would insist that he do something he didn't want to. His cheeks all blustery and his voice loud enough to make Paolo quake under his blanket.

For one moment, I thought I might have won our argument. That he would let me go and accept the limitations on what I could offer as his friend.

Then he reached for my hand, a bittersweet touch, as he twined his fingers through mine. He wasn't going to let me go.

"How about you spend the night at my place? It's pretty close. Edwin will be there, and whoever he drags home after the last set. Definitely Gabriel and Brooks. You can have my bed, and I'll sleep in the living room on the couch. You can leave in the morning. How does that sound?"

As I gazed into his handsome face, considered his compromise and the empty apartment at home, I thought his idea sounded as good as the music I'd heard him play tonight.

CHAPTER THIRTEEN

MARC AWOKE TO a room dark except for an electronic glow visible through a doorway. A computer? He could barely see through eyelids that felt swollen shut, couldn't shake off sleep. Someone had placed a blanket over him.

He tried to roll over, but his leg rebelled, faint spasms that made his muscles shiver and twitch. Not quite to the level of pain, but uncomfortable enough to chase away more of the fog in his head.

The flight to Atlanta. He remembered now. Spasms so bad, he had chowed down on muscle relaxers before the plane had even begun its descent. Too many, obviously. He could barely remember landing, had only the vaguest memory of getting to this hotel.

But even drugged and disoriented, Marc recognized Courtney's silhouette in the silvery glow, her features in profile, beautiful. She had gotten him into this room, had put the blanket over him.

Would life *ever* get back to normal? Would he ever be in a hotel room with a beautiful woman for the only reason he should be in a hotel room with a beautiful woman?

There were countless things he would rather do with this woman than burden her with his problems.

She had offered to drop him off at the terminal, but he had declined. He had refused to make concessions, had been determined to travel the way he had traveled a thousand times before. He remembered the way she had looked at him in the airport, though, remembered her threatening him.

"If you can't make it to the cab, Marc, I'm going to call for a wheelchair right now."

He had made it. Barely. Then must have passed out in the cab.

This was his fault. He'd been weaning himself off all the pills, even the muscle relaxers. He had needed to think clearly, had been trying to take back his life. A joke.

"This is why I'm not working." His voice ground out like jagged glass in the quiet dark, broken like the rest of him.

She glanced up, startled. "I'm so sorry, Marc."

He couldn't walk across an airport to get on a plane, and *she* was sorry. The joke was on him. He glanced around, away from the gaze he couldn't see, but could feel in the dark. Clear gray eyes that saw everything.

She had set his cane against the bedside table. Probably to be considerate, so he could easily get up. He had the absurd urge to kick that cane under the bed. If he couldn't see the damned thing, maybe he wouldn't feel the way he felt right now. As if he wanted to be anywhere in the world but here in a hotel room with this woman who knew what a mess he had become.

"I am sorry," she said again, her gentle whisper tore at the quiet, tore through him.

"Don't be."

She had only asked him to do something he had once been capable of doing.

"We made it, Marc. There wasn't a problem."

Wrong. There was a problem. A big one.

She couldn't let it go. "Are you feeling any better?"

If she wasn't paying a lot of money for the services of someone who couldn't do his damned job anymore, he might feel better. If he had a crystal ball, maybe. If he could see what came next, if he knew when life would get back to normal, he could wait it out. But every time something monumental happened, something *humiliating,* he couldn't be sure life ever would.

"Have the spasms stopped?"

He nodded, and silence settled between them again, drawing his attention to the fact that they were alone in a dark suite, even smaller than the cottage, without the possibility of her escaping across the yard to her big house.

He couldn't get away without her help, couldn't get home, even if he knew where that was anymore. Colorado? New Orleans? This woman knew so much more about him than he wanted her to know. And Courtney, with her bleeding heart, felt sorry.

For him.

All he had needed to do was get to the plane, sit in a seat then get back out again. Not a big deal.

Glancing at the bedside table, he noted the time glowing on a digital green display from the clock. Almost ten.

"I didn't mean to waste the day." He was sorry for that, too. She was shelling out cash left and right, and he wasn't worth it.

Apologies should have been coming easier nowadays. He should be getting used to making excuses for not towing his own weight and burdening everyone who crossed his path.

"The day wasn't a waste." She stood and headed toward him, slim curves backlit by the computer's glow as she crossed the distance between them.

He resisted the urge to reach for his cane and get up, to meet her on common ground in the living room, or at least standing. But the earlier muscle spasms, though faint, were still there, and he would probably fall on his ass. So he cut his losses and lay in bed, as helpless as he could ever remember feeling.

She moved fluidly without making a sound, her lean body graceful in motion. She bypassed the chair near a dresser and sat on the bed. He could make out the worry on her beautiful face, even in the dark.

She handed him a water bottle. "The hotel has room service. Are you hungry?"

"No." Cracking the lid, he took a swig that went a long way toward easing the fuzz in his throat. Now he needed a toothbrush. "What did you do while I was sleeping?"

"Picked up the rental car."

"Great." They could have done that at the airport if he hadn't overdosed on the plane.

"And we know Araceli was enrolled in the Atlanta Public Schools system within a month of the evacuations, but she never attended school the first year she was here."

"Really?"

She nodded. "I spoke with the school and found out a Declaration of Intent form was filed within weeks of when Araceli enrolled."

He did not want to ask, didn't really want an answer. "How do we know all this?"

"I didn't want to waste the day, either."

Such a simple reply. There was no rebuke, no emotion at all. Maybe it was the lack of emotion that felt like a kick to the gut. Courtney didn't want to make him feel bad.

Could he feel any worse?

Setting the water bottle on the bedside table, he mentally braced himself. He had only two choices here—table this conversation because he was too damned pathetic to deal with reality or move past the way he felt. He'd screwed up. Simple. He needed to let it go. Courtney had.

The seconds ticked by in time with the throb of his heart. Finally, he asked, "What's a Declaration of Intent?"

Another simple question, but this one cost.

"Documentation that Araceli's guardians had to file with the Department of Education so they could homeschool her."

"I don't remember reading anything about homeschooling."

She shook her head. "That's because there wasn't anything about it. Not in the court documents. Not in Nanette's notes. In fact, Nanette remarked at the conclusion of each semester that she'd spoken with Mrs. Aguilar and received a progress report about how Araceli was settling into school, her grades, those kinds of things."

The weirdness between them was over. Their conversation moved on, all business again, and somehow the transition felt monumental. Marc didn't understand why, but he ran with it. "Do you think the Aguilars didn't file paperwork with the court, or that Araceli didn't attend school because she *couldn't?*"

"Only the Aguilars can answer that. I don't think it's possible to confirm anything from our end because we were rebuilding our system all that year and well into the next. And to complicate matters, so was the family court. They lost a good bit of their hard-copy storage in the flooding, too."

"Brava, Courtney. You have narrowed down the time frame a lot more."

His eyes had acclimated to the barely there light. Her features were a study of shifting shadows, but he could make out the nuances. The dip of her head as she acknowledged his praise. The quick glimmer of white as a smile played around her mouth.

At least one of them was proud of their actions today.

"That's what I thought, too," she said almost breathlessly. "So I took a page from our compliance officer's book and contacted the photography company. They have no record of Araceli for the first year she was enrolled in Atlanta, which could support that she was homeschooled. But they did have her on file for the second year."

He could hear the breathlessness of her voice, knew whatever she'd learned was big. "And?"

"They faxed me a proof. Not Araceli. Jane Doe."

"Bingo."

Her smiled widened, a quick slice of dazzling whiteness in the dark. "Bingo."

Marc was impressed by her resourcefulness. But there was anger, too. She'd left him to sleep off a drugged drunk while she'd done the job she was paying him to do.

Anger at himself for being so stupid.

She was being completely decent about his screw-up, as if slacking on the job was totally understandable and expected given his physical limitations.

Marc faced another choice. Shut down this conversation because his pride stung. She hadn't waited around for him, but had simply moved on without him. She'd known what to look for and gone after it. But this had nothing to do with him, and on some level he knew it. She hadn't intended to make him feel bad with her competence. Knowing Courtney, she had just wanted to help so he wouldn't feel bad for wasting their time.

"Looks like you've got the time frame down to the year after the hurricane," he said, managing his anger, dismissing it because his anger was his. Courtney didn't deserve it. To do anything else would have wiped the smile from her face. She was proud of her discoveries today and had every right to be. He was not, but that was on him. "You've given us something to work with. We'll go after the Aguilars and the family they stayed with tomorrow. Any thoughts on the school situation?"

He didn't reach for a light, found the darkness consoling, as if light would only reveal his defects and showcase the bed where they sat together. He didn't need *those* reminders right now, either. Not when he'd proven himself so unable, so incapable of doing the job he'd once excelled at.

Shrugging lightly, she drew her legs around and tucked them beneath her. "I think the time frame is strange. The Aguilars enrolled all their foster kids in school, then decided not to send Araceli. Something must have happened within those few weeks to make them change their minds."

"Speculate." She'd earned that right.

"I was just going through Nanette's remarks again to see if anything stood out in light of all this new information. Mrs. Aguilar said the same thing that Mrs. Perea had about Araceli—she was having a hard time adjusting."

"Is that unusual?"

"No. On the contrary. Kids pulled from difficult situations can transition easier at first because they're ending some sort of violence or abuse. Those kids tend to feel relieved. Araceli was pulled from a loving home, and that's a whole different ball game. Her situation would be much harder to accept."

"So she only reacted the way most kids would?"

Courtney nodded. "Given the circumstances, I would have made the same call Nanette did and filed the documentation with the court to allow Araceli to stay in Atlanta. She hadn't yet had time to bond with the Pereas, so staying with the Aguilars made sense considering what awaited her in New Orleans. Temporary housing wasn't pretty. That's exactly why the Aguilars decided not to return. They were going to have to start from scratch no matter where they were. They had family here, so it was easier to put down new roots where they landed."

"What were the chances of Family Services and the judge allowing Araceli to be homeschooled?" Marc tried to wrap his brain around potential motives, to start working again.

"Could that be the reason the Aguilars didn't go through the normal channels—because they thought they might be denied?"

"It's possible, but I don't think so. Mrs. Aguilar had been certified to teach in Puerto Rico. Even though she can't teach here, her education would have been factored into the judge's decision. Mrs. Perea wouldn't have had that much instant credibility. Given Araceli's circumstances, I can't see why a judge would have denied the recommendation. Or at least allowed a specific time period to see how homeschooling would work out. Her progress would have been easily monitored."

"Who does the monitoring?"

"The virtual schoolteacher and Nanette mostly. The judge would review, too."

"So the Aguilars would have been more closely monitored if Araceli had attended virtual school, not less."

"You think they just used homeschooling as an excuse?"

"A lot easier to forge a few report cards than it would be to keep up with online work that teachers and social workers and judges are overseeing."

She faced him, eyes glinting in the dark. "That makes total sense. The Aguilars told the school they were homeschooling Araceli and they told Nanette that Araceli was going to school. The school would have been satisfied with the explanation they had been given, and so would Nanette. The chance of them making contact and catching the fact that they were both operating under different assumptions was pretty slim during those first months after the hurricane."

"And by the time the next school year started, Araceli was back as far as everyone knew." The scenario was not only plausible, but manipulative, using Mrs. Aguilar's background as a teacher. Clever. "What do we know about the Aguilars?"

"I don't know them personally. Neither did Nanette. But

they were foster parents for quite a number of years, so their performance had to be adequate at the minimum."

"Were? Past tense?"

Courtney nodded. "They never came back to New Orleans. Their kids were placed in new homes as they became available. In Araceli's case, she came home once the Pereas were able to inhabit their house again. Or was supposed to."

Marc couldn't fathom why anyone would become a foster parent for any reason. From what he'd read, the money wasn't enough to seriously attract anyone, especially in light of the potential behavior problems.

Why would a person become a foster parent then?

He looked at the woman beside him, hair sluicing over one shoulder, long silky hairs snagged on her arm, barely noticeable in the shadows. No question that people took in kids for too many shitty reasons, but there were probably more who took in kids because, like Courtney, they cared. Special people. The kind of people the media didn't report about because stories about caring, decent people didn't sell newspapers. Courtney was a *special* kind of person, he decided.

A woman who believed in others, the way she had believed in Nanette. He'd read the documentation himself, had become acquainted with the woman who'd originally written the reports, a woman who by all accounts appeared thorough and competent.

But the FBI had assumed otherwise. They had considered her a weak link in the chain and the most obvious target.

Marc understood why the FBI would start their investigation there, why finding Jane Doe seemed more urgent than tracking down Araceli. It was the obvious strategy.

Courtney hadn't been willing to settle for obvious.

Marc had read through Nanette's account of tracking down Araceli through the chaos of a natural disaster and ensuing evacuations. He had a decent read on the situation.

New Orleans was his hometown, and watching the after-shock affect his family... The FEMA trailers. Insurance nightmares. Money hadn't made a difference when there had been a shortage of contractors to repair the damage to a city crippled by the storm. Marc and his brothers had all helped his mother put the house back together.

But Marc hadn't understood. Not from the perspective of kids and their caregivers. Kids lost who were too young to know who they were, let alone the names and addresses of their guardians. Kids plucked off rooftops and highways by helicopters. Kids carted off in opposite directions from their parents and guardians, sometimes shipped states away with total strangers.

He could guess what Courtney's life had been like afterward. Her stories probably weren't much different than Nanette's. Courtney would have detailed her efforts as meticulously, the way she had moved heaven and earth to track down her kids.

She was still tracking down those kids. No matter what the cost, no matter what the risk.

Because she cared so much.

Enough even to make concessions *for him*.

COURTNEY REPLAYED THE voice mail. She listened to Giselle relay the information the FBI had discovered about Jane Doe. A solid connection to the Aguilars, Marc would say. Motive even. Courtney saved the message and stood in front of the window, staring out at the city. Dawn faded, the sun washing the mirrored windows of a nearby office building in silver.

Reality kept chiseling away all her hope at finding Araceli alive. Marc would likely redirect their efforts in the light of this new information. She hoped that redirection wouldn't involve returning to New Orleans immediately.

After witnessing the effects of travel on him yesterday,

she had felt terrible, had been convinced Mama and Vince had been wrong about pushing Marc. How could she think forcing him to work, to physically struggle the way he had during that flight, was the answer to anything?

Guilt had been what prompted her into the rental car to go off in search of answers without Marc. Guilt and the hope of accomplishing something that would bring the speedy end to this search. That was the only way Marc's obligation would end. He certainly wouldn't give up until they had discovered the truth, even if it killed him. And after witnessing the physical effects of Marc's injury yesterday, Courtney feared it might kill something important inside him—his will to keep fighting.

The only thing that had ever been important was finding Araceli. But now, as she stared out at Atlanta in the morning, a city she'd always liked, Courtney had to face another reality.

Marc mattered, too.

Not only for his abilities, but for making her feel as if she wasn't all alone in a situation that felt much bigger than she was. And she had been alone, cut off from her life—Giselle, her coworkers, her kids.

That was her life.

But now she had Marc.

With his matter-of-fact common sense, he'd reminded her that she couldn't control the outcome, shouldn't get ahead of herself. He helped her refocus on the facts and acknowledge that sometimes things weren't fair.

And he kept tackling his own limitations.

She watched him struggle, watched him face down his pride every time he was forced into a situation he couldn't easily maneuver, every time they were forced to make accommodations to deal with his injury.

Courtney knew he would much rather disconnect from

life the way she had and not be forced to test himself until he felt ready. But he had been bullied into helping her, and he did, working impossibly long hours when he could have been taking painkillers and resting, sitting in front of a computer or on the phone when he might have been keeping up with his physical therapy.

He didn't blame her for needing his help, but had come to care about finding Araceli.

He came out of the bedroom, looking recovered from yesterday's trials with his wet hair and unshaven cheeks, determined as he made his way to the breakfast cart that room service had delivered earlier.

"Anything?" he asked in his morning voice, a gravelly sound she knew would eventually disappear with the passage of time and another cup of coffee.

She was getting to know this man so well.

Bracing herself, Courtney met his whiskey gaze. "Our Jane Doe is a girl named Carmela Herrera. She's from Medellín, Colombia, which happens to be where Mr. Aguilar is from."

"She's family." Not a question.

"His niece." Courtney nodded. "You're not surprised."

He arched a dark eyebrow and ran a hand through his hair. "Alien smuggling is big business," Marc said as he reached for the thermos of coffee and poured himself a cup. He sipped, looking thoughtful. "You okay?"

No, she wasn't okay. She suddenly felt raw about a little girl who'd lost everything she loved, a child who had cried herself to sleep every night and had begged a woman she'd cared about to take her home. A child who had been missing for so long, maybe waiting for someone to come find her. And no one had bothered for all these years.

Courtney understood what it felt like to be alone.

But not like Araceli, who had been a child without a

choice, and the reality that someone had simply replaced her felt so overwhelming, her heart was breaking. How could anyone just substitute one child for another as if they were interchangeable?

As if they didn't matter?

"This wasn't premeditated," Marc said with a gentleness to his voice that was unfamiliar, as if he understood. "That much I can tell you. The Aguilars couldn't have planned the bus situation during the evacuations. They couldn't have known the Pereas were going to need them to take one of their kids. They enrolled Araceli in school, which probably means they'd meant to send her like they were sending the other kids. There's a lapse of a good ten months before Jane Doe surfaced. Something happened during those first weeks here in Atlanta."

But reason wasn't going to assuage the way she felt right now, so close to the edge she could only say, "She was only a little girl, Marc."

"Courtney, don't—"

She heard him move toward her and glanced around in time to catch his surprised expression as his arms came around her.

And in that one instant, everything changed. She wasn't surprised by the way his arms felt around her, strong and capable of blocking out the despair that engulfed her. But only by the way she felt so right against him, as if this moment had been inevitable and on some level she'd always known.

Resting her face against his shoulder, Courtney did the only thing she could in that moment. She inhaled the clean scent of his skin, savored the warmth of him through the shirt, the way her nose fit against the curve of his neck.

She felt his surprise disappear in slow degrees, in the way his arms relaxed, the steadying throb of the pulse in his neck, the unexpectedness of his action yielding to the reality of two people so aware of each other.

And he was aware of her. Courtney knew in that moment she wasn't the only one who had been resisting.

Marc was just more skilled at hiding what he felt.

Courtney supposed she had known all along. His actions had revealed what his words had not. The hints had been there—in the small kindnesses that had broken through his aloof manner, the verbal reassurances, the determination to track down Araceli even if it meant traveling when he wasn't ready to.

She had thought he only wanted to finish their search so he could get back to his life. She had thought he had only wanted to get away from his family, and she had provided him with a way to do that. And maybe those had been his only reasons at first.

But small revelations had been slipping through all along, she realized. Tiny cracks in the veneer of distance he wore like armor, small revelations that allowed her to see the real man he didn't share with many. The man his family and Harley had once known, the man who could come to care about Araceli, and care about her enough to bridge the distance between them and wrap his strong arms around her.

She hadn't realized, but maybe she just hadn't been able to admit that she'd known all along. To admit would have threatened the control she had barely held in check.

And she had known that caring for this man would be a bad bet from the start. That much she'd known without any doubt.

She exhaled a sigh that lingered in the stillness between them, a sound of relief and revelation, of inevitability.

One tiny sound that broke the moment between them, ended the exquisite and fragile awareness that was no longer content to remain hidden.

Marc's arms slipped away and he stepped back, his expression closed.

No, there would be no more denial.

The earth had shifted. She knew that by the way he turned away from her, grabbing a cup from the room-service cart so unsteadily that coffee sloshed over the rim, by the all-business tone that suddenly asked, "Did Jane Doe have any clue what happened to Araceli?"

Everything between them would be different now. There would be no more pretending. No more avoidance. They could deny the awareness between them, but they'd only be lying.

"Giselle didn't say, so I'm going to say no. She would have told me if she'd heard anything about Araceli. No question." But what felt even more disappointing was how Marc retreated, distancing himself and getting straight back to business.

The whereabouts of a missing child should have felt more critical than his decision to ignore the awareness between them. Far more critical.

But Courtney couldn't deny the emptiness she felt as she forced herself to blow right past the truth the way Marc had, unwilling to dwell on the feel of their bodies pressed close. There would be nothing more between them but this search. It was for the best. He was fighting hard to regain his life. Marc, once a heartbreaker, would no doubt be a heartbreaker again, and Courtney couldn't lose herself to a man who distanced himself from everyone who loved him. Not when loneliness had taken over her life and she'd been too busy, too foolish, to realize it. She was consumed by the search for Araceli. She was vulnerable right now. Far too vulnerable.

"Then we can scratch the Aguilars off our list. The FBI will be on their way. That's if they didn't already send an agent from the field office here in Atlanta."

"They've got to track the Aguilars down first."

The cup poised at his lips. "You think you tracked them down before the FBI?"

She shrugged lightly, a casual gesture when nothing felt casual anymore. "I know what I had to do to find them, and it took me over a week of dead ends. Mr. and Mrs. Aguilar aren't involved with foster care here. Apparently, they applied and were turned down because they didn't meet the state's criteria. They're off the grid. No government benefits. No subsidized housing. No health-care assistance. All my normal channels were dead ends."

"You tracked them down without the FBI's resources."

Once she might have felt good about that. Right now she only felt overwhelmed and a little scared. "The FBI has made searching for Jane Doe their priority. I don't know what resources they've devoted to tracking down Araceli yet, but the Aguilars have moved four times since they sent their last child back to Louisiana. No utility records since the house all those years ago, which means they've been apartment-hopping. The only way I found them was through Mr. Aguilar's cousin, who has four kids with three different last names and only one in her care. The house she lives in belongs to her boyfriend's mother. I don't care who is doing the looking. It is going to take time to unravel *that*."

"Enough time to give us a chance to get there first if we leave right now?"

Courtney shrugged. "Might be worth a shot."

Marc set down the cup, obviously as eager to put action and distance between them, and said, "Then let's go."

And the search was firmly between them again. Even though Courtney knew this distance between them was for the best, she didn't feel it inside.

CHAPTER FOURTEEN

Normal people probably didn't have heart attacks when they found yellow notices taped to their front doors. I wasn't normal. Not for as long as I could remember, so the sight of that thin sheet of paper made my blood pump and my head dizzy.

I should have known to expect something like this. Today was going to suck no matter what I did.

Reaching for the notice, my hand trembled. *My* hand that controlled a pencil boldly, or a marker, or a paintbrush. It shook as I took the notice from the door, careful not to take paint with the tape.

The words were handwritten, an artistic scrawl. I did not expect that. My heart pounded so hard I could only hear a loud *bump, bump, bump,* so I jumped when a voice said, "Rent check bounced. Where's your aunt?"

Dead, dead, dead.

Spinning toward the person who had caught me unaware, I realized the super had been stalking the floor waiting for someone to come home.

"Working." The strangled sound that came out of my mouth made him look at me weird.

The superintendent was a thick-featured man with an accent who always smelled like booze. Debbie used to say he probably used vodka as aftershave. If I were sketching him, I would have decked him out like Russian mafia, someone who would get the job done with a lead pipe and his beefy hands. Not sure why that image stuck when he never wore anything but dingy T-shirts and jeans that didn't cover his butt. To be fair, he was effective at evicting deadbeat tenants.

Which I was *not*.

But he had startled me, and threw me off. I usually reacted faster, but I didn't like being surprised.

"Your aunt, she's working a lot. I never see her." He waited for me to fill in the blanks.

I shrugged, trying to pull off an act as a stupid kid who didn't know anything, but I was coming across as nervous. He sensed it. I could tell by the way he narrowed his gaze.

"So there's no trouble with the money?" he asked. "You and your aunt, you have it to pay the rent?"

"Yes, yes. I don't know what happened." That much was true. The money was in Debbie's account. I transferred it there myself. "I'll tell her. Something must have happened with the bank. She'll fix it. Can she give you another check?"

He considered me with his googly eyes, deciding if I was trustworthy. Debbie's checks had never bounced before. I didn't know what had happened, but we both knew the bank had already closed.

"If the money is there, I'll tell the bank to put the check through again tomorrow. You owe me thirty dollars for a late fee. If it bounces again, that'll be another thirty. And your bank will charge you a fee every time also. Better to pay the rent on time."

That announcement seemed to make him happy. Misery loves company, Debbie used to say. I agreed.

"Do you want a check for the late fee?" I asked. "My aunt will want to know."

"Cash only."

He would pocket every dime for his trouble. The bank would get another thirty for theirs. Not to mention I'd have to go to an ATM, which would cost me another five bucks unless I went to the bank.

Nothing like wasting my limited resources.

"Okay. I'll tell her. Sorry. I don't know what happened."

He grunted, finally satisfied, and trundled off on his plastic slides. I waited until I heard the stairway door shut behind him before unlocking my door. I didn't bother flipping on the light, just unloaded my backpack on the table.

One glance at the dark apartment and I knew I wouldn't make it through the night obsessing about the rent check. I needed to know what happened, needed to know if someone was onto me and if I should grab my emergency bag and hit the road.

Leaving behind everything I had left of Debbie and our life together.

She'd died six months ago today.

There was no way today wasn't going to suck.

I stared at our living room, with the thrift-store furniture we'd bought after coming to Nashville.

Quirky bedroom lamps. A sofa that might have once belonged to an old lady with cats. It smelled of dust and fur and had been covered with plastic and a ton of tiny pinprick holes. We'd pulled that off and the floral upholstery underneath had been in pretty good shape. Couldn't beat the price, even though the sofa made Debbie sneeze.

No televisions. No telephones. No computers.

That was the rule. Nothing to connect the outside world to our home and risk my return to foster care.

Or send her to jail for helping a runaway.

She had tried so hard to hang on until I turned eighteen, so I wouldn't have to hide anymore.

Because of me, *she'd* had to hide.

I always felt so guilty because of that. She used to call me silly and said God had brought us together to help each other. Since I brought so much love into her life, the little inconveniences and big risks were nothing at all. She thought her leukemia diagnosis only proved it.

"We're all living on God's time," she used to say. *"He gave me the chance to do something worthy with mine since I wasn't going to get a lot of it."*

I was her something worthy.

She was everything to me.

Mother, sister, aunt, friend, teacher, guardian, partner in crime, partner in laughter, partner in prayer, my cheerleader, my manager and my support staff.

Even now, when she'd been gone for six long months, all her careful planning kept life running.

The only thing she had ever asked of me after all she had given was that I would remember she was home with God and being taken care of better than I was. I wasn't supposed to forget that. I could be sad. I could miss her. I could even cry. But I always had to be grateful for the time we'd had together and trust that she was in a good place.

She had been a free spirit and always would be—in this life and the next. She promised to keep her angel eyes on me if she could, and to see me again when I got up there.

We had both hoped that wouldn't be for a long time, so I was on my own until then, trying not to *rock the boat,* as she always said. If I could stay under the radar, I might ride out the next year and a half with a roof over my head and my plans unchanged.

If not…well, a year and a half wasn't that long. God would provide. She'd believed that with her heart and soul.

And I missed her so much it hurt.

Being inside the apartment right now depressed me. Even a trip to a pay phone and an ATM would be a welcome distraction from being alone.

Had I been a normal person, I would have called up a friend and said, "Let's do something."

I would have called Kyle.

Of all the people I knew, he was the one I wanted to be with now. He had started guitar lessons today. Not to learn but to teach. He was so good, the Venue had offered him a deal—teach free guitar lessons one day a week, and get time in the recording studio and free promotion for his performances.

I thought he got a sweet deal, and was dying to know how things went on his first day.

He said once he got in good with the directors, he was going to pitch me. He wanted the Venue to display my work in the coffee shop, like a gallery showing. He kept telling me that my stuff was better than what was hanging there now. He wanted to share his good fortune. That was the kind of boy he was. Generous and kind. I liked that about him.

But I couldn't call Kyle. I couldn't let anyone too close because they always expected normal things, like phone calls or knowing where I lived.

Normal things, and I was not normal.

Having close friends had never been a problem because Debbie and I had had each other, and we'd always been on the move. Until she'd gotten sick and everything changed. Then there'd been doctors' appointments, hospital visits and chemotherapy treatments. We'd been in Nashville ever since.

I steered clear of some hoods from the building behind mine and headed past the chain-link fence that surrounded the apartment complex. The night was dark now. I'd stayed at the library until it had closed at six, then sprang for a cup of coffee at Starbucks, working on a paper until well after eight. Debbie wouldn't approve of me going out now. I knew it, but I also knew I wouldn't be able to sleep until I found out what had gone on with the bank. If I didn't sleep I would lie awake and obsess all night and get nothing done tomorrow.

The streets in this fringe part of downtown weren't too

desolate yet. It was only a few minutes past nine. Debbie and I had taken women's self-defense classes when we'd been in Florida, so I kept my eyes open. I knew how to stay safe, knew what to do if I wasn't.

The pay phone wasn't far from the bank anyway, and I didn't want to draw any more attention from the super. If he watched my place too closely, he'd realize Debbie wasn't there, and then I'd be in trouble. All her careful planning depended on two things—no one noticing I lived alone or that she had died.

She had come up with that plan. It gave her some control. She had lots of faith, but withering away from leukemia wore her down. She didn't care about dying for her, but for me.

I was thankful I'd been able to care for her the way she'd always cared for me.

We had needed each other. I still did.

But, thankfully, one phone call to the automated service with all her passwords solved the mystery.

The stupid bank had frozen all account activity because there'd been a security problem with the ATMs. This had nothing to do with me, and everything to do with the bank. All I had to do was go inside or online to access my account and confirm all my transactions were authentic.

If I'd have had a phone, I would have received their call and avoided this whole mess.

At least they wouldn't charge me for the bounced check on their end. I would still be out thirty bucks to the super, and since my account was frozen, I couldn't even withdraw the money. I could go to the library in the morning, get on-line and take care of everything to reactivate the account.

Which left me nothing to do but head back home, feeling lonelier than ever.

I took off in the direction I'd come, only this time I didn't walk on the sidewalk but in the street. There were hardly any cars and no moon, so I could see who might be coming at me from both sides.

Debbie would have approved of that, at least. And I gazed into the night sky as I walked along, knowing she was among all those stars. Tears blurred my vision as I waved.

I just wished I could see her.

CHAPTER FIFTEEN

COURTNEY SAT IN the rental car, barely recognizing Marc. He sat beside her, stripping off his button-down to reveal the muscle shirt below. His strong arms flexed, and Courtney instinctively leaned against the door to put some distance between them. She'd rented an SUV specifically for the roomy interior, but in the face of those broad shoulders and well-toned chest, this SUV might as well have been her Mini Cooper.

He twisted around to toss his shirt in the backseat, and she glimpsed some inked design through the lightweight fabric of the T-shirt. A sizable tattoo.

Add temporary hair coloring that had turned tawny hair to a muddy brown and a few days of stubble on his cheeks, and Marc DiLeo had become a stranger.

Especially when he pulled a pistol from his laptop case and tucked it into the waistband of his jeans.

"Marc, what are you doing?"

Slanting his gaze her way, he frowned as if he didn't understand the question. "What?"

"You have a gun," she said unnecessarily.

"I'm licensed to carry."

"In Georgia?"

He scowled. "Yes, in Georgia. Did I ever mention my job involves traveling?"

Courtney stared at him, refusing to back down. She hadn't known he carried a gun, but she knew he couldn't be lying about the license. All airlines had strict guidelines that regulated traveling with firearms. Marc would have been arrested and slapped with insanely high fines if he hadn't followed the correct procedure. She hadn't checked a bag, but he had. She had assumed he didn't want to trouble with a carry-on and his cane. She might have assumed wrongly. He had been alone at the baggage counter and could have declared a firearm, and she wouldn't have known.

She didn't know what he was trying to prove, but he'd been so remote ever since their earlier encounter, purposeful as he had urged them out the door to question the Aguilars before the FBI brought them in and turned an important connection in their search into a dead end.

The Aguilars lived in the southern part of the city in a duplex complex not far from the federal penitentiary. There was a window box with bright annuals in the front. Two plastic chairs sat beside the door in a plot of grass as if husband and wife enjoyed sitting outside and conversing with the neighbors. A narrow hedge bordered a low wooden fence, and the Aguilars' home was one of the more well-maintained duplexes, welcoming even, with a wind chime suspended from the shingled overhang.

"Are you sure you want to take *that* with you?" Courtney tried again, but didn't want him to think she was questioning his judgment or freaking out.

But she was. Approaching anyone armed just begged for trouble. A thousand different things could go wrong, and people could wind up hurt or dead.

Marc could wind up dead, and if she didn't die with him, she'd wind up facing Mama and his family. And feeling guilty for the rest of her life because she'd involved this man in her problems when he'd said he wasn't ready to work.

Did he think he had to prove himself?

Everything had changed this morning. She had known it would be impossible to ignore.

But she didn't want him taking unnecessary risks. She didn't know if threatening the Aguilars with a gun would officially turn their private search into obstruction of an investigation.

Could the FBI prosecute them?

Marc obviously wasn't thinking. If he was, she wouldn't have had to explain the potential consequences of approaching anyone—particularly someone they didn't know—with a weapon.

She attempted reason. "You're going to antagonize these people, and they won't help us."

He inhaled, the sound of painstaking patience. "I'm not looking for help. I'm looking for information. I won't intimidate anyone with my cane. Not unless I beat them. You would rather I start a fight?"

"Of course I don't want you to fight."

"Then let me do my job."

He *was* trying to prove himself. Somewhere between yesterday's difficulties on the flight and this morning's embrace, Marc had decided to come out swinging, and they were all going to suffer the consequences.

Courtney. The Aguilars. Araceli.

"You're clear on what you need to do, right?" he asked.

"Keep the windows up and the car idling. Keep my sunglasses and hat on in case anyone comes close enough to see through the windows," she repeated his exact instructions.

Not freak out because he had a gun.

"Keep the doors locked until I get back."

"Marc, this isn't smart."

His eyes fluttered shut for a brief instant. "You are paying me good money to do my job. Will you please trust me?"

He didn't wait for her reply, just reached for the door handle and flashed a grin in profile. "Duck if you hear shots."

The man was *so* not funny. Breath trapped in her throat, she watched him maneuver out of the seat and shut the door—and made out his tattoo as he pulled on a leather jacket.

Christ hung on a crucifix between his shoulder blades.

Jesus and a gun? Who was this man?

Locking the car, she slipped on her sunglasses and tried not to panic as Marc opened the gate and made his way down the concrete path to the door.

He was definitely steadier on his feet today. She didn't know what it cost him to put on such a show, but he moved along at a fair clip, not giving the impression of someone who had recently had to drug himself to walk through an airport.

She studied Marc to see what a stranger might see. The man who looked so much like his brothers suddenly looked the part of street thug, who could have been involved in a multitude of unsavory situations that could result in the use of a cane.

God, she hoped nothing went wrong.

A man with salt-and-pepper hair opened the door, early sixties maybe—Mr. Aguilar? She couldn't be sure. He and his wife had been assigned to another coworker for the years they had been foster parents. The Aguilars had been adequate guardians with no reports or inquiries against them.

Courtney had to wonder if Nanette would have been sitting here while the armed bounty hunter she'd hired interrogated a foster parent. Would Nanette have risked her family to take action, or would she have waited for the FBI to conduct their play-by-play investigation?

Courtney risked only herself.

And the man she was responsible for involving.

The man with the gun.

She willed herself to take deep breaths, to manage the anxiety making it hard to sit still. The two men conversed back and forth rapidly. Courtney couldn't hear what they said, but their actions revealed the tone of the encounter, a muted performance. Mr. Aguilar's expression morphed from a blank stare to irritation before the man visibly blanched. His features were suddenly stark as he stepped through the door and pulled it shut behind him as if not wanting whoever was inside to overhear.

Marc lifted his jacket, presumably to reveal the gun.

Mr. Aguilar's motions grew urgent. She clenched the steering wheel until her knuckles were white. Her mind played a looping litany.

Don't get killed. Don't get killed. Don't get killed.

The reality of the situation she'd placed everyone in hit hard. She was responsible if anything went wrong because she couldn't wait for the FBI to do its job.

She'd chosen instead to consult with Marc, who should have been distant, *safe.* And would have been if not for Mama, who had pushed the situation beyond Courtney's control.

And yet she had gone along with the plan, so desperate, until Marc was off proving himself *with a gun...* And she cared what happened to him.

Then the confrontation ended.

With one anticlimactic breath, Courtney watched him motion to the car with his cane. She watched Mr. Aguilar shake his head, then duck back into his house so fast he stumbled on the step.

She had no idea what had transpired. All she knew was that the relief flooding through her as he walked back to the car was so intense it left her weak. With effort, she reached for the door locks, depressed the button, then put the car in gear as Marc climbed in.

"Go." His command filtered through her heightened anxiety and kick-started the adrenaline again.

Courtney drove.

Marc smiled.

And relief melted away to reveal anger simmering below the surface, as unbidden and unexpected as everything that had been happening in her life lately, as out of control.

"That was reckless and uncalled for." She should have blasted him backward with her hostility, but he didn't flinch.

"What?"

"The gun, Marc. Confronting that man armed. Jeopardizing yourself. That old man. Anyone within range. Me. *Araceli.* If the situation had gotten out of hand, we might never find out what happened to her."

He didn't say she was overreacting. He didn't say anything. The way he just calmly shrugged out of his jacket and reached into the backseat for his shirt spoke volumes.

"Sorry I scared you."

That only made her angrier. "This isn't about me being scared."

He arched an eyebrow.

Or was it?

She felt wildly out of control, so caught up that she still sat at an intersection after the light had turned green. The car behind her beeped its horn, startled her into action. She gunned the engine, and they took off.

"I'm not law enforcement, Courtney," he finally said. "Burden of proof is not my problem. I find people, and I need information to do that."

His tone brought her around to glance at him. His expression was stoic, distant. She'd offended him.

"You hired me to do a job. You should trust me to do it."

She wanted to ask if he'd gotten what he needed, but she was still too rattled to back down, too emotional.

Because he was right.

She hadn't trusted him to do his job, hadn't trusted his judgment or his abilities.

FOR ONE STELLAR MOMENT, Marc had been normal again. As he'd engaged Aguilar, he'd been caught up in the chase, tuned in to the man's surprise, his fear.

And for that moment, he had felt back in control. Of the situation. Of the future. Of himself.

Marc had gotten what he'd gone for, but withheld the information. He wouldn't spill until Courtney asked. She wasn't stupid enough to think Señor Aguilar would volunteer what he knew about Araceli, but the weapon had spooked her.

No, not the weapon.

Him having the weapon.

She thought some old man would knock him on his ass and take his Ruger, and she'd get caught in the cross fire.

Had she been wrong?

No one could miss Marc limping along with his cane. No one would overlook such an obvious vulnerable point. Any confrontation would have wound up with his opponent going straight for his weak spot, and Marc would have been on the ground, scrambling to get on his feet again. Unable to even get up without something to hang on to. A cane. A fence. A helping hand.

Anyone could have laid him low.

Even the old man.

That was reality. Marc had known it. That was why he'd gone in with his weapon.

He'd taken a risk. Courtney was right there. The way he'd worked six months ago wasn't the way he could operate now.

Six months ago he wouldn't have considered packing to question an old man.

But Marc was a liability now.

Courtney knew it. Had been scared.

Marc closed his eyes. He could block out the city whizzing past in a blur, but he couldn't escape the way the future stretched before him as blurry as the passing landscape, every second marked by the reality that he may never again function normally. Could life the way he had lived it be over? He hadn't considered that before. Hadn't allowed himself to.

What if it was? What would come next?

He didn't have a clue. The only thing that felt normal right now was the pain. Not the Ruger tucked against his waist. Not when it suddenly felt too important, too necessary.

Not the woman seated beside him. She was the whole reason he felt this way right now. Her problems.

And his family. They were responsible, too.

Not a damned one knew what was involved in his work. Not a one. Yet they'd pushed him, and he'd allowed himself to be goaded into attempting what he wasn't ready to attempt. Some pathetic part of him wanted to rise to the occasion and show them all, to prove to himself he wasn't as pathetic as he felt.

But Marc was pathetic, even more so because he couldn't accept reality, clung to a desperate hope.

No different than Courtney.

She had driven them back to the hotel, obviously realizing he needed to costume-change before he could interrogate anyone else. He didn't think he'd need to visit the Aguilar family anymore, which left the church people. He shouldn't need a gun to get information from people who spent this life trying to work their way into the next. That should please Courtney.

She looked stoic when pulling through the circular drive at the lobby entrance. Bringing the car to a stop, she said,

"You go up. I'll park in the guest lot so we don't have to valet."

Another concession.

Rage warred with the relief at not having to walk all the way around the hotel. He'd already pushed his leg to the limit by trying not to look like the cripple he was.

And he still had to get to the fifth floor, and their suite was not close to the elevator. He could not afford a repeat performance of Monday. Right now he needed to accept the limitations that defined his reality and deal with them. Period.

Marc made his way upstairs and straight into a shower. He stood beneath scalding water and didn't move again until the constant pounding on his leg finally loosened up the muscles. Only then did he turn off the spray and get out, the heat soaking away the strain in his muscles and his head. He felt capable again, less rebellious.

Until he came face-to-face with Courtney.

She stood in the living room, visible through the doorway as he emerged from the steamy bathroom. Suddenly, all he could hear were her stupid questions.

"Are you sure you want to take that with you?"

She should have been asking him whether or not his busted ass was up to interrogating anyone. If he wanted her to protect him from the big bad old man.

Suddenly everything about her was a dare.

From the glossy black hair that would feel like silk to the touch to the clear eyes she raked down the length of him.

He stood wrapped in a towel.

Her gaze traveled over him again, surprise all over her face, widening her eyes, parting her lips.

But she didn't look away. She only stood there for a protracted moment, a deer stunned by headlights, and by the time she'd rallied, mumbling something unintelligible and turning away, it was too late.

Marc had seen everything.

This felt normal. A beautiful woman looking at him like he was a man, with want in her eyes.

Yet she turned away, and that action only proved she didn't think he could perform any better than he had at his job.

His Ruger couldn't protect him from that failure.

"You were wrong about me." His sharp words were a slap to the quiet.

She turned back, surprised, no less than he was because he couldn't stop. Anger ripped through him like an explosion, blasting out of his mouth in a hot accusation.

"You could at least admit you were wrong to go along with my family. You asked for my help, and I turned you down. You should have taken me at my word. You should own it."

More slaps. Only these landed.

She looked so vulnerable standing there. Every inch of her raw with guilt. Every slim curve making him raw, reminding him that he was a man who couldn't do anything anymore.

Even be a man.

He was acting like an asshole. He knew it, but he couldn't stop. Not when she was as aware of him as he was of her.

But she'd turned away.

He was so tired of fighting for something he couldn't achieve, tired of fighting the truth of what a joke he had become.

"I'm so sorry." Her voice was a broken whisper between them, a sound that tore at the quiet, *at him*.

Her gaze pierced the distance, clear eyes glinting moistly, sobering him in one brutal instant.

More reality.

This was about him. All about him. Not her.

"Hey, hey." He sounded as broken as she had. He covered the distance between them in a few halting steps. "No, I'm wrong."

She gazed up at him, so close, and her tears made her eyes sparkle like diamonds. And just to prove that he was a busted, useless idiot, Marc did the stupidest thing he possibly could.

He touched her.

Slipping his hands on her arms, he gave her a slight shake. "Don't."

His voice was a plea. He hated everything about himself. He couldn't handle hating himself because he'd hurt her, too.

Tipping her head back, she gazed up at him with shining eyes. And everything vanished, everything but her parted lips and her surprised breaths.

That awareness in her exquisite face.

The want.

Somehow all the frustrations and fears, the recriminations and regrets, vanished. Feelings gave way beneath a purely physical need, awareness that he was standing close to a beautiful woman who wanted him.

There was no thought when he lowered his mouth to hers.

Their lips met, a glance of soft skin to skin, and her delicate sigh. He tested her response, the way her mouth yielded beneath his, the mingling of their breaths, in sync.

She trembled, so slightly he would have missed it had he not still been holding her, but he clung to her, poised between testing and taking, so unsure.

Courtney's hands fluttered between them, as if she, too, hadn't committed to any course.

Push him away? Pull him close?

The moment was torture.

Then her hands glided over his chest, just a whisper of a

touch, and her fingers slid into the curve of his neck, coaxed him closer as she leaned up on tiptoes to deepen their kiss.

Then there was nothing but fire inside him, the knowledge he was still a man who could make a woman want.

COURTNEY KNEW MARC had something to prove. He was a child trying to provoke her, a man whose pride had taken a beating. He wasn't interested in her. Not really. She was just a convenient target to inflate his confidence, to appease his masculinity.

She should have shut him down.

But there'd been something in his anger, something she had never seen before.

And it was that glimpse of *something* that drew her closer, made it impossible not to kiss him back, to explore this awareness even though it made no sense whatsoever.

She didn't want to like Marc or understand what drove him. He had way too much baggage for her to deal with. She was at a difficult crossroads in her own life. She was out of sorts and vulnerable to someone she didn't trust herself to be vulnerable with.

But the feel of his mouth on hers vanquished that horrible loneliness. His broad, broad shoulders blocked out the world. Courtney couldn't deny him or herself in that moment. Not even if it meant they would have to face each other awkwardly across Mama's dinner table for the rest of their lives.

He didn't come to town that often anyway.

Why shouldn't they give in? They were both adults, both needy right now. For entirely different reasons maybe, yet their need was still the same.

To be together.

That was all the rationalization she needed.

Courtney stopped resisting.

Leaning into their kiss, she swept her tongue through his

warm mouth, explored the taste of this man who should be nothing to her but was suddenly everything.

He tasted of boldness and intensity, a man with so much simmering beneath the surface. And now with the freedom to touch… Skimming her fingers along his throat, she traced the hard line of his jaw, the cheekbones, the skin around his eyes, his brow.

His laughter burst softly against her mouth, but he never stopped kissing her. Sliding an arm around her waist, he locked her against him, and she melted a little inside at the feel of his hard body, all that muscled strength. She was surprised by how neatly they aligned when he was so much taller.

But with her head tipped back, her mouth slanted beneath his, the world narrowed down to the breadth of his shoulders, the heat of his bare skin. The way his fingers slid into her hair until he cupped her head, maneuvered her closer, enticed her mouth wider with his tongue, their passion exchanged on each breath, each sigh that broke against his lips.

Longing sizzled between them. Like everything else about this man, his passion was intense, evoking exactly the same response. Her body grew molten with anticipation, with the promise of discovery.

There was no will to resist, only to yield, to shed all inhibitions, rationality and anything else that might seem like sanity outside this hotel room.

She cared only about right now.

Running her hands along his arms, Courtney explored the strength of his biceps, dragged her palms down the hard lines of his back. The towel clung moistly to his hips, daring her to touch. So she did. She pressed him close, nestled his hardness against her tummy.

His groan broke against her lips, a ragged sound, then suddenly he was in motion, dragging her toward the bed, tempting and teasing her with half kisses because their stumbling steps didn't allow for anything more. She clung to him eagerly, helping to balance them as they covered the distance. His steps awkward. Her legs nearly liquid beneath her.

Her pulse raced hard with excitement as she tugged at his towel. It fell away as Marc hit the bed. Their kisses broke and he went down on his back. A good thing because her feet tangled in the damp fabric. She was the one who lost her balance, came down on top of him, unable to break her fall until she lay stretched across all that naked male perfection.

He seized the opportunity, his touch sparking a fire that clearly hadn't been stoked in too long. And she was no different. How long since her body had felt so alive? How long since her breaths had burst from her lips in tiny gasps, the ache deep inside annihilating any inhibition?

And Marc knew. He recognized the eagerness of her response, and his mouth was on hers again, hungry kisses that tangled their tongues and distracted her so his hands could run wild over her body. He molded her hips, and when he bunched up her skirt until he could run velvet-rough fingertips along her thighs, Courtney wouldn't have dreamed of resisting.

Dragging his hands over her bare bottom, he discovered the thong that left her exposed to his caresses. His throaty growl reverberated through his body, his pleasure alive in a sound that filtered through her in a physical way. Tracing the edge of silky fabric, he explored her intimate places with a skilled touch until she was breathless and trembling against him.

He never stopped kissing her. He never stopped touching her. And somehow in the haze of excited desire, she'd forgotten he was a man on a mission, a man determined to prove he could make her come unglued in his arms.

His fingers sought out her oh-so-sensitive places,

teased and explored, *aroused,* until she gasped her pleasure against his lips, amazed by how he could tease such
responses from her body when he was the one naked and
on his back.

And when she came undone in his arms, Courtney melted
against him, and he chuckled softly, showering light kisses
down her throat, inhaling deeply of her hair, resting his
cheek against hers in such a tender display.

Who was this man with the expert touch and gentle spirit?

Not the bounty hunter who was closed off to the world,
so distant from his family.

The heartbreaker Harley had warned against?

Yes, and no. As Courtney came to awareness, she knew
that Marc's touch revealed unspoken tenderness. She hadn't
known him this way, suspected not many did.

But she was so drawn to him, to the glimmers of that
caring man. His eyes were closed, the black fringe of his
lashes striking against his olive complexion. Resting her
head against his shoulder, she pressed her face into his neck,
felt the throb of his pulse against her cheek. Brushing her fingers over his mouth, she trailed them along his stubbled chin,
learning his beautiful face in a moment when he seemed at
peace.

Had she ever seen him so at peace?

Courtney didn't think so, but the moment was tranquil,
unexpected, exquisite in its fragility. She sensed it, in tune
with him as their bodies curled close, as he reveled in some
private thought he didn't choose to share.

When he pressed a kiss to her fingertips, she thought her
heart might break.

She didn't know why. She only knew he touched her in
some place she hadn't realized could be touched.

And how much she wanted this peace to last.

Brushing her fingers across his lips as she rolled away, she was careful not to jostle his leg. She stood, her skirt swirling around her legs, concealing her from his gaze. He moved, and she was determined to provide a distraction to help him forget anything but enjoying this moment.

Turning away, she shook out her hair.

She could hear his weight shift on the bed as she stepped out of her shoes and unfastened the clasp on her skirt. Releasing the zipper was all it took to send the skirt floating to the floor. There was no sound from behind her, nothing but their breaths in the quiet. Hers shallow, his ragged, as she peeled away her blouse and bra and dropped both onto the floor.

Glancing over her shoulder, she hid her face in the fall of her hair, never before so grateful for its length. She was exposed to him completely where he lay, stretched out on the bed in all his naked perfection, propped up on an elbow with his good knee bent.

His molten gaze devoured every inch of her.

He extended a hand, and she took it, allowed him to draw her toward him, still shy beneath his gaze. He may have touched but he hadn't seen, and now, the gentle expression on his face made her feel beautiful.

Wearing only her thong, she stretched out beside him, curled against him, breathless with anticipation, heart racing as he propped up on an elbow. To her surprise, he didn't kiss her again, but she wanted him to. No, he raked his gaze along her body, a heated look that sparked fires in its wake. He didn't touch her, only traced a hand over her mouth, around her chin, down her throat, a barely there caress that made her tremble.

He lingered around her breasts, skimming his fingers along her sensitive curves. A smile played around her lips as he leaned forward. She braced herself. Her chest rose and fell sharply, but he only blew on one taut peak, a warm burst of breath that penetrated her skin, made her breasts swell heavily and a tingling begin deep in her belly.

Her mouth parted around an "Oh!" and he arched a dark eyebrow, clearly enjoying her response.

Then he continued his assault on her senses, exhaling along her waist, nibbling his way to the hollows of her hips, her tummy, becoming acquainted.

His erotic exploration started the shock waves building again, until she shivered and stretched beneath his touch, couldn't stay still, involuntary attempts to ease the ache inside. She was almost embarrassed by the wanton display she presented but anticipation drowned out reason.

Far in the recesses of her lust-soaked brain, she again remembered Harley's warnings to keep the bedroom door locked. No joke. This man had a gift. Not an artist who might create masterpieces from nothing, but a musician who cajoled sweet sounds from an instrument.

And when he finally wound up *down there,* he met her gaze across the expanse of her body. Courtney knew what he intended, knew he was proving himself at her expense, knew he wouldn't stop until she came unglued again. Stretching her fingers toward his face, she stroked the tawny waves at his temple, wanted him so badly she would allow him anything.

CHAPTER SIXTEEN

THE HOURS BLURRED for Courtney. They made love once, twice, *three* times before the sun had set. They dozed in each other's arms. They awakened each other with hungry kisses. They explored each other's bodies and responses, and satisfied their yearning for the extraordinary way they came together.

Now, as Courtney lay curled against Marc, the comforter pulled over them, cocooning their weak, sated selves together, she wondered if he had proven himself. He'd left no question that he was an inexhaustible lover.

But had he proven himself to himself?

His range of motion had seemed more an annoyance than a limitation. True, his leg hadn't supported his body weight, but she grew breathless thinking of all the other ways their bodies had fit so neatly together.

She hadn't known what to expect of a leg so badly battered, but when he'd finally permitted her the freedom to explore him in the fading sunset, she had acquainted herself.

The marvels of medical technology had not added insult to injury. In addition to the damaged skin, only a webbing of thin surgical scars along his thigh and behind his knee hinted at all the damage below. Crushed bones, mangled cartilage and torn muscle. Still, she found herself grateful he was alive. For him. For all the people who loved him. For herself and what they had discovered together.

Whatever this was.

This was foolish. That much was a given. This morning they had been determined to ignore the awareness happening. Marc hadn't been ready to work by his own admission. She was vulnerable and lonely by her own admission. Not a winning combination to begin any relationship.

But this wasn't a relationship. This was nothing more than two people who needed each other. Circumstance had brought them conveniently together, and so long as she remembered that's all this was, she had no worries.

There was no ignoring the awareness any longer.

The next time Courtney awoke, night had fallen completely. There was no lamp on in the suite, not even the sliver of light beneath the door from the hallway. Only the silvery glow of stars through the bedroom window.

And the feel of Marc all around her.

His strong arms tucked her close. Her hair was a crazy tumble across the pillows. The hollow between his shoulder and neck made the perfect place to rest her head. Her breasts pressed against the raspy hairs on his chest, measured the steady beat of his heart. One knee had slipped under hers, the other he held apart carefully, safely.

"I shouldn't have gone armed today." His drowsy admission filtered through the quiet, a surprise.

Courtney hadn't realized he was awake and didn't know if she should ask, if the answer would be out of bounds. She asked anyway. "Why did you?"

His chest rose and fell on a deep breath, a sigh. "Limping to the door wasn't going to intimidate anyone."

"Did you need to intimidate him?"

Marc nodded.

She didn't have answers. Not for him. Not for herself. They were in uncharted territory. The only thing she knew was that she didn't want to sacrifice the way she felt right now.

Savor the gift of the moment.

"Araceli ran away," he said softly, another gift. "The first time they were staying in the shelter. Apparently, she had taken a liking to a woman from the church, followed her home and accused the Aguilars of mistreatment. The woman brought Araceli back and confronted them. Aguilar and his wife swore it was a lie. The woman warned them she had been watching the way they treated their kids. She threatened to go to the police, but the Aguilars finally left the shelter with Araceli. This time when she ran away, no one brought her back."

"You believed him?"

"He was answering my Ruger. It's a safe bet he was telling the truth."

There was nothing simple about the way Courtney felt just then. All drowsy satisfaction evaporated, and she lay there blinking in disbelief.

Araceli had run away. Because of abuse?

She had run away at the Superdome, too, but Mrs. Calderone had cared enough to return her to the Pereas. Even though she would have rather kept Araceli with her.

"If it had been in her best interest…"

What kind of person didn't return a distraught little girl?

What kind of person didn't even try to find her?

Courtney couldn't wrap her brain around any possible answer. She had devoted her life to dealing with the problem of vulnerable and throwaway kids, helping them find safe places to feel loved, one by one by one.

Even though there was no end of the line.

There would always be *just one more* child who needed a safe place, who needed to feel loved. Because there would always be one more unable, selfish, uncaring or truly evil person who would hurt the kids who relied on them for everything.

So why did it seem like all her efforts combined didn't make the impact of one horrible person making horrible choices?

She didn't know, didn't think she would ever know. But Courtney knew foster kids, knew some were runners.

Marc rested his chin on top of her head, secured her with those strong arms, as if he sensed her struggle, understood the impact of what he'd learned about a young girl who hadn't wanted to live with strangers.

"How could he let her go?" There was no answer. Not one she would ever comprehend. "How could he not call the police to find her?"

"According to him he was afraid they would be accused of abuse that never happened. They didn't want to lose their other foster kids because they needed the money. They'd lost everything in the hurricane, and Louisiana was cutting checks. So was FEMA. He looked for Araceli, and was convinced she had gone off with a woman from the church shelter."

"The woman who brought her back?"

"Debbie. He didn't remember the last name. She left Atlanta the same time Araceli vanished. He lied to his wife and said he sent Araceli back to New Orleans because she was trouble. When his niece was being recruited by a Colombian gang, Aguilar saw a chance to solve his problem and help family at the same time. Identity theft. If it helps any, he said the gang nearly killed his brother when he made a stand to protect his daughter."

How would knowing Aguilar's niece had been cared for in Araceli's stead help? Courtney muscled her way through the pieces, tried to fit this information into the larger puzzle.

She couldn't get past people being okay with a missing eight-year-old girl. How did they sleep at night? "Jane Doe knew the truth. But once she came to Atlanta, how could Aquilar's wife *not* know?"

"I didn't ask. I didn't think it mattered. Maybe he was trying to protect her. What was she going to do at that point? Turn him in? They were looking at criminal charges—identity theft, fraud, who knows what else? If she was an accessory, she'll still be facing charges if the FBI catches up with them."

"Not if. *When*." If Agent Weston couldn't figure this out on her own then Courtney would explain it.

"I don't have a problem believing Mrs. Aguilar would go along with whatever her husband said," Marc continued. "What real choice would she have had? Turn him in? He kept a roof above the family's head. But there's still hope. The FBI picked up Jane Doe, so she's off the streets. One kid down. One to go. And we know where to look next. Beats the hell out of IDing her body."

Courtney pressed her eyes tightly shut against the image. Was there really hope that this "church lady" still provided a home to Araceli after so many years? There were too many pieces missing, too many questions that needed answers to make sense.

But Marc had hope, and he had compassion to consider how Mrs. Aguilar might have been stuck with her husband's choices, understanding about trying to save another young girl from being recruited into a gang. Courtney liked what that said about him.

"Ironic that Jane Doe got caught up with a gang here, when that was what she came over to get away from. I'm glad the FBI tracked her down." Courtney gazed up at him, made out his profile in the darkness. "Do you think Aguilar abused Araceli? Why else would she run away?"

He shrugged. "We don't have enough information to answer those questions. I'm sure Aguilar wouldn't have volunteered the information if he had abused her, and I didn't ask."

"What did you say? Your gun didn't do *all* the talking."

That made him smile. "I told him I was looking for the people who smuggled his niece over the border."

"How did that translate into information about Araceli?"

Marc rolled his eyes, but she could tell he liked that no matter what his future held, no matter what mistakes of the day, he had come away with the information he'd gone after. He had something to hang on to. She understood.

"I implied Araceli was dead and he would get nailed for the murder of the kid whose identity his niece stole. He was quick enough to explain what happened and reassure me she had been alive the last time he saw her."

Courtney had witnessed the scene, could imagine the man's shock that the truth was coming to light after all these years. Had he thought they'd gotten away with their crime, or did he live in fear of being caught?

Was he still in touch with his niece?

"Knowing what we know of Araceli, I can think of any number of scenarios that might make her run away," Marc said. "She was one determined little kid. But I don't think she would keep making the same mistake."

"What mistake is that?"

"She kept trying to get away. Mrs. Calderone brought her back and the church lady brought her back, too. The first time at least. If Araceli went for round three, she would go for a knockout. I don't know what she would do, but my gut's telling me she would make it very difficult for anyone to return her."

"Oh, my God, Marc. You're right. But how could she do that?"

He shook his head. "Who knows? But according to Aguilar, she wasn't above lying."

"So you think the third time might have been the charm?"

He pressed a kiss to her brow, a sweet gesture that did so much to reassure her. "If she was lucky. If we're lucky."

Against every sane thought in her head, Courtney felt very lucky right now.

MARC PLACED THE Ruger in the room safe and withdrew the key. He didn't need to be armed to interview church ministers.

"I'm ready to go whenever you are." Courtney appeared in the bedroom doorway, gorgeous in a linen skirt and jacket that emphasized the long lines of her body.

Sex agreed with her. She was an exquisite woman, had always been even when he didn't like her. But this morning, with her hair pulled back from her face and her eyes sparkling, she made it a struggle to think about anything but stripping off that business-chic ensemble and getting her naked again. He didn't think she would have minded. There was a contentment about her he hadn't seen before, definitely not since they'd begun searching for Araceli.

He'd been very instrumental in putting a smile on the lady's face. And making her blush now. The color rose in her cheeks the longer he watched her; one glance and the memory of being naked together was between them.

When he slipped an arm around her waist and pulled her close, she went liquid in his arms, molding against him.

Exactly the reaction he was looking for.

With her heels, she lined up differently against him. He could press his mouth to her smooth brow without bending. So he did. She tipped her face up, ready for a real kiss. He obliged.

Marc liked this vantage, he decided. In heels. Barefoot. She felt good either way.

Then they were on their way to get the car, riding down

in the elevator in companionable silence, but they hadn't made it to the third floor before he slipped his hand around her waist.

He couldn't seem to stop touching her.

"I need to check with the desk to see if there are any faxes," he said when they arrived in the lobby. "Why don't you go deal with the valet?"

She took off with a wave, a delectable sight of smooth strides and swinging hips.

He had to tear his gaze away.

"Room 512," he told the desk clerk while retrieving his wallet from his jacket pocket and sliding out a credit card. "Run this card instead of the one you have on file."

"Of course, sir." The clerk stepped away from the counter and vanished through a doorway.

When she returned, she gave Marc his card and assured him everything was in order. He thanked her. For the first time in too long, he was back on familiar turf.

No woman he slept with had ever paid a hotel bill.

Courtney still waited outside, but the valet brought around the car within minutes. Marc briefed Courtney on their cover on the trip to the Evangelical Mission Church, which had served as an emergency shelter for the nearby Gulf states during Hurricane Katrina. For once, his cane worked with a costume, lending him the eccentric air of literary elitist.

They met with Tamara Bradshaw, the church's ministry director, a high-energy woman with the practiced graciousness of people in the business of evangelizing.

Marc handed her a business card that read "Manning Dumaine, critically acclaimed author of *Expelling God from School*."

He introduced Courtney as his assistant, and launched into his spiel. "I'm an author writing about the essential function of NGOs during national crises. For the chapters on natural disasters, I'm collecting data about the specific role of churches, going back as far as Hurricane Andrew and as recent as Superstorm Sandy. Your church was listed as a shelter during Hurricane Katrina."

"We run a long-term shelter mission here," Tamara explained. "The largest in the Southeast."

"That's why we're here. I need to understand exactly how you serve the needs of evacuees. My new book raises awareness on the function of churches during crises. It's impossible for the federal government to provide services without support from nongovernmental agencies. Sadly, churches are getting a bad rap in the media nowadays. Too many people don't recognize how they serve the community at large."

Within minutes they were in a golf cart.

"We're a vibrant church community here, and our campus is close to a hundred and fifty acres," Tamara explained.

She'd obviously noticed his limitations, but the concession didn't irritate so much when Marc realized the shelter was clear across the campus. Or maybe he was just in a better mood today.

The worship center dominated the property. There was visibility with parking lots stretching in three directions, but still a hundred different places for a child to hide.

"So Pastor Waters wasn't the pastor during Hurricane Katrina?" Marc asked.

"No, our dear Pastor Morris was at the helm then. He was our pastor for over twenty years and through two church relocations. He retired a few years ago."

"He would have been the one to involve your congregation in the shelter mission."

Tamara nodded, and waved to a landscaper as they drove past the child care facility. "We have seven thousand members in our congregation. We're eager to do God's work in our local community and distant communities. Pastor Morris arranged for disaster relief training with the Red Cross after Hurricane Andrew. We opened our first shelter in the fellowship hall back when it was still a separate facility from our worship center."

Shifting around in his seat, Marc glanced at Courtney in his periphery, the breeze lifting her hair. So lovely.

"I'm interested in specifics about the services you provide," Marc said. "If you served as a drop-off location for relief supplies from the Red Cross and FEMA or provided supplies. How you staffed the shelter. That kind of thing."

"Once we opened the doors to receive the first buses of evacuees from Mississippi and Alabama, we didn't demobilize until nearly five months later."

She launched into a narrative of transforming church facilities into makeshift dormitories, staffing the shelter with teams of volunteers who worked in rotating shifts, cooking to provide hot meals, collecting linens, towels and clothing to launder, providing ongoing child care activities.

"Some of your families wound up staying with you for months, isn't that right?" Marc asked.

She nodded. "Many became our brothers and sisters. Quite a few who stayed in the area have become a part of our church family." Tamara wheeled up to the curb at a side door of the vast worship center. "We'll go through this entrance."

They disembarked, and she unlocked the door, allowing him and Courtney to precede her inside. Flipping on lights as she went, she led them down a hallway with doors on both sides.

"Our long-term families required a different kind of care," she explained. "More outreach. People had left home without medications, so we needed to connect them with physicians and pharmacies. We had volunteers dealing specifically with children. Those who wound up remaining for over a few weeks needed to get to school. Enrollment in the area schools increased by close to five hundred."

Marc guessed that the Aguilars hadn't been the ones to enroll Araceli in school. He could tell by Courtney's expression, the heightened interest as she jotted notes, that she suspected the volunteers of the church shelter had been responsible, too.

"We did a lot of counseling and spiritual direction and praying, of course. So many of our evacuees wanted to go home. Too many had no homes to return to. Others had no way to get there. There was a lot of depression, a lot of souls that needed uplifting and hope." She pushed open doors to a massive hall. "Here we are. This was our hub."

She guided them through the open auditorium, an industrial kitchen, restrooms, classrooms.

"What do you do with this space when you're not housing people?" Courtney asked.

"Rent it for banquets and conferences. We have an event coordinator on our staff. The room partitions, so it's multifunctional. And we were able to create dormitories to give our evacuees some privacy."

Marc rattled off statistics about other shelters he had researched over coffee this morning. He asked about their volunteer structure as he noted exits and mazelike corridors that led away from the main auditorium.

"Four hundred volunteers." Marc smiled at Tamara. "That's impressive. How did you schedule your staff? I know some of the larger shelters we've spoken with utilized coordinators. The occasional smaller one, too."

"We came across one church that opened the doors to an old convent, and housed maybe a dozen evacuees," Courtney added. "They ran a shelter with only four volunteers. Of course, they also had outreach. Parishioners providing laundry services and bringing meals, et cetera. I don't think the entire parish had four hundred parishioners total."

Tamara gestured to the facility around her. "God provides. We're blessed with so many generous people. They're the ones who make all this possible."

Marc had been waiting for just this opportunity to ask personal questions about the volunteers. "I hope to get across that exact message. It's vital people realize they're the ones who must make this happen, not the faceless bureaucracy. We have to work hand in hand with government, not look to them for everything so we lose the ability to do for ourselves."

"Well said, Mr. Dumaine." Tamara shut off the lights in a hallway of classrooms and led them back to the auditorium.

"We came across quite a few names connected with your shelter. I assume they're coordinators or people instrumental in running the shelter, because yours was one of them." He glanced at Courtney. "Read me some of the names on the list please."

Courtney rattled off a number of names they had pulled directly from the church website.

"A few of those are coordinators." Tamara laughed. "But you also have the executive pastor, the secretary and the ministers of Biblical training and athletic outreach."

Courtney chuckled. "I even have one with no last name. Debbie? Do you have one of those around here, too?"

"That would, no doubt, be Debbie Abercrombie, but she's not here. We borrowed her when we learned we would need to keep the shelter open for longer than anticipated."

"Borrowed her from where?" Marc asked.

"From our association," Tamara explained. "We belong to a movement of churches dedicated to spreading the Gospel of Jesus Christ and making disciples of all nations. Debbie comes from a family of one of the founding ministers."

"I obviously didn't research enough," Marc admitted.

"You may simply not have gone back far enough. Our association began in the sixties with a group of congregations dedicated to fruitful mission work here and abroad. We're still a tightly knit group of churches."

"A network, hmm. That would certainly expand your abilities. So you needed extra help and reached out to another church and they sent you Debbie?" Marc asked.

"Sort of," Tamara explained. "We can bring in volunteers from other churches, but most people have families and roots, which limits their time commitments. That's when we call on our church planters. They start new churches in places where they're needed, so they live more mobile lives."

Marc held the door as the ladies passed, but once they were outside again, it was Courtney who asked, "Okay, so Debbie was a church planter? Do I have that right?"

"Indeed you do. Debbie was a second-generation church planter to be exact. She was reared in our missions in Mexico, South America, Africa. I'm not even sure where else. She's quite the free spirit. I met her on a mission in Mexico years ago. As soon as I heard we needed to keep our shelter open long-term, I tracked her down because she possesses two qualities that I value highly—she's extremely organized and such a cheerful giver."

"Tracking her down? Sounds like it wasn't easy."

"Not with Debbie." Tamara smiled fondly. "When she was on deputation, she was easy to find. Our network circulates a newsletter, so we can pray for our missionaries' special needs. But Debbie hasn't been out of the country in a few years, so she just flits around from church to church to church."

Marc knew they had the next step in their search even if it encompassed a lot of area. He happened to specialize in big areas. Things were looking up. "Has she been back in Atlanta since Hurricane Katrina?"

Tamara shook her head. "No. I haven't seen her since I put her on a bus to Arkansas when we closed our shelter."

"Was she going to the shelter in Little Rock?" Courtney asked. "The longest-term shelter was there."

"That's right." Tamara nodded. "The church that ran the shelter is one from our network. The central location made it a hub for Louisiana, Texas and Mississippi, so they couldn't seem to shut it down. Their program ran several months beyond ours. Debbie helped me wrap things up here and then headed there."

They piled back into the golf cart and made the trip back to the offices. Marc thanked Tamara for her help and then chatted idly. He finally asked, "So what's your cheerful giver doing nowadays?"

"Funny you should ask." Tamara shifted her gaze his way, and she shook her head. "I spoke to someone from one of our northeastern churches who asked me about her recently. They had wanted her help during Hurricane Sandy."

"Did she help?" Marc asked, curious.

"No. Strange, but no one could seem to track her down."

CHAPTER SEVENTEEN

WE SAT ON the riverbank in the park. Kyle worked on his new song while I sketched him. The *perfect* afternoon. Sunny and cold. No work. No homework. Just the riverboat cruising past, big paddlewheel churning the water until it sounded like part of the music. Of all the places I might have gotten stuck, I didn't mind Nashville. It reminded me of home in so many ways.

The music. The river. The tourists.

Kyle.

He hadn't been part of New Orleans, had never been there as far as I knew, but he was the best part of Nashville.

With his throaty voice and feelings that came out in his music, he made everything better, pushed all the loneliness I'd been feeling to the edges where I could barely see them. When we were together, anyway. Or when I thought we would be together, which was happening more and more often. We weren't official yet, but we'd kissed.

I think he somehow sensed I needed to be around him, so he hung around more, made himself available. He was profound that way. I could hear it in his lyrics. He wrote the way I drew—noticing details others overlooked, insightful about people. I thought he was as talented a musician as I was an artist, and that was saying something.

Even though I was used to sketching in natural light, the sun reflected off the riverboat's windows, creating an interesting play of light and glare on his handsome face that

I toyed with in my sketch. I couldn't be too daring because this was a commercial sketch, a poster promoting Kyle's next gig at the Venue. I had already done one for him, and the feedback was so positive, I decided to sketch another for his next performance. I thought using real art to advertise added a special touch.

Since I'd taken a bunch of classes online for graphic design, I knew how to put things together. Some classes were really great. Others not so good. But Debbie always said that no effort was wasted if I came away with one little something.

"So always make sure you come away with one little something," she used to tell me, laughing.

I missed her laughter. But I remembered her advice, and always learned something. I was glad I could put those *somethings* to use for Kyle. The best part of creating his promotional posters was how thrilled he was. So thrilled, that after his gig he'd hung the first on his bedroom wall and planned to frame it when he got extra cash.

The music stopped.

"You going to do it?" he asked suddenly, letting me know what was on his mind.

A conversation I didn't want to have right now when the day was peaceful and perfect and we were together.

It was a gallery showing at the Venue.

Kyle hadn't been the only one thrilled with my poster. The Venue directors had asked about the artist who'd sketched him, and Kyle had done what he had promised and told them about me.

They'd wanted to see my work, so I brought by some pieces from my portfolio and got invited to do a gallery showing if I had enough work to display. I did. But I also had a problem that was ruining my excitement about my first official gallery.

"I suppose I can be 'the artist known as no one'." It was a joke, but Kyle's frown told me he didn't find it funny.

"I don't understand what the big deal is about your name. It's pretty. Different."

"It is pretty different," I said mildly, making him scowl even harder because that hadn't been what he'd meant.

Pretty *not mine,* which was why I didn't want to talk about this until I figured out what to do.

Kyle set aside his guitar and stretched out on the blanket. At first he stared across to the other bank. The riverboat had passed and wouldn't be back for another few hours.

Then he shifted his gaze to me, and I pretended not to notice. I was working on my sketch, hoping he would drop the subject. I had told him I would think about what to do because I wanted the gallery to happen. This was a really big deal, but the details had to be worked out.

I appreciated his support. But he didn't understand the problem. And I couldn't explain.

Until I turned eighteen and could use my real name, I would not sign my art.

It was a matter of principle.

I hated that he was so put out with me. He'd been really generous and encouraging. And he wanted to make me feel better because I'd been so bummed lately. He wanted to be my hero. A guy thing, but really sweet. I think he wanted to share all the exciting things that were happening in his career, too. He wanted exciting things to happen to us together.

I wanted that more than anything, too.

"We're alike, you and me," I finally said. "On our own a lot." *Always.* "Sometimes I'm surprised at how alike our lives are. But there are some things that are different, Kyle. You're older. You've graduated already."

"I don't have a clue what that means, because you're like

a closed book." He sounded sulky. No longer the guy with the voice that made my heart ache.

I wanted to make him happy, to avoid this subject, which seemed to be coming up more since we kissed. My secrets were bugging him. He didn't call them that, but he knew I wasn't inviting him home for a reason, wouldn't tell him where I lived. Like him, I came and went as I pleased. But he'd already graduated high school and was on his own.

He knew I still had a ways to go.

"What if I show my work under a pseudonym?" The idea just popped into my head. A compromise.

"What would you use?"

"ARO. All caps. One word."

"A name?"

"Yeah. Not Aro, but *A-R-O*." I tested the sound out.

"Sounds like initials."

My initials. Some teeny-tiny part of me. "It's different, right?"

He shook his head as if to clear it. "*Now* different is good? What's up with that?"

"I want special." I wanted *real*.

I knew he didn't get it. He wouldn't get it without knowing the truth, especially since he was a musician all about putting his name out there. He wanted credit for his music. Wanted recognition. I did, too.

But it was more than that. For the first time in so long I couldn't remember, I wanted someone to call me by my real name.

CHAPTER EIGHTEEN

COURTNEY CAME FACE-TO-FACE with a few realizations. The first was that she hadn't felt alive for a long time.

A very, very long time.

Though she and Marc had barely left the hotel during the past few days and had been existing on stolen naps and room service, Courtney had come back to life during days and nights fueled by incredible sex and the urgency of a chase conducted in front of a computer, on a phone and at a fax machine as Marc did what he did best—track down adults who were trying to hide.

His first break came in the bus rosters of evacuees.

Fifty-five passengers boarded the bus in Atlanta. The Little Rock church recorded the arrival of fifty-six evacuees.

Marc tracked down the name of a church volunteer involved in the administration of the shelter, only to be informed the discrepancy had been a clerical error.

"A child was accidentally counted twice," she said.

There was no record of an additional child at the Little Rock shelter, and Debbie Abercrombie was reported to have remained there until the shelter had been demobilized two months later. But Marc wasn't so quick to accept the clerical error explanation, and cautioned Courtney not to get too disappointed. They considered the possibility Araceli had stowed away on the bus, attaching herself to a family upon their arrival in Arkansas, then vanishing.

They tracked down Debbie's living arrangements during that stay, but the documentation for the church-owned housing also appeared to be in order and made no mention of a child.

Contacting neighboring tenants at the time proved tedious and time-consuming and didn't yield any mention of a child. But a conversation with a woman who had been in between short-term missions at the time did produce unexpected information.

Courtney had been the one to make that call, so she engaged the woman to learn Debbie was the great-niece of a man who had once been a church pastor and a founder of the network.

One call and they clarified the relationship Tamara had previously mentioned, and learned Debbie's parents had died in a bus accident in Mexico, not long after Debbie had married. She and her new husband had continued establishing a church there, then continued their mission work in the Fiji Islands and Bolivia. The woman couldn't remember what had happened, or the husband's name, but she knew Debbie had returned a widow.

"Do you know how to get ahold of her?" Courtney asked.

"Afraid I have no clue. She used to pop in every few years, but I haven't seen her or even her name in our prayer rosters for quite a long time."

"By any chance do you know where she went after you closed the shelter?"

"That I do know. She went to South Carolina to visit her great-uncle. He was a former pastor of our church in Columbia and a very good man. Her only family left, I believe."

Courtney thanked the woman and faced Marc, who had been listening over speaker, and received a kiss for her efforts.

"You're hired." He massaged her neck with strong hands,

and she leaned into his touch. "Saved us tons of work on that call."

He liked to touch her. She liked when he touched her. And in between all the touching, he hadn't missed a chance to romance her. A rose on her pillow. A box of gourmet chocolates when he'd thought she looked like she could use a sugar rush. He'd been clever with arranging these surprises because the only time they left the room was for the fitness center so he could keep up with his therapy.

"You're welcome," she told him, and meant it.

The great-uncle proved a gold mine of information once they found him. Turned out the former Pastor Fitch had moved into an assisted living facility four years before. A few phone calls to senior living homes in the area located him and confirmed he was still a resident. But attempts to speak with him produced a nurse who informed them Pastor Fitch wasn't accepting telephone calls. She transferred the call.

Marc motioned to Courtney to handle the call. "Probably another nurse. You'll have better luck than I will."

Courtney reached for the notebook and pen she'd been using to compile notes, and when connected, she greeted the woman on the other end. "I was hoping to speak with Pastor Fitch, but I understand he isn't accepting calls."

There was a good-natured chuckle. "That's one way to put it. He hasn't taken a call in a year. He gets confused, you see. Is there anything I can help you with? I'm his care tech."

"I'm trying to track down his great-niece, Debbie. We served together at the mission in Bolivia, but she moves around so much, I can't find her most recent address. I figured Pastor Fitch was my best bet."

"She used to visit and call all the time to check up on him," the woman said. "But we haven't heard from her. Good thing he doesn't notice anymore or he'd be hurt. Especially since I'm still making sure his checks get mailed for special holidays."

Courtney nodded to Marc, heart beginning to race. "That doesn't sound like Debbie. If you have her contact information, I'll get in touch with her and see what's up."

"I've got it in his address book. Give me a second."

Marc sank back in the chair, idly stroking her hand that held the pen, a casual gesture that didn't feel casual at all.

"I had a number but I don't think it works anymore because someone scratched it out. There are a lot of scratched-out numbers and addresses for her. But here's the one I've been sending checks to."

Courtney scribbled the address of a post office box in Nashville. She asked for the phone number, too, on the off chance it might still be in service or somehow provide a lead. After thanking the woman, she disconnected the call.

"Post office box in Nashville, hmm." Marc glanced at the information she had written down, considering.

"Can you do something with that?"

"No problem." He smiled.

Courtney marveled at how he transformed right before her eyes. Where was the sarcastic jerk she'd had no use for?

The man in front of her had become an excited lover who kissed her breathlessly whenever they added a new piece to the puzzle. A man who touched her casually. Marc had said he was on familiar turf again, that he was getting to know his prey.

He was getting to know her, too. During the lulls between faxes or awaiting return calls, he discovered what made her sigh and melt in his arms until she was the one to strip off his clothes, to hop into his shower, to curl up beside him in bed, to savor every moment they had together.

He inspired a wild abandon in her she had never known before. But as much as she reveled in the feeling, she felt anxious. Which led to another realization—she should always trust her gut. She had known from the start getting involved with Marc would be a bad idea.

She had been right, if for very different reasons.

Courtney had been able to resist the jerk he'd been, even though she had been attracted to him. Resisting this thoughtful lover he'd become was *much* harder.

"Why don't you get on your computer and track down the network churches in Nashville while I work on this address?" He pulled his notebook computer across the desk toward him.

Harley had warned Courtney to keep her bedroom door locked. She hadn't thought she would be in any danger of falling for Marc's moves.

She'd been wrong.

What she knew in her head wasn't what she felt inside. Her inside was having no part of rational warnings that this seduction was exactly that—not the start of a relationship.

She did not understand what demons drove Marc to live the life he had been living before his accident, but she needed to remember he was still the same man, a very attractive man who shunned commitments.

She did not want her heart broken.

The search for Araceli was an emotional roller coaster, and she was defenseless.

Against his kisses, his smiles, *him*.

So she threw herself into the search, determination renewed to protect herself by staying realistic even though she had no real world to hang on to. There was only her and Marc in this suite, and their united efforts to find Araceli.

A few more hours of research yielded information, but not what Marc had expected. "I should be able to find a physical address attached to this post office box."

"No luck?" she asked.

"Yeah, I've had luck. The bad kind. If I didn't know better I'd say Debbie had a history as a con. She doesn't miss
a trick. I've tracked her to Nashville, but I can't pinpoint
where because everything that should lead to her is smoke."

Courtney rubbed her temples and reached for the bottled
water. Adrenaline was the only thing keeping her going. "In
English, please."

"Every connection I find to this woman jerks me around
a bit before leading to a dead end. That's intentional. I've
got addresses for post office boxes and bank accounts that
lead to empty lots on Google Earth. No car insurance. No
utilities. No phones. No internet. But I've got email accounts
with more fake addresses and backup email accounts used
to verify accounts. Everything about this woman appears
in order on the surface, but she exists only on paper. Makes
you wonder why, doesn't it?"

Courtney nodded.

"Especially when I start looking at the deviations from her
established routine. She normally contacted her great-uncle
but hasn't recently. She normally bounced around from mission to mission. Church people saw her or heard about her
but now she seems to have dropped out of sight. Harboring
a runaway child might change someone's normal behavior."

"Any mention of a child?"

"No. But she must have a reason for going through this
amount of work to make herself invisible."

Courtney leaned her head against the back of the sofa and
closed her eyes. For the first time since this nightmare began,
real hope replaced desperate wishful thinking. They were
unraveling the events of the past eight years, and each revelation that didn't lead to the worst-case scenario suggested
that maybe Araceli's luck factor had been of the good variety.

"What do you think?" Her voice was a breathless whisper.

"Debbie Abercrombie is hiding in plain sight," Marc explained. "Everyone knows her. Everyone knows she gets around. People have even seen her. But if someone tries to track her down, she's no longer there. We're not looking for someone concealing her movements, but someone blending in."

He repositioned his leg and the tension on his face eased. He was as tired as she was. Probably more.

"We still don't have a solid connection to any child," he continued. "Not the normal stuff. School enrollment. Child services. We need another angle. The art is bugging me because we still haven't fit it in. Araceli was attached enough to her father's drawings to run away because some kids damaged them."

"Mrs. Calderone said they were the only things Araceli's mother would have cared about."

"The art factors somewhere if we've got a kid—the *right* kid—we just have to figure out where."

Courtney recalled their visit with Mrs. Calderone and the caricature Araceli's father had drawn of his daughter. "What churches did Debbie visit during the past eight years? After Little Rock. Read me the list."

Marc pulled the notebook computer toward him. He pulled up a browser window and search engine.

"Okay, here goes," he said. "We've got St. Louis. We've got Miami. We've got Columbia. And Baltimore. New York City. Cincinnati. Nashville."

Courtney sensed his gaze on her but kept pulling up window after window on her own laptop, fingers flying over the keyboard, heart racing. "Guess what all these cities have in common."

"Mission churches."

"Marc, they allow busking." When he continued to stare at her blankly, she pulled a face and said, "Street performing."

"What Araceli's father used to do in Jackson Square?"

"What he was teaching Araceli to do in Jackson Square."

Understanding dawned on his handsome face, transformed into excitement. "You get a raise."

She laughed, pleased by his praise. "We know Debbie. What would she do if she decided not to return a runaway artist to foster care?"

Marc's smile reached his eyes. "Vanish, for starters. Make them invisible, and maybe even foster her runaway's talent."

"That's what I'm thinking."

Marc considered. "You said these cities 'allow' busking. Does that mean street performing is legislated?"

"They usually have ordinances with the guidelines delineating where, when and what. Every city is different. Buskers can perform all over New Orleans but cities can designate specific areas, encroachment or noise volume. Most cities make money by charging for permits, so performers can keep busking under some control with fees and penalties."

Marc's expression transformed. "Really?"

She knew what he was thinking and zeroed in on her computer and pulled up the busking laws for Nashville.

"If Araceli is drawing caricatures like her father, she would need a street vendor's license to sell them. Do you have any way of finding out if she has one? Under Debbie's name maybe? It says here they only issue a certain number annually."

"Let me see what I can do. That info will be with the county clerk. I've got connections, but it'll take time." He glanced down at his computer display and started typing.

Courtney took the opportunity to stand and get her blood flowing. She went to the window and moved aside the sheers, glancing at a sunny afternoon. Would they have their answers soon? What would happen when they did?

Marc would move out of the cottage and on with his life,

and she'd go back to work. Not long ago that had been all she wanted. Now...

"All right," he finally said. "Cross your fingers. We should know something by tomorrow."

She turned back to face him, found his gaze traveling appreciatively over her, and she actually tingled in response.

Now she couldn't allow herself to think past *now*.

"Should we contact the National Center for Missing & Exploited Children?" she asked. "They could put an age progression photo on billboards and milk cartons."

He frowned, folding his arms over his chest. "I'd be afraid that using the media to flush them out might drive them under. If we're right and Araceli is with Debbie, then she has kept that kid off the grid for a long time. If Araceli's alive, she's sixteen now. She'll reach the age of majority soon. They could keep running that long."

"Well, that's not what we want."

"No, we don't. The FBI hasn't picked up the Aguilars yet. If we tip our hand now, we could be stepping right in the middle of whatever it is they are doing on their end. Not a place I'd care to be."

"Ugh. I forgot about them." A testimony to how this cocoon of sex had consumed her. She was in so much trouble here. "What do you think they're waiting for?"

Marc shrugged. "My guess is they're angling for a bigger payoff. They have the niece in custody, so they know she was brought into the country illegally. They might be attempting to bring in whoever smuggled her across the border. They'll want something to show for their efforts, and the odds of locating Araceli after eight years aren't great."

"I don't want to get in their way."

"Our best weapon is the element of surprise. Time is on our side for once," Marc pointed out. "After eight years Debbie probably isn't expecting an active investigation, so if we move fast, we could bring in Araceli. *If* we got this right and she's around to bring in."

When Courtney caught Marc's gaze this time, neither of them were smiling.

MARC TOOK PREVENTIVE measures for the flight to Nashville. Courtney suggested dropping him off at the terminal before she returned the car to the rental agency. He managed to get past the knee-jerk reaction that fueled his pride and accepted that he could save a lot of steps by avoiding the shuttle back to the airport.

More preventive measures came in the form of muscle relaxers, and not enough to annihilate him. He hoped that with luck, and getting up to move more during the flight, the trip to Nashville would go without incident—the way he'd made a thousand other flights during his career.

Marc got his wish. He popped one more muscle relaxer midflight for good measure, but arrived at the airport without Courtney needing to put him on a gurney.

Another concession to accommodate his physical limitations came when Courtney arranged for the rental agency to deliver the car to the terminal. She signed the papers and they left the agent to take the shuttle back to the agency.

Marc wasn't sure if he was learning to compromise or was desperate to avoid a repeat performance of muscle spasms that could register as seismic activity. He wasn't hiding anything from Courtney. She'd seen the good, the bad and the ugly.

And still melted against him when he touched her.

His phone vibrated on their way to the hotel. After glancing at the display, he connected the call. "*Hola, mi amigo.* Perfect timing. I just got off the plane."

Courtney shifted her gaze from the highway, crossed her fingers and mouthed the words, "Good luck."

As Marc's longtime associate briefed him, he watched her in profile as she maneuvered through traffic. His chauffeur. She had braided her hair today, and he idly twined the silky hair through his fingers, enjoyed the connection between them.

Every person who had played his chauffeur had only amplified the reality Marc couldn't drive himself anymore. Even Courtney. But today she felt right seated beside him, not as a reminder of his lost autonomy but as his collaborator in their search. While he listened to what his investigator had turned up, grateful for the timing, grateful he had made the trip without creating a scene, he was surprised by how at peace he was with her. As if she'd been beside him all along.

When Marc disconnected the call, he was smiling.

"Good news?" Her voice had that breathless quality that reminded him of when they lay in the dark naked.

"Good news." He tugged lightly on her braid. "No licenses or permits in Araceli's or Debbie's names. He hit the same smoke I did, so he went after her financials."

Courtney blinked. "Nothing's private, is it?"

Marc pulled a face, but he liked how impressed she seemed when all he'd done was make a phone call. "There's always a paper trail. The trick is getting to it. Way easier with government agencies than with private banking."

"That's scary."

"No shit. But lucky for us because we've got checks to the clerk for permits and licenses for one Beatriz Ortero."

Courtney's expression dissolved on an audible breath. "Omigod, Marc. Do you think it's her?"

He shrugged. "As soon as we get to the hotel, I'll run some databases to see what I can come up with on the name. But I can't think of any other reason why Debbie would need a street vendor license. Unless she has taken up busking."

Courtney laughed excitedly, visibly forced her attention

to the road where it belonged. "I can't believe it. After all this time, maybe it is possible that this nightmare won't turn into a horror story."

He hadn't understood how responsible she felt. That hadn't registered with him because he knew she'd only recently inherited Araceli's case. She wasn't responsible for overlooking the events of eight years past, events that had let a seemingly determined little girl slip away in all the commotion of natural disasters and switch-offs with foster families.

He had thought Courtney was a lot of things—impatient and controlling among them. But the woman seated beside him, the woman who felt as if she belonged there and always had, was neither of those things, and both.

Courtney cared enough to do whatever it took to find a missing child, regardless of risks. She was competent enough to know she needed help and to get it.

Marc was struck by the comparison to his own situation. He had needed help, too. But instead of reaching out, he had resented the help he had gotten.

That didn't come as a surprise. How could it? He had only been looking at how everything affected him. He hadn't thought about how freaked his mother must have been to almost lose a son. No, he had thought only about how she had seized the chance to drag him back to New Orleans, to get him at the mercy of his crazy family when he was down and out.

And thinking about every person who had gone out of his and her way to help him... Marc stared at the unfolding city as they crossed a bridge over the Cumberland River. The river threaded off into the distance, not unlike the river he'd grown up around, and he wondered why he could suddenly see his actions for what they were, as if the fog had cleared away to reveal the truth of the choices he had made.

The fact that he could barely walk wasn't nearly as pathetic as the way he had treated people who had helped him, people who loved him.

He hadn't seen it, had been so wrapped up in his own angst that he'd been blind to everything and everyone but himself.

"Hey, you okay?" Courtney asked.

He glanced at her, found her eyeballing him with a frown. "Yeah. Why?"

"You got quiet all of a sudden."

"I was piecing in what my contact told me about some collection agencies going after Debbie," he lied. "She had some hefty medical bills."

"She was sick?"

Marc shrugged. "Privacy laws make medical info tough."

But what he found even tougher was acknowledging his actions. The way he had been treating everyone who cared. Most people came in and out of his life, not around long enough to care about. Or so he'd told himself. His family was different. When he looked at his life reflected against the mirror of Courtney's actions, he had to ask himself: How had he never seen how lame that was?

CHAPTER NINETEEN

THIS WAS THE proudest time in my life. I glanced around my first gallery, my sketches displayed from a wooden molding that hung about three-quarters up on the wall. Low enough so whatever hung there could be seen, but high enough not to invite anyone to mess with the art.

There were a lot of kids in the coffee shop. It was the place where they hung out between shows and stopped in between skating sessions. There was a small stage that was used for open mic night and readings. Preaching, too. Sometimes I forgot this place belonged to a church.

Jesus sort of fit in around here. One of the crowd.

The youth directors had prayed over my gallery to officially open it, had asked Jesus to bless my talent and guide my career. There were lots of "Amens!" and "Hallelujahs!" from the kids who'd been sitting around, and I thought it was the perfect start.

I thought I would feel close to Papa right now, but I felt my angel Debbie all around me. She would have been running around fussing, oohing and aahing over every piece up on these walls. She would have reassured me the mats were perfect, that real frames would have only detracted from my art.

She would have skipped right past the fact we couldn't have afforded to display my art more conventionally anyway. She had never cared for things or convention, didn't think they mattered. Only people were important things, and being together, supporting one another and having love.

She had been so like Papa that way.

"Do you have a favorite?" Kyle came to stand near me, slipped a hand around my waist casually, a little possessively.

I leaned into him, so happy I could die and go to heaven right this very second. And it was funny because the feeling wasn't all about seeing my art displayed.

A lot of the way I felt was about Kyle sharing this moment, as if I were a real artist. Not that I wasn't a real artist all the time. I was. But this was different than hanging my sketches in my pitch. This was different than making money sketching caricatures or painting faces.

Real artists had galleries.

Art by ARO. Getting closer.

"All of them," I admitted softly.

He rested his cheek on my head, and I knew he understood.

"I fall in love." I sighed dramatically, but I meant every word. "Each one started with an idea that came alive with my imagination and through my hands. Sometimes that happens like magic and other times it's like torture, but while I'm creating, each one of these pieces is the love of my life."

Pencil sketches. Pastels. Watercolors. Acrylics. The mixed media I had created with scraps from a subway construction site in New York City. I even displayed my masterpiece to date—a landscape of the District street where I set up my pitch. But I worked during the day, and this scene was all lit up in neon at night. Debbie had given me the expensive canvas for my fifteenth birthday. We had eaten spaghetti and rice for the next month, and neither of us had cared.

None were framed. All were a part of me.

Each one marked a different time in my life. A step along my journey. A new skill. A developing skill. A mastered skill. Some kids had school photos. I had art. And who wanted a reminder of missing teeth and bad hair?

Kyle tucked me a little closer, as if we might blur the boundaries between us and blend into one. Sfumato in real life instead of the canvas, I thought.

"My music is like that," he said. "Except when some lyrics are giving me a hard time. Then I can't even listen for a while. I won't hear it because all I remember is how it felt."

"Problem children. I know all about those."

He glanced up at a watercolor I had done a very long time ago in Miami. One of Debbie's favorites. She had always made me keep it as a part of my portfolio, said it was special.

"At least I can play with my lyrics until I'm satisfied," he said. "Melodies, too. But you commit to the canvas."

"You'd be surprised how much playing I can do," I admitted. "I just play before I commit to my medium. Lots of preliminary work. Sketching is different."

"How?"

"More spontaneous."

"I've watched you sketch those cartoons. You're fast, and if you screw up, you don't get paid."

"Caricatures," I said with a huff. He could never resist teasing me. "I've been doing this a long time."

My whole life practically, but I didn't get a chance to explain because Ryan, one of the youth directors, came over to congratulate me.

Then it was a blur of excitement and congratulations and praise until the show began. More sfumato. Kyle had a set tonight and always drew a crowd. He was sweet enough to give me a shout-out, so everyone knew to look at my work while they were there and tell me how talented I was.

He could talk tough, but he was really so kind.

I didn't even care that I had to drop my online calculus test in the morning when the library opened. I wouldn't have missed one second of tonight, *our* night, because as much as it was my night, it wouldn't have been special without him.

He had made it possible.

Which was why I was unprepared when the night tanked.

Maybe it was all the emotions—so many soaring highs made the lows even lower. But when we finally left it was well after midnight. I don't think either of us had thought about what would come after when we had been having so much fun all night. Dancing together. Kissing and sitting close as we drank coffee and discussed with friends the work of Gabriel García Márquez, minimalism and abstractionism, the pros and cons of blurring boundaries between music genres.

So when we were suddenly outside in the night, the moon silvering the street with a dewy glow, I was still so high on the night, I didn't even realize we had a problem.

"Oh, man." Kyle shifted his guitar around to his back. "How are we going to do this?"

I knew exactly what he meant and tried to sidestep trouble. "I'll go with you tonight, okay?"

"Can't." He shook his head. "Edwin's sister and girlfriend are here for the weekend. He cleared it with all of us, so we told him no sweat, we wouldn't bring anyone over. They're your age, and he promised his parents to keep them low-key."

My mood crashed. If I would have had a brush in my hand, black would have been all over the canvas.

I knew we were headed for trouble before I even opened my mouth. This was going to be a power struggle, and that was the last thing I wanted for this amazing night.

"It's not that late yet."

His expression darkened, reminding me of the way storm clouds gathered right before the tornado sirens started to shriek. "Are we really going to do this again? *Now?*"

After *everything*. After he thought we meant something to each other. He didn't say that aloud. He didn't have to. It hung in the air between us.

"Please," I said. "I don't want to ruin the night. Not tonight, when everything is so perfect."

He motioned to the bus stop. "Fine by me. Let's go."

Every fiber of my being wanted to be a normal person tonight. Not someone who had to hide. Not from Kyle. We'd hop on the bus and ride to my stop, I'd kiss him goodbye and wave as he rode off again.

And I might have done just that, but I wasn't so sure he'd stay on the bus, didn't want to risk it if he insisted on walking me to my door.

Then we would have only delayed this confrontation, moved it into my neighborhood where I couldn't draw any attention.

So I stared at him, mentally debating the consequences. So what if Kyle knew where I lived? I trusted him. He would never put me at risk. I knew that with my whole heart.

Not intentionally anyway.

I could hear Debbie in memory, always mentally calculating the risks, controlling everything she could control but knowing there were still a thousand things she couldn't.

Everything about my life depended on staying hidden, and I had lived that way for so long, I didn't know how to live any other way. I was afraid, *too* afraid to take a chance.

"Why can't you just put me on the bus and wave goodbye? Why can't you trust me that this is the way it has to be right now?"

Because *this* was between us.

He didn't have to say that, either. Everything about him looked hurt and angry, from his tone to the way he shoved his hands inside his jacket pockets.

"Is anything ever going to be real with you?" he asked. "Or are you going to keep blowing me off."

What could be more real than hanging my art on the

Venue walls? I wasn't blowing him off, but I understood why he felt that way. "You don't know what's at stake, Kyle."

"I would if you would tell me instead of making this some big freaking drama."

I stepped away, not so much stung by his words, but by his anger. There was no way he could understand. But bringing him home would risk all Debbie's efforts. She had set up everything because I needed an adult to sign off on even the simplest things. She had sacrificed everything for me, even made her own funeral arrangements. Cremation. No service. No death notice. She passed from this life with no one but me to notice, so I could still live in the apartment, access her checking account, spend all the checks she had signed in advance.

Someone would eventually realize she had died, of course, but she had hoped that wouldn't happen until after I had reached majority and could go to school.

That was the plan.

And if I didn't get an education, how was I ever going to make enough money to get to Colombia and find Mama and Paolo and bring them back here?

What if I wound up in foster care again? I would be dragged back to Louisiana.

Away from Kyle.

"Kyle, please." My voice broke. "You must trust me."

Which was the stupidest thing in the world I could have asked for. I wouldn't trust him, but I wanted him to trust me.

The bus hissed in the distance, jolting both of us, saving me from asking for anything else stupid, and him from another angry reply. From things we would regret later.

"Oh, look, it's *your* bus." He fixed his gaze on the approaching vehicle and wouldn't look at me.

The bus ground to a stop. The doors rushed open.

"Kyle, I—"

But he was already walking away. And I had never felt so alone. I climbed onto that bus, tears blinding me as I slid my pass through the scanner and sat down.

I saw him passing under a streetlamp as the bus drove off. And my sobs almost choked me.

CHAPTER TWENTY

MARC REALIZED THEY needed a new plan. Unless Courtney lucked out and drove past a street artist fitting Araceli's description, they would drive around Nashville all day and not learn one damned thing. Of course he couldn't walk the streets asking questions, so they had a problem.

"What do you want to do?" she asked.

Yesterday, after they'd checked into the hotel, they'd taken the time to research what they needed to know about Nashville street performers. Since there had still been some daylight, they'd ventured out.

No girl fitting Araceli's description had been on the streets last night then, either.

"I was hoping we'd have some luck," he admitted.

"Probably not the best day for street artists. At least until the weather clears."

He hadn't considered that. He should have. Wasn't rocket science to realize someone who drew pictures wouldn't want to get caught in the rain. But he was distracted today. Exhausted from yesterday's flight and disturbed by his revelations.

Accountability for his actions bit, particularly as it meant Nic had a point about the pity party. Never fun admitting his big brother might be right and that Marc deserved an ass-kicking. But pity wasn't the problem. Anger was. He'd had a shitty attitude since the accident. Not because of the accident—he took risks. Bringing in a skip wasn't the same as tracking down a kid. The anger was all about being forced to stay put when he wanted to keep running.

But what in hell was he running from? His family?

That didn't make any sense. Pains in the asses though they could be, they were still his family. He wouldn't keep in touch or come home to visit if he didn't want to.

So what was with all this anger?

"I've got to clear away the smoke." From his head and from Debbie Abercrombie's whereabouts. "We need our next break. We need to find out who ran up the medical bills."

"Sounds like a plan," Courtney said. "What do we do?"

"I've got a guy digging. He can get into places most people can't." Or wouldn't risk getting into. That, too. "If there's anything, he'll find it. It's going to take time."

She didn't look reassured, was worried Debbie had been sick. Or Araceli. They'd rushed to Nashville only to run into a brick wall. Marc dug through the financials of Pastor Fitch on the off chance Debbie had been assisting with her great-uncle's bills. No dice. The situation appeared to be just the opposite. From what Marc could tell, Pastor Fitch had been throwing small change at Debbie to supplement a trust fund that yielded only a small monthly dividend. Not enough to live on, but enough to make a free-spirited, missionary lifestyle possible.

But they were getting nothing done by driving around on a drizzly morning. Worse still, if they kept circling these streets, they would draw attention from the beat cops.

While passing by a Western wear store with a huge cowboy boot above the awning again, Marc had a brainstorm. Using the GPS on his phone, he located the addresses of nearby vintage clothing stores and pawnshops.

"Make a right at the next light." He directed Courtney to drive to the next block before making another right. "Look at that. There's a place to park right in front of the store."

"We're going shopping?"

"Come on. It'll be fun."

She climbed from the SUV, eyeing him narrowly. "You, have fun? Not buying it."

He liked that about her. She didn't take his shit. "All right, I admit it. I hate shopping."

"Then what are we doing here?"

"No point in driving around, and I can't exactly walk the streets unnoticed." *Or walk at all.* "I've solved our problem."

Grabbing the door, he allowed her to precede him inside. She took one look at the hippie-type store with beads everywhere and enough burning incense to make his sinuses go berserk and asked, "Um, what are we buying?"

"New clothes."

"Okay, I'll bite. How does that solve our problem?"

The clerk behind the counter, a kid with more metal studs than a biker jacket, looked up and grunted. Marc scanned the layout, separated into idiot-proof sides for guys and girls.

"We're going to become street performers, so we can get out of the car and interact with people without being obvious."

She asked the obvious question. "What are we going to perform?"

"You can be a mime." He raked his gaze down the length of her, taking in all the creamy skin exposed over the collar of a shirt that subtly hinted at the curves beneath. The jeans that rode low on her hips and clung to every inch of her lean legs. "You wear, what—size four?"

"Very good. I'm impressed."

"Don't be." She wouldn't think much of the way he'd honed the skill. "I've been running my hands over every inch of you. I know what you feel like."

She arched an eyebrow and he chuckled. Leaning over, he pressed a kiss to her warm skin, the simple contact suddenly chasing everything else away. What was it about touching her that dulled the edges of his mood?

More questions. No answers.

Maneuvering through a few racks, he set down his cane and searched until he found the rack with her size. Plucking off a hanger, Marc eyed the floral-print dress someone's grandmother might wear to an Easter parade. Passing it to Courtney, he kept looking.

"What do you think I'm going to do with this? Make throw pillows?" she asked.

"Ha, ha. You need something quirky but not too out there. We want to blend in on the street, not be too memorable."

Retrieving his cane, he headed across the narrow shop. The one thing he wouldn't be was *un*noticeable no matter what he wore, which was why he planned to park himself in one spot.

There were the usual oddball items he might expect to find in a vintage store—the brocade cigarette jacket, the fringed suede vest. Marc chose items in his size that weren't so over-the-top. A Hawaiian shirt in a bright print that a tourist might wear. The sort of short-sleeved button-down that old Latino men seemed to favor. And a cool fedora. That was a keeper. *After* he sprayed the inside with disinfectant.

Peering across the racks, he found Courtney considering a lace dress with a high collar that looked like someone's budget wedding dress. "Too memorable."

Glancing over her shoulder, she nodded and returned the dress to the rack. Her hair would be noticeable. He made his way to the clerk and dropped off his items. Then he looked through a hat display, choosing a floppy crocheted number that would work with the Easter dress.

"Do you need to try on anything?" he asked when she caught up with him.

"I don't think so. Everything should fit well enough for what we're doing."

She sidestepped him and went to pay for their purchases, but Marc got his card to the clerk faster. Then he held the door while she passed through, and they emerged on the street.

"Used clothing should not be that expensive," she said on the trip back to the car.

"Not used. Vintage."

"*Previously worn* no matter what you call it."

His phone vibrated. He connected the call and said, "That was fast," while tossing his purchases into the backseat.

Maybe luck was going to make an appearance today.

"Came across something I thought you'd be interested in." Bill was the current nom de plume of a guy in his mid-twenties who had been running information for a decade. He would drop out of sight every few years, then reinvent himself, contacting a few select clients willing to pay big for his specialized services.

Marc climbed in the car. "Make my day. I need it."

"Maybe I can do that," the voice shot back. "Just depends on whether you wanted to bring this one in dead or alive."

Damn it. Luck, all right. All bad.

Glancing at Courtney, Marc found her watching him with the keys still dangling in her hand, waiting to hear good news. Out of the blue, he had an image of the way she looked when she was about to fall asleep. Her lips would part around a deep breath and she would nuzzle her face in the crook of his shoulder. Her body would relax and melt around his.

He wasn't sure why he thought of her that way now, but the ache inside was acutely physical. The last thing he wanted to do was douse the hope that made her eyes sparkle.

Courtney sat in stunned silence, trying to make sense of what Marc was saying.

"Debbie died?" she repeated, still unsure she had understood him correctly.

Marc nodded. "Six months ago."

They had covered the distance of eight long years only to miss out on learning the truth about Araceli by *six months*.

God, she didn't even know how to begin processing this, how to understand they had come *this* close to learning what had happened to Araceli. Suddenly everything was changed.

"What do we do now?"

He idly stroked her hand. She wanted to lean into his touch, to feel his strong arms around her. He was upset, too. The edges of his expression raw.

"We keep looking. A sixteen-year-old girl won't be able to cover her tracks as efficiently as Debbie."

"Unless she vanishes on the streets like Jane Doe."

"The FBI tracked her down within weeks. We can, too. Be a lot easier than what we've been doing."

Courtney didn't want to hear that. Not when this latest turn felt so unfair, so horrible. Debbie had *died*.

Motive no longer mattered. Whether Debbie had thought she was keeping Araceli safe, or simply filling a void in her own life, she had lived her last years erasing her existence, and that was so sad. Courtney hoped they were right, hoped Debbie had done all this for Araceli. Hoped they had found something special together—a young girl who had been torn from her life and a giving woman who had lost the people closest to her.

Please, please, please let there be a happy ending.

"How did she die?" Courtney asked.

"I don't know," Marc admitted. "There's no death certificate on record. My money is on an illness, though. The medical expenses were incurred over the span of two years."

"Marc, how can there not be a death certificate? Unless there's a body lying around." That stopped her cold. Thoughts of happy endings evaporated as every horror story about missing kids resurfaced. "Oh, God. There isn't a body lying around?"

"No bodies, but a lot more smoke. I don't have many details yet. Apparently, with a home death, once the death certificate is signed by a physician, it's up to the family or whoever's responsible for the arrangements to file the paperwork with vital records and handle the documentation for beneficiaries."

"She died at home?"

He snorted. "Of course not. That would have been easy. Transportation would have had to be arranged, which meant the funeral home would have called the police because they can't move a body otherwise. It's the law." He shot her a frown. "No, Debbie died with a death midwife."

"A what?"

"Something called an end-of-life consultant."

"You have got to be kidding me."

"Apparently not. End-of-life consultants. Death midwives. Call them what you want, but they allow families to care for their dead instead of turning them over to funeral homes that are expensive and treat death like big business."

Courtney tried to wrap her brain around death without a funeral home. Her Great-Aunts Frances and Camille had died twenty-four hours apart. Frances, the elder, had waited for her little sister to pass before she went, too. That's what the family believed, anyway. Close in life. Close in death. It had been the craziest situation, but the most peaceful one for everyone who had loved the elderly sisters.

Courtney could not even fathom what would have been involved in dealing with their deaths at home. The funeral home had been so wonderful at walking them through every step of the process from arrangements and flowers to filing the death certificates and dealing with insurance companies.

"With all the laws about everything nowadays, I can't even imagine how that could be legal," she said.

"Give me a second and I'll tell you how. Why don't you drive while I research?"

"Where are we going now?" She guessed their shopping excursion was over.

"To go talk to this consultant. I've got an address."

Courtney inputted the location into her phone's GPS. According to the business description, Sacred Goodbyes was a hospice-type facility in the northern end of town. She pulled away from the curb and headed back toward Broadway.

"We shouldn't be surprised," Marc finally said as she merged onto the highway. "From everything we know about Debbie, this sounds right up her alley."

"I still can't believe this is legal. How can they not legislate the disposal of people? How is that even possible?"

"My guess is not too many people would do this, so it's not that big a problem."

Courtney frowned, but Marc wasn't looking at her. He was still squinting at his phone display.

"From what I'm reading here, death midwives are just holistic versions of funeral directors. They provide hospice care and make death a celebration of life, encouraging loved ones to create a sacred environment that lets memories and loving conversation flow to ease a person from this life to the next. That was a quote." He gave another snort.

"Apparently they arrange green funerals and provide earth-friendly urns and caskets. They even provide bereavement services after the death. But they still have to get the death certificate signed by an authorized person. In Tennessee, that's a physician or coroner."

"Then why isn't there a death certificate?" Courtney braked to avoid being cut off.

She had to focus on the road so they didn't wind up needing an end-of-life consultant themselves. When Marc didn't respond, her thoughts raced, all the urgency to piece together eight years, and they had missed Debbie by *six months*.

"I see where the glitch could be," he said. "The death midwife would have to get the death certificate signed by a physician, then get it to a crematory or funeral home to have the body dealt with. That's it. The next-of-kin would be responsible for filing the death certificate with Vital Records."

"That's a bit of an oversight."

"Not if someone was stalling or trying to keep anyone from knowing Debbie had died for say, maybe a year and a half."

She gasped. "You mean until Araceli turned eighteen?"

He shifted in his seat, turned toward her. "Most people trip over themselves to get the death certificate filed and issued so they can claim insurance money and cash out assets. But what if Debbie set up her death so life would keep ticking along as usual for as long as possible? Her trust fund would continue to direct-deposit into her checking account. That could explain why Pastor Fitch hasn't heard from her."

Courtney shifted her gaze off the road and found him looking at her with hope in his gaze. No response was necessary because they both knew the answer.

"Sounds exactly like something Debbie would do."

JOCELYN SOMMER WAS not what Marc expected of an end-of-life consultant. Eccentric, yes. Quirky even. But not the woman who emerged into the reception area, wearing Hello Kitty scrubs and looking like a busy nurse off a floor in any of a thousand hospitals, nursing homes or hospice facilities. The nameplate on the desk verified that she was a nurse practitioner.

"Hello," she said warmly, a voice that was generic frenzied nurse rushing around from room to room.

"We wanted to speak with someone about services."

Courtney leaned in over the desk, desperate for hope. "We got your name from a friend, the family of a woman whose death you handled not too long ago."

"Who was that?"

"Debbie Abercrombie," Courtney said.

"Oh, I loved Debbie." Jocelyn smiled fondly, as if everyone who'd died with her was a friend, which made them friends of a friend. "I didn't know she had family."

"A great-uncle who isn't able to travel. He's in the same nursing home as our grandmother, and his nurse was the one who gave us your name. We're considering handling our grandmother's passing ourselves. Our mom is having a tough time dealing with all this—she won't even discuss the subject, let alone make prior arrangements."

Marc was impressed. Courtney lied so easily it was disturbing. "We hadn't known you could handle deaths anywhere else until the nurse mentioned Debbie and what you do here," he added. "We're hoping it might be something our mom can wrap her brain around before this gets ugly."

"Your mother's is a common reaction, I'm afraid." Jocelyn circled the reception desk, sounding sympathetic.

She fished through some brochures about preparing for death and caring for a loved one at home. "Take these. They might help if you can get your mom to read them. Maybe ask her if she would rather your grandmother pass away alone with strangers or surrounded and cared for by the people who love her. She might feel reassured enough to at least listen."

"Good idea," Courtney said. "She's in total avoidance mode. It's difficult."

Jocelyn smiled thoughtfully. "So many people don't want to think about death. But babies are welcomed into life surrounded by love. We should send our loved ones from this life the same way. It's natural and beautiful that way."

Home death seemed a lot less crazy.

"Sounds like Debbie thought that," Marc said.

"Absolutely. She knew the end was near, so she oversaw every aspect of the process. I think she felt more in control."

"We understood she'd been sick a long time."

Jocelyn nodded. "I provided hospice care at the end. She died here, very peacefully. Exactly what she had wanted right down to the green funeral service. She chose a wicker urn because it's better for the environment. A caring lady."

"So it was just you and Debbie?" Marc glanced at Courtney, tried to look worried. "I'm not sure Mom would want that for Grandma. She'd want us all there."

"You could be with your grandmother. Having people around is actually more the norm." Jocelyn pulled open a drawer and riffled through the contents until she found a color booklet, which she flipped open to reveal photographs of rooms filled with people and decorations. "We provide individual services. Some people hold court while everyone they know visits to say goodbye. Sometimes the closest people stay around the clock. Our suites are set up to comfortably accommodate guests."

Courtney glanced at the booklet and said softly, "Mr. Abercrombie can't travel, so Debbie didn't have anyone to be with her when she died."

"She had me and her neighbor. A lovely girl. They were dear friends. She stayed with Debbie right until the end. Whenever I walked through the door, they were together, chatting, laughing, crying. Debbie passed surrounded by love."

"Her neighbor?" Courtney glanced up at him, feigning

surprise. "That must be the girl Mr. Abercrombie was telling us about. Do you even remember her name?"

"I think you listen to him more closely than I do," Marc admitted. "He likes to talk."

Jocelyn smiled knowingly. "That would be Beatriz, and she's a lovely girl. In fact, see that painting on the wall behind you? She did that herself as a thank-you gift."

Marc's pulse kicked into gear as he and Courtney turned in unison. And there, showcased on the wall, was a sizable canvas in an elaborate frame, a field of wildflowers beneath a blue sky. He and Courtney shared a beat of stunned silence before she moved forward as if drawn by the painting itself.

"Omigosh, it's amazing," she whispered reverently.

Even if Marc hadn't known anything about art, he would have known the landscape had been well executed.

"I finally had it framed," Jocelyn said. "Just got it back maybe six weeks ago. Took me a while to decide what I wanted to do with it. I wanted to complement but not detract."

"Mission accomplished," was all Courtney said.

The perspective was what made the scene so unique. Wildflowers dotted a green field in wild confusion. The result of vibrant colors and skilled brushstrokes with the perspective created a sense that the wildflowers were reaching toward the blue sky with puffy clouds, eagerly trying to get up there.

The painting was unsigned.

COURTNEY UNDERSTOOD MARC'S PLAN. She understood they were going undercover, so they could interact with the buskers and try to get information about Araceli. Marc couldn't walk the streets, so he would stake out a street corner.

She could walk the streets. The actual area that comprised the District was manageable. Her vintage purchases were in the backseat. She would park the car in a lot off the main drag, easy to get out of sight. She had a purse large enough to carry a costume change, and had pinpointed places where she could use the public restrooms to change.

The soda shop.

The tearoom.

The park.

She would stroll through the streets, marking every busker she could find, checking in with Marc after every costume change that would—hopefully—keep her from drawing notice.

Just another tourist....

Marc was going undercover as a busker. He had taken her to a pawnshop this morning to purchase a saxophone. She hadn't known he could play, but he'd found a half-decent one by his estimation for a reasonable price.

He took her to a corner on Broadway. "Drop me off here."

Courtney turned onto the side street and pulled along the curb to let him out. He reached into the backseat to grab his gear, slid on a jacket and placed a fedora on his head.

"What do you think?" he asked. "Do I look the part?"

Courtney dragged her gaze over him, considering. The man was a heartbreaker is what he was, with his whiskey eyes and handsome face, those broad, broad shoulders and strong arms that could envelop her until the rest of the world didn't matter.

Until nothing mattered but the feel of him against her.

The way she had come back to life.

But such an admission had no place between them, so she said, "You're going to make a fortune."

If people paid him for the way he looked, he'd probably score enough to quit his day job. She had no clue if he was any good as a musician.

"We'll see. Haven't picked up one of these in forever." He grabbed the saxophone case and winked, shutting the door.

She smiled as he headed toward the corner of a brick building, a spot clearly chosen for visibility. Propping the cane against the wall, he opened the sax case.

Courtney pulled away from the curb, her own need to take action overwhelming. She needed to move, to do something, otherwise her thoughts looped through everything that could go wrong with a sixteen-year-old working on the streets.

A visit to the crematory revealed that Debbie had arranged for her own final disposition.

Ashes to ashes...

Courtney made her career evaluating people who cared for children who weren't their own. Debbie had crossed every *t* and dotted every *i* so a lovely young woman who went by the name Beatriz wouldn't have to risk herself by claiming remains. Those actions told Courtney everything she needed to know about the kind of caregiver Debbie had been.

So, too, with the young girl who had painted an exquisite thank-you for the end-of-life consultant who had made a peaceful death for a loved one.

Not a horror story, but a love story.

So along with her plunging mood swings, Courtney felt a relief so profound it stole her breath. Because along with the relief that luck of the good kind had been with Araceli came a fear that the girl had vanished in the six months since Debbie's death.

Fear they wouldn't find her.

Courtney hit the streets and noticed every street performer she passed, from the juggler who drew a crowd in front of a record shop to the violinist dressed like Elvis walking down the street, playing a popular Mendelssohn concerto. Courtney startled every time she turned a corner, thinking she might catch sight of a dark-haired young girl sitting in front of an easel...

She came across Marc instead.

She heard him long before she recognized him. Heard the music, the twisting, intricate sound of clarity on a noisy city street. For a stunned moment, she could only hear the music.

He was "killing jazz" as it was known in their hometown, improvising with a skill that someone born and reared in the Crescent City would understand. He'd said he hadn't played in forever, but she didn't think that was possible. Not when he played as if that sax wasn't an instrument but an addiction.

She saw the man on the street corner in a fedora, the man she had only glimpsed in the dark, the man who played her body with such tender skill, evoked so much more than a physical response, made her yearn in so many ways. Just seeing him now made her heart ache, glimpsing this exquisite ability. Courtney suddenly understood that the brooding, dissatisfied exterior she saw wasn't the same man his family knew, or Harley.

They remembered a different man.

She didn't understand why he had become a man who distanced himself from everyone who cared, a man who risked himself with his work, who could be so brutal one moment yet so kind the next.

But she understood why everyone put up with him.

Loved him.

Because he had sucked her in, too, the way he sucked in the people who were crowding around to abandon themselves in his music, and he just stood there, braced against the wall for support, his body liquid with the sound, so absorbed that nothing else mattered.

She had no idea why this man was such a mystery, but she knew then that Marc's secrets went far beyond his accident,

far behind the limitations of his injuries. And she wanted to
know why more than she had ever wanted before.

The moment was so surreal she hadn't realized she was
still walking. But she didn't stop. Her heart would break
right there if she stopped, the soulful sounds of his song
and her wild mood overwhelming. Slipping cash from her
pocket, she leaned over to drop the folded bills into his case.
He caught her gaze and winked, so cavalier, so charmed by
it all, but she kept going.

By the time she'd passed, tears blurred her vision.

How could she have known?

She had seen through this man, seen what he let so few
saw about him, his kindness, his *marshmallow center,* but
not at first. At first she hadn't understood. How could she
have known the distance wasn't about protecting himself
but those he loved?

From what?

She didn't know but knew she was right, knew it on some
soul-deep level. He had appeared so callous, as if he didn't
care about anyone or anything.

But he cared too much.

He was the DiLeo son who had taken off for a career that
made big money. Courtney knew this part of the story. After
Marc's father had died, Mama had worked around the clock
to make ends meet. They'd all banded together, working, caring for the younger kids, but Nic's and Anthony's careers had
taken time to establish. A police chief and successful business owner had once been a beat cop and an auto mechanic.

Marc had been the one to leave town for a career rak-
ing in the big bucks—and she knew just how big—to send
home to his family.

Not so different from the way Araceli's father had left
Colombia with his pregnant wife, taking unimaginable risks

as an illegal alien to provide for his loved ones here and back home.

Courtney had glimpsed Marc's caring in his determination to find Araceli, his stubborn pride in the way he'd been throwing money around so she wouldn't pay, his resurrection as their lovemaking coaxed him from that dark place he'd been because of the accident, because of his physical limitations.

And it was while she walked along, her head crowded with thoughts that tumbled in on her worries and fears about what might happen to this man if he didn't recover completely, that she absently noticed a poster that had been nailed to a tree.

There were others along the streets, but this one caught her eye because it wasn't the usual printed reproduction.

Courtney stopped.

Sure enough, it was a pencil sketch of a young man with dark hair. His profile had been depicted with bold detail, the hollows in his chiseled cheeks, the full curve of his lips. He was a handsome boy. His head bowed low, his expression both thoughtful and intense, and Courtney knew he was slouched over a guitar even though the only other image was a hand curled around a stretch of strings, the finely drawn fingers pressing a chord.

An interesting perspective.

The detail was skilled, the sketch so exquisite it seemed a tragedy this fragile paper should be exposed to the elements for a short-lived life on the streets. She searched for a signature, a hint to who had drawn the poster, but it was unsigned. All she learned was that Kyle Perez would be playing at the Venue on Friday night.

Suddenly all her tumultuous thoughts of Marc vanished beneath an urgency as wild as her feelings had been all day.

Keying the address into her phone, Courtney waited impatiently for the map to pop up on the display.

The Venue was only a few blocks off the main drag of the District. She headed that way with brisk steps, barely noticing anything along the way. There were no dark-haired young girls sitting in front of an easel, and nothing else mattered.

The Venue was a large complex that spanned more than a city block. There was a skate park, the musical venue, a used-book store, a coffee shop.

Crossing the street, she approached the front doors, where she found another hand-drawn sketch promoting Kyle Perez. This one was behind plastic in a marquee by the door. He stood in this rendering, drawn from the waist up, playing his guitar on a street corner, much like the man she had just left behind.

Courtney knew the artist was the same. There was no question in her mind, especially when she scanned the sketch to find this one was also unsigned.

Pulling open the front door, she was greeted by a man walking past the foyer.

"Where's the coffee shop?" she asked.

"Straight through there." He inclined his head, smiled a friendly smile. "Can't miss it."

"Thanks." She hiked the purse over her shoulder, scanned the notice board as she passed, noted some featured events—a Bible study, a prayer ministry, a service organization. The Venue appeared to be a youth complex belonging to a church.

Courtney passed from the foyer into a courtyard-type area not unlike a mall food court. There were tables, sofas, chairs and benches set up in conversation areas. On one wall was a stage, on another a coffee bar, and on yet another, the entrances to the small bookstore and a larger auditorium with

a sign above the door that simply stated The Venue. No sign
of the skate park. That must be a separate building.

But that was all Courtney noticed before she saw the art
displayed over the walls and an easel that announced that
the gallery featured Art by ARO.

Her heart throbbed hard as she stood and stared, tried to
take in everything at once. Sketches. Acrylics. Watercolors. Mixed media. Glass. *Caricatures.* All displayed on the
walls. All unsigned but for the easel that read Art by ARO.

A-R-O. Araceli Ruiz-Ortiz.

CHAPTER TWENTY-ONE

FOR AS LONG as I could remember, I had been preparing for the day I might need to run away. Debbie and I always had a backup plan. Always. Not only after she got sick, but for most of the time we had been together.

Since I had told her the truth, anyway.

We had been living in South Carolina for a long time. I think she had really liked being around her uncle. He was getting old, she said. He looked ancient to me. I wasn't sure how he was even still alive. But I understood how leaving her uncle made her sad.

He was her only family, and I knew how that felt.

I loved her so much that I didn't want to see her sad—especially since her being alone was my fault. I hadn't understood until then the sacrifices she made for me, but I did know enough about feeling alone to feel horribly guilty.

At first I was too scared to say anything because I was afraid she would send me back to foster care. I loved our life so much. If I couldn't have Mama and Paolo, I wanted Debbie with her silvery laughter and big hugs.

But I could remember Mama being disappointed with me when I had lied to Papa. He had his portable gallery all packed to go to Jackson Square, but I told him I was too sick to work because I wanted to go to the river with my friends.

Mama had told me sternly, "We don't treat people we love that way, Araceli."

And I loved Debbie with my whole heart.

I told her everything. How the police took me away from Mama's friend and said I couldn't live where I wanted. How they had put me in a prison for bad kids then sent me to strangers' houses until the judge gave me a new home where the kids were mean. I told her how they ruined Papa's sketches—the only thing I had left of him—and made fun of me for crying.

The foster people didn't stop them. They didn't care about me or Papa's sketches. I told Debbie how I had seen Mama's friend again when we were hiding from the hurricane and went to be with her. But she didn't want me, either. She took me back to the foster people, but they gave me away, too.

I had hated those strangers the most. The man had scared me. He screamed at the woman and the kids. He slapped the oldest boy when the boy stood up to him.

But he had never hit me. Not like I had told Debbie.

I sobbed in her arms and admitted I had lied. It was my fault she had to leave the old uncle, and I owned it. That was what Papa and Mama would have wanted.

Debbie didn't get mad. She didn't yell. She only held me and let me pour out my heart.

Then she told me she had seen the way the strangers had treated me and all their foster kids in the church for all those weeks, and she hadn't liked it one bit. When I ran away the first time, she brought me back because it was the right thing to do, and she always tried to do the right thing because that was what God wanted. She warned the man to be kinder or else she would tell the police. She said she would pray for him, too, because Debbie was kind and knew God would help the man be kinder.

Debbie told me that after I followed her on the bus, she knew I must have been scared of the stranger for a reason. God brought us together because he wanted us to be together. And sometimes doing God's will was more important than doing what seemed to be right. We had to trust that He would work it all out. He had given her a chance to help, so she would do her best to give me a good home and an education because she loved me as much as I loved her.

I never felt guilty after that. Not ever.

God wanted us to be together, so we were together, and Debbie did exactly what she promised. Even though we had to hide, she helped me develop my art so I could carry on my family talent. She helped me learn in school so I would have a good career to make the money to find Mama and Paolo.

When Debbie had been sick, she worried about what would happen after she died. She knew eventually someone would notice, that the money would stop and they wouldn't let me live in the apartment. I told her not to worry because we had prepared. I knew what I would need to do to keep up my schooling.

I told her I wasn't scared. I had been fearless at eight, and I was much older now, much better prepared.

But for someone who lived with an emergency bag packed, I was terrified. I knew in my heart it was time to run when I saw the man on the corner across from me, knew seeing him again wasn't coincidence.

I had been so wrong. Being prepared didn't mean I wasn't scared. I was terrified.

He had come into the Venue that morning while I was dropping off a sketch for Kyle's next performance, even though he still hadn't spoken to me since *that* night.

I had gone early because I knew he wouldn't be there. This sketch was a peace offering because I missed him so much.

It was also an excuse to check on my art. A quarter of my portfolio hung on the walls, and I had to keep my eyes on it even though I trusted the directors. I would never have left so much of my work with them if I hadn't.

The man had come into the Venue with a woman, so I hadn't thought anything of him. I wouldn't have even noticed him if it hadn't been for the cane and the limp. But I was standing at the coffee bar, so it was hard to miss him.

He struggled to get through the door and hold it open for the woman. She had such pain in her face. I knew she loved him. But she didn't try to help. She walked through as if knowing she would only make him feel like less of a man because he had such stubbornness. I had seen that same look with Kyle.

Pride.

He thought I didn't trust him, and it made him act even more proud. I understood. But when the man and woman stopped to admire my work, I couldn't think all men were stupid, not when I felt so much pride of my own.

I grabbed my cup of coffee. Ryan had offered it to me for free. He said being a gallery artist meant I got perks. I took a hot sip and thanked him. Then I grabbed my case that contained my easel and supplies and headed out. Today was a workday.

"I'll make sure Kyle gets it," he told me.

I wove through tables to get to the front door, catching the woman's gaze as I passed. She was looking at Debbie's favorite watercolor. I had named that painting *Glad*. Not because I had painted gladioli, but because they were Debbie's favorite flowers. They might not smell as beautiful as a gardenia or a hyacinth, but she was never happier than when she would pinch the tops to coax tight buds to bloom all the way up the slender stalk. Each blooming bud had been a triumph.

I smiled at the lady. She looked surprised at first but smiled. The man turned, too, greeting me with a nod. "Good morning," he said in a throaty voice.

"Good morning," I said.

He had been admiring an acrylic of the victory arch in my

neighborhood when I had been a normal girl with a family. Before life had gone wrong.

Papa had told me the arch had been built so everyone who walked by would see the names of the people who had died in the great world war and remember the sacrifice they made for freedom. I had felt so sad, so I painted that memory in case I never saw the arch again. My way of remembering.

Then I left the Venue and got about my busy day. I wouldn't have thought about that couple again, except that I noticed the limping man a few hours later. I wouldn't have seen him except that when Faffi had dropped by to say hi on her way from school to the library, I had put her in charge of watching my pitch so I could go grab a soda and use the bathroom.

I saw him then, braced against the brick wall with the cane beside him. He wore a hat and played a saxophone. A street performer like me. I realized he had been playing the music I had been listening to all day. He was a really good musician. Way better than the usual street performers. Except Kyle, of course. The songs had made me think of home. My real one.

Maybe that's what gave me the weird feeling. The limping man had been looking at my painting called *Always Remember,* and now I listened to him and thought about home again.

I couldn't remember when the music had started. I didn't know how long he had been there because I couldn't see him from my pitch—the angle of the building blocked my view. But I was pretty sure he could see me over the cars.

The woman wasn't anywhere around, but I had the feeling I shouldn't take chances. I had intended to get a drink so I could pee and work a few more hours, but I turned back around and told Faffi I would go with her to the library.

"Give me a few minutes to pack up," I said.

She slipped the sketches I had for sale off the rack, which

folded up neatly with the easel. I arranged everything into the travel case. I was glad Faffi was with me, because we talked the whole way and I kept my worry down.

But I paid attention to see if anyone followed us. When I got to the library, I signed up for computer time, so I could stay in the common area and see the door. I hadn't brought all my school stuff, only my AP art history to read in between customers. But I could check my virtual school and Debbie's account to make sure everything was in order in case I had to hit an ATM on the way home to get my things.

I always knew running was a possibility, had prepared for it, but deep down inside, I must have thought it wouldn't really happen. As the afternoon passed, I used up my time limit on the computer, then curled up in a chair where I could still see the front doors. I didn't see the man or the woman.

Faffi decided not to leave until the library closed, but I didn't want to run into dark. I told her goodbye, then left. I'd catch the bus from here, which would force me to transfer once. I usually sat in the front of the bus near the driver. Much safer for traveling alone. But today I grabbed the very last seat so I could see everything behind the bus, see if I noticed anything weird. I was still close enough to the back exit if I needed to hop off in a hurry.

The bus drove through town, stopping at every single stop along the way as it headed toward the transfer station. I paid attention to all the cars around, most going the same way since we were all inching through rush hour, never pretty.

By the time we pulled into the transfer station, I was convinced I had gotten spooked for no reason. Maybe I was keyed up because of my fight with Kyle, my excitement about having so much of my art out there. I was probably just jumpy.

I made my way onto the bus that would take me to my stop, but I sat in the back again, just in case. I'd already blown half the day being paranoid. Wouldn't make sense to stop now. It wasn't dark yet, but day was fading. By the time I got home it should still be light, which meant a long night ahead.

The driver finally closed the doors and took off. We left the transfer station, but I noticed an SUV with tinted windows pull into traffic only a few cars behind the bus.

I was on immediate red alert.

I had seen this car when I had been on the other bus. I was pretty sure it was the same SUV because I had noticed the shiny rims. Not the normal hubcaps that would fly off cars when they hit a curb accidentally, but the expensive kind.

I shrank against the seat, not sure how easy it would be to see through the bus windows. They looked tinted, but…I tried to make out who was driving. I thought I could see a woman. The woman? No good. The SUV was too far away. So I just watched, heart thudding dully in my chest. I had to get off this bus.

Think, think!

I knew the drill. I had to stick to the plan. That meant I had to think clearly, get to safety.

If I was being followed, I wasn't about to lead anyone home. I forced myself not to panic. As long as I was on this bus I was safe.

For right now.

Think, think!

I had seen the couple at the Venue this morning.

I had seen the same man playing the sax after Faffi had gotten out of school, so that had been midafternoon.

I had noticed the SUV on the bus from the library.

I tried to remember which leg had given the limping man trouble. I couldn't, so I closed my eyes to visualize him—my brain was wired to work that way. I could finally see him trying to get through the door of the Venue.

His right leg. He had struggled to walk, so he might not be able to drive. Was the woman driving that SUV? I needed to get someplace safe.

I didn't have too many options, because with every passing minute, the sun went down. I didn't want to be caught in the dark toting my portable studio, which slowed me down.

There was only one place to go. I would be safe there, and more importantly, my stuff would be safe there if I had to run.

And that couple already knew that place.

Okay, I had the start of a plan. I felt a little better. The SUV was still there, a little farther back maybe, as if another car had pulled in front.

Perfect. Luck was with me because the bus that ran to the stop nearest my house passed the Venue, too, so I knew all the stops. But I couldn't get off at the Venue. That stop would leave me way too visible.

Think, think!

If I passed the Venue and got off at either of the next two stops, the cross streets were really busy, and it was still late rush hour. If I waited until someone else got off, I could hide between the cars on the street and the buildings, duck into a store to see what the SUV did before circling back on the next block to get to the Venue. At the very least, I could ask Ryan to store my gear in his office, which he kept locked.

I hung on to my gear, prepared to move, feeling better, more in control.

I could handle this.

The driver noticed me in his overhead mirror, probably thought I was about to pull the bell. I forced myself to relax. I had a plan, it was all good.

We cruised past the Venue. Tonight was open mic so the place would be packed. That worked for me. Meant all the directors would be there. The skate park would be jammed, too, because it was half-price admission. More people meant more places to hide.

Kyle might even be there. God, I hoped so. If Ryan had given him my sketch, I felt pretty sure he would at least say thanks. I could give him a big hug and tell him I was sorry.

For not being able to be honest with him.

And for dropping out of sight.

He wouldn't know I was leaving yet. I had to see him again, not leave with bad feelings between us. The thought of him being angry at me hurt so much.

Several people prepared to get off at the next stop. An old lady tucked a big purse safely under her arm. A hood rat stood, hanging on to his waistband, so his pants didn't wind up around his ankles. I decided to go with them. I could get into the record store with only a few steps, and there was a big window. I should be able to see what the SUV did.

"Excuse me," I said to the guy holding his pants.

He shot me a dirty look as if he didn't understand why I didn't get off behind him at the back exit since I was already there. I made my way to the front with the old lady.

We got off the bus and I bolted for the outside foyer of the record store so I wouldn't be seen. I got inside just as the bus was preparing to take off again.

The car in front of the SUV went around the bus, but the SUV slowed almost to a stop to let the bus into traffic. It was the law.

Or the SUV could have assumed I was still on the bus.

I waited until I was clear, although I'd drawn the attention of the clerk behind the counter, who glared at me as if I were there to cause trouble.

I left. I didn't head down the street, even though that would be the fastest route to the Venue. Instead, I stuck close to the building and down the alley to the Dumpster. From there I could cut to the next street and come at the Venue from the skate park.

I cased the street but didn't see the SUV. I resurfaced and hurried toward the skate park, clinging close to the building. There was still enough light to see me, but I made it.

I was barely through the door when I ran into Kyle.

He was coming from the hallway where the classrooms were. He looked so handsome with his wavy hair and dark eyes that I swallowed hard. I could only stare at him like I would never see him again, when I wanted to so, so much.

He stopped short when he saw me, obviously surprised, and for one terrible instant I thought he was going to keep walking.

Instead, he rushed to me and demanded, "What's wrong?"

CHAPTER TWENTY-TWO

"Marc, she got off the bus," Courtney hissed, speaking into the hands-free device. Pulling against a curb, she willed the rental car to blend in with the other cars parked along the street and waited to see if Araceli emerged. "She waited until the stop after the Venue but then she ran inside a record store. I think she was onto me."

"Sounds like it," he said. "One thing's for sure. This isn't the place for a confrontation. I'll try to blend in until I can get out. It's not easy, to tell you the truth. Everyone is young around here. Even management. I'm noticeable."

Anxiety was making her nauseous. Or maybe that was because she hadn't eaten anything yet today, hadn't had a thing since a cup of coffee at the hotel before they'd left this morning. She didn't know. She only knew they had found Araceli alive, but now had to get her so she couldn't run.

"Marc, we can't lose her."

"She'll either look for help here or be back," he said. "Her work is hanging on these walls. I'll see if she goes for it, and if she does, she won't be carrying all this stuff anywhere without help."

Courtney wanted to feel reassured. She only felt frayed from spending the day playing hide-and-seek.

And extremely grateful Araceli was still alive.

"What should I do? I thought I would be able to see both streets from here, but she must have headed toward you."

"If she marked us, then she knows we've already connected her to this place. She's either not expecting us to pick her up or she thinks we'll be deterred by all the people." He hesitated a moment, considering. "Head this way and park somewhere you've got a vantage to see if she leaves."

Courtney could cope as long as she stayed in action. "On my way."

She wasn't sure what the plan would be from here. They had hoped to establish Araceli's routine and discover where she lived. Then they were going to figure out how best to confront her without panicking her and driving her underground.

Epic fail on all counts, because their plan had been moot when they had unexpectedly run into her this morning.

Courtney had known the instant she had seen the beautiful girl with the warm eyes and dark chocolate hair this was who the snaggletoothed child in the school proof had grown up to be. Not so much because her features were recognizable, but because the earth had shifted when their gazes met, as if on some gut level Courtney and the girl had registered that the search was over.

And not worst-case scenario. *Yet.*

They had clearly underestimated Araceli.

Courtney didn't know what the best thing to do was. She didn't want to call the police, because then the situation would roll right into Agent Weston's jurisdiction. But Courtney also knew that confronting Araceli wasn't likely to be productive. The girl had moved heaven and earth to get away from foster care. To expect her to simply agree to return to New Orleans wasn't realistic. She had a few ideas, but to even present them, she needed to talk with the girl, try to reason with her.

Courtney found a place to park in the lot between the Venue and the skate park. It wasn't exactly a space, but she had no problem hopping a curb and making a place in the bushes.

From here, she could catch most of the action, see the side doors and the back area of the skate park. She couldn't see the front door of the Venue, but she could see the street. That was the best she could do. Maximum coverage that would allow her to pull out and follow Araceli quickly if necessary.

Lowering the windows, she idled the engine, prepared to leap into action, but she hadn't sat there for more than five minutes when the side doors shot open with a crash. A group of noisy kids burst through, some jeering, others yelling, a few even catching the action on their cell phones.

A fight.

Courtney's heart throbbed a single hard beat when she recognized the man who appeared, grabbing on to the swinging door to balance himself as if he'd been shoved from behind.

"I don't know where you're from, old man," a boy growled from behind Marc. "But you don't stalk women. You need to take off and not come back."

"No one is stalking—" The words weren't out of Marc's mouth before the kid went at him.

The boy might have youth on his side, but Marc had a man's strength and a lot more skill. He defused the attack by pulling the young hothead into a headlock.

"If you'll stop swinging and listen—"

"Loser," someone yelled.

There was more cheering and shouting, kids circling until Courtney couldn't see Marc anymore.

"Get him, Kyle!"

Courtney thought about moving the SUV and using the horn to break up the crowd. Instead, she grabbed her phone and scrambled out.

A kid shoved Marc from behind, and that was all it took

for the boy named Kyle to break free. When he went at Marc this time, he went straight for Marc's leg.

Marc went down. Courtney could see the pain on his face, the way he tried to roll to manage the impact. The kids cheered.

"Break it up!" Several older guys burst through the door. "Break it up!"

One grabbed Kyle while the others broke into the crowd. Araceli peered out the doorway behind them, the fear on her face, warning Courtney that she was going to bolt, so she did the only thing she could do—went after her.

"You interested in pressing charges, sir?" Officer Langston asked.

Marc's leg throbbed so hard he thought it might explode. He glared at the stupid kid, who fought smart and dirty. He wouldn't mind beating this kid with his cane right now. If he'd had one. His had gotten lost in the scuffle, so he had been relegated to half hopping from wall to table to chair to desk to get to the director's office inside the club.

"No. I'm not." Pressing charges would only make this situation worse. No cops. No running.

No damned way to do his job.

That was Marc's takeaway from the whole situation. He listened to Araceli explain to the beat cops how she had noticed "the limping man" this morning here in the club and again in the District. When she saw the SUV following her, she had come back here for cover because she knew she would be safe around people.

Marc had blown his own case. Courtney had thought she had been marked, but he was the one who had been noticed. He had tailed more people than he could even remember, people who had known they were being hunted, and not once had he ever been marked. Until tonight. By a sixteen-year-old girl.

Nowhere in Araceli's explanation did she mention her real name. Marc felt bad for her. She looked as if she might collapse on top of her boyfriend when Courtney flashed identification and explained she was a social worker from Louisiana, who was in town tracking down a lead on a missing child.

"Did you find that missing child, Ms. Gerard?" Officer Langston jotted down a notation on his pad.

"I think this young lady can help me find out about the child I'm looking for. Officers, would it be possible to speak to her privately? I'm going to have to contact my department soon to let them know what I've found out."

Officer Langston collected their identification and headed out the door. His partner warned, "We'll be right outside."

As if anyone was going anywhere. Not only were they buried deep inside the Venue, but Marc didn't have a damned cane.

Araceli was crying now, tears streaming down her face, her sobs making it hard for her to breathe.

"Who are you looking for?" Kyle demanded, pulling her closer, shielding her face against his chest and beneath the flow of her long hair.

Courtney met Marc's gaze, and he recognized the tears in her eye, the raw edges of her expression.

This was not how she had wanted this scene to go down. He looked around the office for tissues.

Courtney squatted in front of the young couple, hooked her hands together. "I work for DCFS, Araceli."

Kyle looked up, surprised, and Marc knew the kid was hearing that name for the first time.

"It's a really long, crazy story," Courtney said softly. "But no one knew you were missing until just a few months ago.

That's when we started looking for you. We had to work all the way back to the hurricane evacuations."

Kyle frowned. Marc located a box of tissues and brought it to Courtney, who took it with a quiet "Thanks" and made it available to Araceli.

"I know I'm the last person you want to talk to, but it's really important we figure things out now, because there are other government agencies looking for you. As soon as the police run your name, I won't have control anymore."

"Then don't tell them," Araceli sobbed, looking up, her face streaked with tears. "Just let me go."

Kyle took the tissues from Courtney and pulled out a few. He pressed them into Araceli's hand. Damned kid might have knocked Marc on his ass, but he clearly cared for this girl.

"I'm afraid the choice isn't mine. The police are involved. What I can do is make sure you get into a home where you want to be. Even Mrs. Calderone's, if that's where you want to go."

"You know her?" Araceli's sobs were slowing. She was starting to think past the shock.

Courtney motioned to Marc. "This is Marc. He specializes in finding missing people. I hired him to help me find you before the FBI did. We spoke to Mrs. Calderone a few weeks ago. She told us all about how you found her in the Superdome shelter. She wanted to take you with her, and has felt terrible all these years that she had to send you back to your foster parents. She was afraid she couldn't protect you. You remember what things were like back then, Araceli."

No response, only sobbing that tore at a young man whose expression was a mix of anger and helplessness.

"Mrs. Calderone has something for you," Courtney continued. "Marc and I promised we would bring you by her place, so she can give you the things she took out of your apartment after your mother and brother were sent back to Colombia."

"Wh-what?"

Marc half sat on the edge of the desk. Life signs finally. Good for Courtney.

"Your father's sketches. There were four. One of you and your brother reading a book, and one of your mother. She is beautiful. Your father drew one of himself, too. And there's a caricature of you with a ponytail in front of an easel. Mrs. Calderone believes it was a miracle they survived the storm, so she saved them all these years, hoping she would get a chance to return them to you or your mother. She showed them to us. That's how we knew you were an artist, too."

Marc had to give Courtney a hand. She was slick, using every trick she could, even the truth, to bridge the distance between the past and the present.

How had he ever thought this woman didn't care?

"What if I won't go back with you?" Araceli asked.

Courtney sighed. "It's not up to me. I wish it was. That's why I wanted to talk with you alone. Before the FBI gets here. You've crossed a lot of state lines, so they're the ones in charge of the investigation. I wanted you to know what to expect and what I can do for you."

"What can you do?" Kyle was showing life signs, too.

"I can come up with a situation that you'll be content to live in until you're eighteen. It'll just take me a little time. We're going to have to go before a judge, but he'll be so relieved that you're okay, he'll work with us to come up with a living arrangement where you can keep up with school and working and your art. You're not eight years old anymore. You'll have a say about where you want to be."

Araceli wasn't buying it. Neither was the boyfriend. Marc could see that all over them. They were probably telepathi-

cally planning to pull a Bonnie and Clyde, so they could ride
out the next year and a half on the run together.

The only thing to do was try to salvage what he could
of the situation. "I want you to listen to me, Araceli Ruiz-
Ortiz," he said. "This is about to get ugly. Once those beat
cops run your name, the FBI is going to be all over us, and
you'll be out of our jurisdiction. You're a smart girl, so listen up. Now is the time to cut a deal."

Courtney shot Marc a look. She had no clue what he was
up to, but she got to her feet, trusted him to have his say.

Marc continued. "We know you want to vanish and ride
out the time until you turn eighteen. We know you don't
want to go back into foster care or else you wouldn't have
been running for all these years. But if you'll trust us, we
can do a lot to make the situation as attractive as possible."

The girl was pale and shaky. She leaned against Kyle,
who tightened his arm around her. "How?"

"I will personally go to Colombia to track down your
mother, and get her to sign the paperwork so the judge will
let you live with Mrs. Calderone, Courtney or any other
adult you care to live with until the FBI investigation is
officially closed and the judge rules on your case. If your
mother wants to come back to the States, then we'll get her
a good immigration attorney. If she hasn't reached the statute of limitations to apply for a visa after deportation, and
you want to go live with her then I'll buy your plane ticket.
How does that sound?"

"You think you can find her?"

"I found you, didn't I?"

That was the best he could offer the girl, because even
if he ever got his leg under control, life as he knew it was
over. He was a liability at the job he had once excelled at.
He would never be back to normal, never be back to one
hundred percent. The life he had known was over. Period.

But he also realized that the only thing that really mattered right now wasn't a job but the way Courtney was looking at him, as if he was her freaking hero.

"GISELLE, I WANT to help Araceli pack her apartment before I bring her back to New Orleans," Courtney said after Giselle had called her back.

"You've got the green light, kiddo," Giselle said.

"Oh, thank God." Courtney rested her forehead against Marc's shoulder, held the phone awkwardly against her ear.

It was two o'clock in the morning. They were still at the Venue, standing outside the director's office door while the officers talked with Araceli and Kyle inside.

Marc braced himself against the wall, probably even more exhausted than she was. But she inhaled deeply of his skin, the scent of him so familiar, so reassuring, like when they lay in the dark in each other's arms.

It was almost over. They would soon be heading back to New Orleans and whatever the future held for all of them.

"I don't have to worry about Agent Weston showing up to put Araceli in cuffs then?"

"You do not," Giselle said smugly. "The judge gave you carte blanche to treat Araceli like an adult who has control over her life. She's been living on her own, and he agrees that needs to be respected. You don't think she'll run, do you? All bets will be off if she does. And we'll never hear the end of it from Agent Weston."

Courtney inhaled deeply again. She had followed her instincts all this time and didn't plan to stop now. "No."

Now Araceli had incentive, thanks to a generous man who understood what it would take to make this young lady happy. The older lady in his arms, too.

"When the judge says the FBI has to wait to interview

Araceli until she gets back to New Orleans, then the FBI has to wait. Best part is that I get to tell Agent Weston."

Giselle laughed, sounding exactly the way Courtney felt right now—giddy.

"Well, you have fun with that, Giselle. I'm going to wrap this up with the Nashville officers. I haven't eaten a bite in over twenty-four hours and the adrenaline is wearing off. Thanks for getting this taken care of."

"Thank you, Courtney, my friend. I knew there was a reason I always give you the tough cases."

"Lucky me."

"Lucky me, too. And Nanette. You're the best."

Courtney ended the call and found Marc smiling. Burrowing her face in his neck, she smiled, too.

When the officers came back out of the room, Courtney explained what was going to happen. "The judge sent a fax. It should be at the station if you want to check."

The officers made a call to ensure everything was in order, then they gave her the address that Araceli had given them. "We'll be escorting you there, but once we check out the place, you'll be on your own."

Marc thanked them for their help.

"Just call us if things go balls-up," Officer Langston said with a laugh. "We'll be on shift. Things won't be as exciting the rest of the night."

There was something about happy endings that put everyone in a good mood.

The officers informed Araceli she would be released into Courtney's custody, and Kyle was free to leave. Of course he wouldn't leave Araceli's side, so the four of them made their way to the rental car for a police escort to Araceli's place.

Her home was in a lower-rent part of town, but the apartment was safe and clean. There was no phone, television or computer, but lots of homey touches. A love note with little hearts on a napkin hung from a magnet on the refrigerator amid photos of Araceli with a lovely woman with soft brown hair and a gentle smile. Art graced every surface and appeared to be an evolutionary yardstick from papier-mâché figurines and sculpted vases obviously made by small hands to a gorgeous sketch of the woman in the photos.

Debbie, the woman who had filled this young girl's life with love. Love was everywhere in this tiny apartment, and Courtney blinked back tears as Araceli showed Kyle around her home, a young girl who was finally going to stop hiding in the shadows and turn her beautiful face up to the sun just like the wildflowers in the picture she had painted as a thanks.

There were two twin beds in the apartment's only bedroom, but Courtney didn't think Araceli or Kyle would be doing much sleeping, so she just left the door open and made her way into the living room to Marc. Looked like they wouldn't be getting much sleep, either. They sat on the couch with their feet propped on the coffee table and their heads together.

"Thank you," she said as they sat there in the dark, the only light the glow from a night-light in the bathroom, listening to the muted whispers that came from the bedroom.

"Thank you for springing me from my mother's," he said quietly.

"We're even, is that it?"

He just nodded, and she snuggled against his warm body.

"You were very generous to offer to find Araceli's mother."

"Gave her a reason to swallow her pride and come back to New Orleans, and that made you happy. I'm a rock star now."

"You are." She pressed a kiss to his throat, tasted the strong beat of his pulse there, wanted so much more than a few days with him. "Whether or not you're talented. Which you are apparently, and I didn't know you even played."

"I haven't played in a long time. Surprised I remembered."

"Marc, seriously." He obviously hadn't learned to play in band class at school. The man had been trained, and she knew enough about DiLeo family history to wonder when.

"Music was once my life. I'd forgotten. Or blocked it out."

She wanted to know why, wanted to know *him,* the things he didn't easily share, the things that made him a caring man.

Because he was, though he worked so hard to hide how much he cared.

"Why?" Such a simple question.

"Other things became more important, I guess."

Such a simple answer for something she sensed wasn't so simple at all.

"Now I don't know what comes next," he admitted.

Tracing the curls at his nape, she made an admission of her own. "All I know is whenever it's time to move on, something better always comes along."

"Does it?"

"Always." Wasn't that what they were doing right now? "Sitting here with you is so much better than being alone."

He was silent for such a long time she didn't think he would reply. But when he pressed a kiss to her hair, his throaty voice gentled the unfamiliar darkness. "You're right."

And the pleasure that filtered through her chased away the last of her reservations. She sat there nestled in his strong arms and remembered the past weeks as this man had antagonized her, proved himself to her—likely to himself, too—made love to her with breathtaking frequency and ridden in on his white horse to promise a happy ending. And Courtney knew why she didn't want to let him go right now. Somewhere along the way, she had fallen in love.

CHAPTER TWENTY-THREE

THROUGH THE COTTAGE kitchen window, Marc could see when the light on the second floor of Courtney's house went out, and when it did, he knew Araceli had gone to bed.

He hadn't needed to make the flight to Colombia to keep his promise after all. With the help of an investigator from Bogotá, Marc had tracked down Araceli's mother and brother within a week. There had been a lot of tears when mother and daughter had spoken for the first time in eight years, and Marc felt a sense of accomplishment that he couldn't remember experiencing before at the part he'd played bringing a family together again.

Or maybe it was just the way Courtney had looked at him as they stepped out of the room to give Araceli privacy with her phone call—as if he were her hero. Marc knew then that he would do whatever he could to reunite this family in person. Araceli's mother had already passed the statute of limitations necessary after a deportation for applying to reenter the country legally, so Marc had hired an immigration attorney, who was currently reviewing the case and preparing the documents to file.

The family court judge had allowed Courtney to formally host Araceli, who had moved in. According to Courtney, the place no longer seemed so big and empty with a teenager in residence. Things were working out smoother than they could have hoped.

Getting up from the kitchen table, Marc made his way

to the door and stepped outside into the brisk night. He and Courtney had made it a habit of meeting after Araceli had turned in for the night, and he had no sooner pulled the door shut behind him when her porch light came on.

Courtney appeared, backlit by the glow, her features cast in shadow but the sight of her causing his heart to throb a single hard beat. Life was changing. Marc might not know where he was going yet, but he was putting the pieces in place one by one. Because Courtney had been right. When it was time to move on, something better always came along.

She was his *something better*.

Tonight she carried two steaming mugs. Might be coffee or cocoa or some foul tea she seemed so fond of. He wouldn't know until he got onto the porch. Some nights she brought a bottle of wine. Whatever struck her fancy. He drank what she brought, because he didn't care what was in the cup so long as she was seated beside him, chatting away about whatever was on her mind, asking for his opinions and listening to his replies.

As content to be with him as she had been during those treasured nights during their search for Araceli.

She sat on the top step and set the mugs beside her, watching him as he crossed the yard. Their gazes finally met, a hello that connected them in the quiet night.

"Hi," she said softly.

"Hi back." He maneuvered onto the step beside her. "Thought you were standing me up tonight."

A smiled played around the corners of her mouth. "I'm actually surprised they went to bed so early."

"They? Violet over again?"

She nodded, passing him a mug.

His niece had been thrilled to have someone her age to hang out with, and Araceli was equally impressed with Violet, who had lived in South America for several years. The two happily conversed in Spanish, a match made in heaven. Or so it seemed, since Violet had been at Courtney's more than she had been home these past three weeks since their return from Nashville.

He sipped from the mug. Coffee. His personal favorite. "Thanks," he said. "I thought Violet promised to help her mother with the wedding preparations. Guess not."

"I'm not really surprised. Nic and Megan are going to be honeymooners. Violet has got to feel like a bit of a third wheel right now. I think Araceli is the perfect distraction."

Marc supposed she was right. "Works both ways."

"You've got that right."

Araceli, too, was facing dramatic changes in her life, and while she was eager for the reunion with her mother, she did understand the need to follow the legalities to the letter of the law. After deportation from this country, reentering became far more difficult. Fortunately, Araceli was more street-smart than most kids her age. She and Violet were a pair that way.

Courtney snuggled close and rested her head on his shoulder. "Got a date today."

"So the FBI officially closed the investigation?"

"About time, don't you think? I'll go in for a hearing on the first of November and should be back to work on the fourth."

"You're relieved." Not a question.

She nodded, and exhaled a contented sigh that reminded him of the way she sounded at night in his arms. He missed having her all to himself. Now that they were in New Orleans, he had to share her with everyone in her life. Her family. His family. Her friends. Araceli. The Department of Children and Family Services. He had gotten spoiled.

"I am," she admitted. "Going to have to play catch-up with my kids. I've missed them."

He wasn't surprised to hear that, not with the way she

cared for everyone around her. "Does that mean you're going to start working nonstop again? I don't see you enough as it is."

She patted his leg reassuringly. "Then we'll have to remedy that, because I've learned my lesson. I'm all about balance and enjoying the moment. How about you? How was therapy today?"

Resting his cheek against her silky head, he stared into the yard, only the stars and the porch illuminating the dark. He felt a contentment that was still so unfamiliar, a peace that things were working out exactly the way they should. As long as he didn't stubbornly fight for the things meant to be let go.

He had to stay focused on *now* and not cling to the past or worry too much about the future.

"Therapy went well, thanks for asking. Streetcar ride didn't wear me out so much. Every day is getting better."

She burrowed her face against his neck, another response reminiscent of being in her arms naked. "I'm glad."

She hadn't been when he had first announced his intention to ride the streetcar to his therapy sessions. Like his mother, Courtney wanted him to accept more help than he was willing to accept. He would ride the streetcar until he could get behind the wheel of a car again, which was the first of his short-term goals to reclaim his life. He was setting realistic goals, and every day that passed, he was getting stronger, figuring out what he wanted.

"Listen, I have a proposition for you," he said.

"This sounds serious." Setting aside her mug, she glanced up at him, her gaze lingering as if she had been missing him, too. And *that* look in her beautiful eyes, a look he was getting used to seeing lately, had done far more toward helping Marc see past now into a possible future than all the therapy he'd had in the months since his accident combined.

Catching her chin between his thumb and forefinger, he tipped her beautiful face toward him.

"I'm not going back to my mother's. I want to work something out with you so I can stay in the cottage for a while. With you returning to work, I don't want to be far away, wasting time we can be spending together. I'd invite myself to move into your place, but you've got a guest who's at an impressionable age. Moving some random guy in probably won't look good to the judge. Then there's the admiral. He's old. Don't want to give him a heart attack."

A laugh slipped between her parted lips. "You're not some random guy."

He arched an eyebrow, resisted the urge to catch her mouth beneath his. "No?"

"No," she said decidedly. "You're the man I don't want to be too far away so we don't waste time we can spend together."

"That's settled then." Lowering his mouth to hers, he gave in to that need to kiss her, to taste the excitement and feel her melt against him, eager and willing. Marc might have no clear idea of what the future would hold for him, but he knew one thing for absolute certain.

He would convince Courtney to be in it.

MARC SAT AT his mother's kitchen table—in the same spot he'd been sitting since his return. Only tonight he didn't feel crammed into a corner to stay out of everyone's way. This was simply his seat because it met his needs, the way Damon's seat kept him out of reach of Nic and Anthony. The way Nic sat at the head of the table where their father had once sat. The way Vince squeezed in anywhere because everyone wanted to be next to him. The way their mother sat closest to the stove.

They had been squeezing in more and more chairs lately.

For Anthony's family. Nic's family. Now Courtney, whose new seat was right beside Marc.

They were going to need a bigger table soon.

Or, knowing his mother, a bigger kitchen.

She had added Araceli to the wedding guest list, believed finding a missing child deserved a celebration. Since Nic and Megan already had one planned...

Tonight they had all gathered around the table for coffee after the rehearsal dinner, rehashing the events of the night and going over plans for the big day tomorrow.

"Are you kidding?" Nic was saying. "I'm going home tonight. Violet won't let me see the bride. She's playing by the book."

Anthony laughed. "No surprises there. She's *your* kid."

"You know about the bad luck, Uncle Anthony," Violet said. "I'm not risking it. No way. Araceli agrees."

"I do." Araceli narrowed her gaze at Nic. "And no peeking, Chief Nic. You promised."

Nic snorted. "Like I could even get past you two. You're worse than bodyguards."

Violet and Araceli exchanged smug glances. Courtney slipped her hand beneath the table and reached for Marc's, and he slipped his fingers through hers, more content than he could remember being in so long. He appreciated having Courtney beside him, knew she appreciated how she and Araceli were made to feel as if they were a part of the family.

His family. All it took was a dinner invitation... Marc had to admit he liked the way they just dragged over an extra chair or two and included everyone.

Even people who didn't want to be included.

He wasn't sure when he had stopped wanting to be included, but he was glad they had never stopped asking.

"Hey, Uncle Marc, I want to know something." Violet

ground the chatter around the table to a halt again and made him the center of attention.

"Shoot, kid."

Tossing her tawny hair back, Violet frowned at him, looking so like Nic in that moment Marc had to laugh. Just what this family needed—another Nic. "Araceli told me she heard you playing a sax in Nashville. I didn't even know you played, but she said you were, like, really inspired."

Courtney gave his hand a squeeze. Tilting her head forward just enough so her hair slid down to cover her face, she tried to hide a smile.

"That's generous, Araceli. And, yes, I used to play, Violet. When I was your age."

If his family hadn't been his family, they would have respected that answer and left it there. But they were his family, so they felt compelled to turn his answer into a damned epic, embellishing and exaggerating and imparting way more information than Marc wanted to recall, let alone share.

"Your uncle did a lot more than play, Violet," his mother announced. "He was so talented that every music school in the country offered him scholarships for college. All the good ones, anyway. Eastman. Juilliard. Oberlin. He even went to a music conservatory for high school. That's how good he was."

When his mother stopped to draw air, he asked, "You done?"

"No, as a matter of fact. Violet missed out on a lot of family backstory. I need to bring her up to speed."

"Grandmama looks out for me." Violet beamed.

But his mother was bringing more than just Violet up to speed. Courtney tried not to appear too eager to hear the story, but failed miserably. Her grip tightened on his, and she leaned forward on the bench, hanging on his mother's every word.

"Your uncle filled this house with music. Inspired music. Sometimes he'd even bring his friends and the house would sound like a concert hall."

"You couldn't even hear to talk on the phone," Anthony agreed. "Had to take calls outside."

"Except this was in the day when phones were attached to the wall with a curly cord about this long." Vince held up his hands about a foot apart.

Damon groaned. "Let me tell you how many times Uncle Anthony ripped the phone right out of the wall trying to stretch it outside to talk to his girlfriends."

"The phones weren't, like, *mobile?*" Violet asked.

"They were not. And your uncle Marc didn't only play the saxophone." His mother seized control of the conversation again. "Although that was always his favorite. He was like Araceli with her art—a prodigy. All he had to do was pick up an instrument, or sit at one, and he could play anything. He has an ear for music. It's an amazing talent. Once he started training, all the orchestras and bands in the city wanted him to play for them."

She went on and on and on. If Marc could have gotten out of this corner, he would have run screaming. If he could have run. As it was, he slid his hand from Courtney's and folded his arms over his chest, feeling self-conscious. He even felt a little guilty because his mother waxed nostalgic with such drama that everyone knew a house without music must be torture.

Even Courtney glanced up at him, mouthing the words, "Really?"

Marc glared. If he didn't say anything, maybe the conversation would turn to something relevant, like the wedding.

But, no. His mother hadn't stopped talking when Nic slammed his hands down on the table so hard the coffee cups rattled. Every gaze around the table shot from Marc to Nic, who held a hand to his ear. "I hear choirs of angels singing."

Their mother must have known what *that* meant because she gasped and looked straight at *Marc*. "Nic, now is not the time."

"It's the *perfect* time. If we wait for him, we'll all be dead. Or he will at the rate he's going."

His brothers got quiet, even Damon—never a good sign.

Courtney frowned up at him to see if he had any clue what the hell they were all talking about.

Marc didn't have a clue, which also was not a good sign. Looked like the time had come to beat a hasty retreat. He inclined his head toward the door, a silent cue for Courtney. They would have to grab Araceli and make a break for it.

"It's my wedding, Mom." Nic held up his hand as if that might stop her objections. "I gave you a grandchild—"

"Hey, I gave her two at the same time." Anthony managed not to pound his chest. "One of each."

Nic wrapped an arm around Violet and pulled her close. She glowed beneath his attention. "I gave her the *first*."

"Does it count since we didn't know about her?" Damon asked, and it was a good thing he was sitting safely out of reach, judging by Nic's expression.

"I. Am. The. Groom." Nic was also used to giving orders. "So we do things my way."

"You know, my ride's heading out." Marc scooted the bench back and pushed himself up. "Peace out, dudes."

Courtney was already in motion, but Nic stopped them cold.

"Oh, no, you don't. Everyone sit. I have a present for my best man. Now put your butts back on that bench. Violet, don't let your uncle move." Nic bolted out of his chair so fast he nearly knocked the damned thing over.

He vanished from the kitchen, and Anthony leaned forward. "I know what's coming, so I'd start walking, gimp. It'll take you that long to get out of here."

"Oh, no, you don't." Violet circled the table and pressed both hands on Marc's shoulders as if she could keep him there by force.

Heavy footsteps thundered up the stairs. Everyone was staring at him, and he didn't doubt that at least half the table knew what was coming. Courtney looked worried, but it was his mother's expression that made him nervous. She could handle anything, but even she looked faint around the edges.

Marc did not want to be here. "You're not supposed to give the best man a gift until *after* the reception, *after* I make the toast. It's bad luck. Violet, are you going to risk it?"

She dropped a kiss on the top of his head and ruffled his hair. "You're not going anywhere, the police chief said, and I really don't want to deal with him."

"So you roll your uncle under the bus?" Courtney asked. "Can't say I blame you."

"Traitor," he told her.

Her clear eyes sparkled. Slipping her fingers over his knee, she patted him reassuringly.

Then the floor shook again as Nic clambered down the stairs. His mother eyed Marc warily, and he braced himself.

Nic reappeared, carrying a big black bag that looked like a trash can liner. "Okay, everyone. Clear me space."

Hands flew around the table, sliding aside coffee cups.

Marc stared as Nic set down the bag in front of him with great ceremony and a weighty thump.

Anthony provided a pocketknife. He wasn't smiling. "Here you go, Marc. Have at it."

Violet was bouncing on her tiptoes with barely contained excitement. "Go on, Uncle Marc. We're all dying here."

In reality, Marc was probably the only one close to dying—maybe Courtney, too, because her fingers were digging into his thigh now. As he sliced away the filmy plastic, he recognized the shape of the case below. And time stopped. Just stopped.

His old sax.

Marc knew the case by heart, the shock-resistant top-of-the-range case that had cost nearly what his father had made in a week. He knew because they'd shopped for it together.

"You've got to have solid equipment, Marc," his father had told him. *"You put an LT5 under the wrong hood, and you're just begging for trouble."*

Marc had no problem understanding the engine reference. What he hadn't understood at the time was how his father was swinging the pricey sax and expensive case. Scholarships paid the tuition, but the conservatory was still a money pit.

Books. Music. Recital fees. Housing. Meal plans.

"Your job is to go to school and do your best," his father had said. *"You leave me and your mother to figure out the rest. We're the parents. That's our job."*

So Marc had done exactly that. He'd studied hard, kept his scholarships and earned more. And owning this sax had allowed him to hold his own at a conservatory filled with overprivileged snobs with parents who threw money around. Marc may have been a scholarship student, but he'd been a damned talented one. He'd made it two full years before Nic had called with the news his father had died of a massive heart attack. One minute he was fine. The next he'd been dead.

Only after the funeral, after the finances had unraveled, did Marc find out how his parents had paid for his school.

By taking a second mortgage on the house.

He'd only found that out as his mother had been about to lose it, leaving the entire family without a place to live.

So *he* could study music.

By the time Marc shook off his shock, he realized the kitchen was so silent he could practically hear the sound of everyone holding their breath. He pushed himself up, unfastened the case by rote, buying himself time to figure out what to do with *this*.

And there it was.

Just as perfect as it had been all those years ago. His first new sax—not a used student version, but a professional instrument with the sweetest, most flexible and centered tone. The brass still gleamed. Whoever had packed it away had preserved it well. His mother most likely. She would know.

Marc ran a thumb along the bell, touched the key guard. His whole life had once been tied up with this instrument. Now he had no clue what to do with it. He only knew *his* sax shouldn't be here, not when he'd hocked it long ago to catch up on the mortgage so his family didn't wind up in the street.

The fact that no one had said a word spoke volumes. The only thing he knew right now was how much his response mattered.

Because his family mattered.

And he mattered to them so much more than he'd been able to deal with. Right now. Back then.

They probably expected him to blow up and storm out of the room. A few weeks ago that's what he would have done.

He couldn't face his mother yet, not when everything felt so fragile inside him. He looked at Nic instead. "How is this here? And how is this *your* best man gift to me?"

"It would still be sitting up in Mom's closet if I didn't go get it."

"Nic," his mother said, but there was no fight in her voice right now, absolutely none.

Nic spread his hands. "All right, I tracked it down."

Anthony nodded. "We all bought back the ticket."

"I saved it during the hurricane, thank you very much,"

Vince said. "I told Mama to take it with her. You saved her life and didn't even know it. She had the thing wrapped up so well, she used it as a flotation device."

That broke the tension with a round of laughter.

"Why would you claim the ticket?" Marc had given up music.

"Because your father wanted you to have that sax." Tears trembled in his mother's voice. "He wanted his incredibly talented son to have whatever he needed to follow his dreams. It was the most important thing in the world to him."

And what had Marc done with those dreams?

Nothing. He'd given up.

He glanced at Araceli, who watched him with big, dark eyes. That kid had moved mountains to follow her dream. But Marc had put making money to help out the family before everything else. Sure, he'd wanted to help, had needed to, but that had been an excuse, too.

Why had he abandoned what had been important to him—to punish himself? Because he felt guilty his family had sacrificed so much for him? Because he felt he might have been responsible for his father working himself to death? Because he didn't feel worthy of jeopardizing everyone for *his* dreams? Because he was afraid he couldn't live up to their expectations?

All of the above?

Or was he way the hell off base?

Marc didn't know.

But he didn't think it would be so hard to figure out why he'd been running all these years.

He finally met his mother's gaze, saw how much she hoped right then. *Felt* how much they all did. Even Courtney beside him, leaning in close enough so her shoulder touched his hip.

Just so he knew she was there.

There was nothing he could say worthy of the sacrifices they had made, for all their love.

So he just said, "Thank you."

Such simple words, but he meant them.

THE REVELATIONS OF the previous night had left Courtney reeling. After they had returned home, and Araceli had gone to bed, Marc and Courtney had sat on the back porch, where he had revealed the circumstances that had resulted in him giving up his private education. What he hadn't said was as important as what he had.

Learning about his past had put some pieces in place about the man she had fallen in love with. The distance he kept with his family suddenly made so much sense. Courtney suspected he didn't let people too close because he felt the responsibility for those he cared so deeply about.

Marc had proven how much he cared by his actions—financing his family, making enough money with his high-risk, high-profit career to see to the needs of everyone who had needed his help.

Unselfishly. Unconditionally.

How had she ever thought he wasn't the same caliber as the rest of his family?

She had discovered that he was even *more* of everything she loved about the DiLeos. The kind of man who could be bullied into a search he had wanted no part of, then move heaven and earth to find a young girl. He had promised Araceli the moon to get her cooperation to return to New Orleans.

And he had delivered.

Their relationship might not be traveling a conventional path of friendship and dating, but the man who was slowly opening up and letting her know him was a man Courtney could respect, admire, trust. Their future would be exactly what it was meant to be, and she was determined to stand beside him and cherish every second of their *right now.*

Marc was officially renting the cottage, a formality on which he had insisted. She didn't argue, although she had been there nearly as much as he was, popping in to visit during the days, bringing Araceli over for dinners at night.

Araceli had been spending a lot of time helping Violet prepare for the wedding this weekend, and on the nights two newfound friends had slept at Violet's or Mama's, Courtney had slipped into bed with Marc, eager to pick up where they had left off.

She had been at his side during every wedding event. Until now at least, when she sat in a church pew with her brother, her niece and Araceli, watching the action at the altar, where Marc stood beside Nic, looking so handsome, the *most* handsome DiLeo brother without question.

Her excitement was palpable, and she wasn't the only one caught up in the love that filled the church. How could anyone not be affected when the bride and groom were beginning their married life together surrounded by so much love?

By the time the newly united Nic and Megan DiLeo kissed for the first time as husband and wife, their guests applauded enthusiastically and cheered uproariously, not stopping for a full five minutes.

There was so much goodwill and laughter that when the guests headed outside the church for the short walk to the reception hall, anyone within earshot might have thought they had crossed paths with a Mardi Gras parade.

The only thing that would have made this perfect day even more perfect was if Courtney had been at Marc's side. But the best man escorted his niece Violet, who was the maid of honor. So Courtney hung back as the guests filed out of the church and stuck close to her brother, niece and Araceli.

Mac and Toni were disappointed Harley couldn't be with

them, so they had gone out of their way to include her in the events. They had brought a photo of her, which had been making the rounds all day.

Guests posed with Harley's photo, smiling cheesy grins. The photo had traveled on a riverboat. A streetcar. Through the zoo for family day. Through Harrah's during the bachelor party. The photo had sat in a church pew and in a reserved seat at the reception. Meanwhile, Mac and Toni and quite a number of the guests snapped pictures, then texted the results to Harley with amusing captions.

Harley battles the privateers, and kicks their butts!

Mom hanging from the streetcar—while it's moving. Gasp!

Harley bringing the groom luck at the blackjack table.

Courtney wouldn't have been surprised if Harley's photo got a dance at the reception.

But Courtney was the one surprised by an invitation onto the dance floor.

Marc showed up at her table, so handsome in his tux and the promise in his whiskey eyes that the horror of the search that had brought them together seemed like another lifetime.

He extended his hand. "I want to dance with my girl."

Slipping her fingers into his, she smiled at Araceli and waved goodbye. Excitement made her tremble as Marc led her to the dance floor.

He hung his cane over his arm. "Don't expect much," he told her. "I'm good as long as it's a slow dance."

"You're good all the time."

His eyes gleamed with a look that promised to show her just how much better he could be.

Courtney couldn't even imagine. She sounded breathless

when she said, "I don't expect anything, Marc, but I want everything." Pressing against him, she savored the strength of his body against hers and followed his motion. "Lean on me."

And he did.

With his cheek against her forehead, the rest of her lined up so perfectly against him, they moved to the music, their bodies alive in that unique way they always were together.

"Everything's yours already." His warm breath burst against her ear, sent tingles through her, a sensation she only felt in his arms. This man brought her to life. "I thought you knew that."

"I do," she admitted. "But I've missed you today. The view from where I sat wasn't a bad consolation prize, though."

She could feel his smile, knew he understood she referred to him. He pressed a kiss to her temple, a gesture that told her without words that he felt the distance the way she had.

"Oh, man. Look at you two." Anthony swept past with Tess. "What's next? The tarantella?"

"Yeah, right." Marc snorted with laughter.

Courtney knew the Italian folk dance. She had actually learned the dance at Anthony and Tess's wedding, where Mama and all the DiLeo boys had taught everyone the dance because no one could marry into an Italian family without dancing the tarantella for luck. That wedding had been another celebration that had set the standard for just how much love could be crammed inside a reception hall.

If possible, today might even push the bar, because love was everywhere Courtney looked, on every smiling face, in the laughter, the dancing, the toasts and the tinkling of silverware against glass that signaled the bride and groom to kiss *often*.

And each time the bride and groom kissed, Marc stole a kiss himself, not shy about showing his emotions.

No one had asked any questions about what was happening between them. Not Mama or Mac or the rest of the family. Mama had probably threatened them all with death by starvation if they opened their mouths.

Courtney would have to thank her.

Only Harley had dared weigh in with an opinion. She had chided Courtney for not keeping her bedroom door locked, then charged her with caring for the DiLeo brother who was the most loving and loyal of them all. Or else she would answer to Harley.

After she recovered from delivering the newest little Gerard, of course.

Courtney had promised, even though she thought Harley was getting way ahead of herself.

Still, she took to heart her relationship with Marc, determined to enjoy the moment and no longer afraid to hope for where the future might lead them.

And while she and Marc swayed together, their bodies deliciously close, she whispered, "You good?"

"I couldn't be anything else with such a beautiful woman in my arms."

She melted inside, couldn't help but sigh. Content.

He chuckled against her ear, an easy sound that assured her he meant what he said. "I got down that aisle all right."

"And to the reception hall."

Lifting his head, he gazed at her, and the desire she saw in his handsome face stole her breath. "We might think about doing this one day ourselves."

And just like that, their *right now* suddenly had a future, and it would be together, filled with so much love.

Tipping her mouth to his for another kiss, Courtney breathed one word against his lips. *"Perfect."*

Because life was just that when they were together.

CHAPTER TWENTY-FOUR

TODAY WAS MY first day back to work. I had waited to start working again, so I could get everything settled. First there had been decorating my new room in Courtney's house. I called her Aunt Courtney now because that's what Violet called her.

Then there had been wedding planning and the appearances in the judge's chambers and arrangements for school— I had decided to switch to a real school with Violet since we were both in the same grade. Then there were visits to the attorney who made arrangements for Mama and Paolo's return.

I couldn't wait to see them again, but the wait wouldn't be terrible because Aunt Courtney and Uncle Marc had given me a special gift. All wrapped up in a pretty box with a big happy bow had been a cell phone that could make calls internationally with unlimited minutes.

They had sent one to Mama, too.

The gift reminded me of something Debbie would have thought of. Papa had said sometimes we had to look really hard to find love, but right now I could see it with my eyes closed.

Love was everywhere, and I was so very grateful.

I filed Debbie's death certificate, after Courtney promised I wouldn't get into trouble for not filing sooner. She said the judge would take care of everything.

We did get a surprise, though, in a letter from an attorney in Nashville. Debbie had visited him before she died to make arrangements for her estate. She had never told me.

When her death certificate became part of public record, the attorney had been instructed to contact me by my real name. It took him a few weeks to track me down, but once he did, he explained that Debbie had created a trust fund for me with what remained of her own trust fund.

It wasn't a crazy amount of money, but it would be enough to pay for my housing and supplies for the whole time I went to art school if I got good scholarships. My angel. The only person who knew how much I wanted to study art. Even now when she was no longer with me, she still helped me live out my dreams.

But far better than the money was the long letter she had left, written in her handwriting and her beloved chatty voice I missed so, so much. She began with:

> *My dearest Araceli,*
> *I always wanted a child of my own. From the time I was a little girl and wished for lots of siblings to play with until the time my darling David went home to heaven. God in his loving kindness gave me the best daughter I could have ever dreamed of. You. And I cherished each and every minute we were together....*

She had touched me from heaven.

Courtney suggested I tell Debbie's old uncle of her passing. So I wrote him a letter about how she had gotten sick and how peaceful her passing had been. I put a copy of her death certificate in the envelope, and Courtney had mailed everything. I also wrote a tribute about the amazing woman Debbie had been to let all the church people know she had passed after a long illness. I told them if they wanted to

honor her they could make donations in her name to the
church's missions.

In some tiny way, I had helped settle her affairs with the
people she loved, and I thought that would have made her
happy.

I had always known Papa watched over me from heaven,
and now I had Debbie as my angel, too. I felt sure they must
both be sending me luck on my very first day back to work
because I was able to set up my pitch where Papa had always
set up his. On St. Ann's close to Decatur Street.

*"You might think to be so visible on Decatur would be
best,"* Papa had explained, *"but people who sit for you will
feel a tiny bit shy. They don't want to be in the middle of all
that craziness with the carriages and traffic. Right here is
perfect. They can see lovely trees and flowers and smell
the beignets."*

I was home again.

Only now a sign hung from my rack.

Art by ARO.

Ryan had sent that with me when we had taken my gallery
down. Now I would proudly sign every sketch with my name.

Araceli Ruiz-Ortiz.

I hadn't signed my name in a long time, so I practiced it
in different handwriting until it looked like art and felt like
mine again.

My first morning was off to a very good start. I was filled
with memories of all the times I would sit in this square with
Papa, watching the people pass by, all sorts of people—
tourists, locals, workers, police.

Papa had taught me how to guess who was who. The police were obvious. Tourists carried cameras and were never
dressed right for the weather. They wore shoes that were not
good for walking or wore long pants on steamy hot days.

Locals usually rushed around on their way to wherever

they were going, not noticing anything around them. They didn't see the beautiful city. They didn't smell the river or the lovely flowers that grew everywhere. They didn't let the excitement that was always in the air touch them in their hurry, missing everything worth seeing.

The workers were easy to tell, like the police, but much more fun because many wore costumes. Pirates from clubs along Pirate's Alley and Bourbon Street. Men in top hats and tails who drove horse carriages. Women dressed as wenches from the museums. Ghost-tour guides who carried scythes.

I had visited many cities, and had enjoyed them all, but there was no place like New Orleans. This city was special.

It was home.

Mrs. Calderone had given me Papa's portrait, and now it hung in a place of honor on my rack. Not the original sketch, but a copy. Courtney suggested we make it, so we could enjoy his sketches and keep them safe at the same time. She made copies to send to Mama and Paolo, too. Courtney was practical. I liked that a lot.

Violet had promised to visit me in the afternoon with lunch, and as I waited for customers, I felt inspired to begin a new sketch. I wanted to draw the view of Jackson Square from this very spot, so I would never ever forget. Not the cathedral or the Presbytère, but a view Papa had so loved.

The slate flagstone street. The oak trees along the iron fence. The carriages lined up along Decatur Street. The horses looking festive with bright bows in their manes. A tiny slice of heaven that my beloved Papa had once filled with his laughter.

That was the view I sketched, and I loved my pencil exactly the way my papa had taught me, and the rest of the world went forgotten until a voice startled me from my work.

"Art by ARO. I might want you to draw me a cartoon."

I gasped aloud. I knew that voice.

And there he was, looking as handsome as ever in his jeans and Converse, as natural as if standing here in Jackson Square was the only place in the world he would be.

My pencil clattered to the ground as I leaped up and threw my arms around his neck. "Kyle."

He held me close for a long time, and I thought he must have missed me as much as I had missed him. But I was too surprised to keep quiet. The questions were bubbling out of me along with my excitement.

"What are you doing here? When did you come? How did you find me?"

He only laughed and looked at the sketch I had begun. Then he leaned back against the wall and stretched out his hand. "The name's Kyle Perez. And you are?"

I understood then that he wanted to start fresh. I shook his hand—very formal for two people who had already kissed. A lot. "Araceli Ruiz-Ortiz. Pleased to meet you."

"So this is your new gig?"

My fingers tingled as his hand slipped away, those calloused fingertips so talented, so capable of creating magic. I had always intended to contact him. Once I got settled with a computer and internet access.

"Not so new. I grew up here. This is where I first started working. A very long time ago."

He looked around, the sun catching his hair, making the black waves gleam. His dimple told me that he approved. "Cool."

"How did you find me?" I asked.

"Marc," Kyle said. "We've stayed in touch. He said there were no hard feelings because of what happened, and I wanted to know how you were doing."

"So you're here to visit?"

He shook his head. "To stay. Until I feel like leaving

anyway. I wasn't drawing nearly the crowds without your sketches to promote my gigs."

I laughed at that.

Thrusting his hands deep into his jacket pockets, he met my gaze. "I've never been to New Orleans. Marc says it's got great jazz, and I won't be stuck playing on a corner. I can play freaking anywhere."

"I'll show you around," I told him.

His dimple flashed, and he looked so, so handsome I couldn't help myself. I tossed my arms around his neck again and gave him another big hug.

Debbie had always believed in happily ever afters, and I decided right then that I would, too.

* * * * *

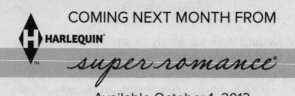

COMING NEXT MONTH FROM

HARLEQUIN®

super romance®

Available October 1, 2013

#1878 HIS BROWN-EYED GIRL • by Liz Talley

Lucas Finlay is completely out of his league looking after his two nephews and niece. Luckily assistance is next door. Addy Toussant manages to make order from the kid chaos. She's also sparking an out-of-control attraction in him!

#1879 A TEXAS FAMILY
Willow Creek, Texas • by Linda Warren

Jena Brooks returns to Willow Creek, Texas, to find the baby who was taken from her at birth. Will Carson Corbett stand in her way...or does he hold the key to solving the mystery?

#1880 IN THIS TOGETHER
Project Justice • by Kara Lennox

Travis Riggs is a desperate man. So he does something a bit crazy: he kidnaps Elena Marquez. His only demand is that Project Justice review his case, but things get complicated when Travis starts falling for his hostage!

#1881 FOR THE FIRST TIME • by Stephanie Doyle

Mark Sharpe has been torn about JoJo Hatcher since he hired her. Yes, she's a great investigator. Yet she tempts him to cross the line between boss and employee—something he's never done. But when his teenage daughter is threatened, JoJo is the one he trusts to find the truth.

#1882 NOT ANOTHER WEDDING
by Jennifer McKenzie

Poppy Sullivan intends to stop her friend from marrying the wrong woman. Problem is her first love—and heartache—is the best man, and he wants a second chance. But there's no way she's giving Beck Lefebvre the opportunity to break her heart again, no matter how charming he is!

#1883 BECAUSE OF AUDREY • by Mary Sullivan

Audrey Stone and her floral shop are thorns in Gray Turner's side! All he wants to do is wrap up his family's business holdings in Accord, Colorado. But every move he makes, she's there...in the way. Worse, now he can't get her out of his mind!

YOU CAN FIND MORE INFORMATION ON UPCOMING HARLEQUIN® TITLES, FREE EXCERPTS AND MORE AT WWW.HARLEQUIN.COM.

HSRCNM0913

Not Another Wedding

By Jennifer McKenzie

"So?" Beck's voice drew Poppy's attention, caused her to turn
before she thought better of it. "Aren't you going to ask how
we know each other?"

Oh, he'd like that, wouldn't he? Though she might not have
seen him for years, she knew his type. He prided himself on
being unforgettable to women. Well, it was time he learned
a lesson.

"No." She couldn't help noting how good he looked. Really
good. However, she'd give up chocolate before admitting it.

She turned on her heel, intending to return to the party and
find someone—anyone else—to talk to, but his hand caught

her bare arm above her wrist. His fingers were warm.

"I guess I've changed. You're as gorgeous as ever, Red." His blatant appraisal of her body should have ticked her off. She was not his to behold, but the attraction sizzling through her was impossible to deny. Poppy shook the thought off. She did not want him looking at her. Not even a little. He'd lost that privilege years ago and a bit of sexy banter and warm hands didn't change anything.

"If you'll excuse me." She pulled her arm free and hurried away before he got a chance to stop her again. As she made her way through the crowd, Poppy did her best to ignore the knocking of her heart. When she sneaked a glance back, Beck was still watching. He even had the audacity to raise his glass toward her as though to toast her running away.

Fabulous.

Will Poppy be able to avoid Beck?
Or is he determined to renew their acquaintance?
Find out in NOT ANOTHER WEDDING
by Jennifer McKenzie, available October 2013 from
Harlequin® Superromance®.

HSREXP0913

REQUEST YOUR FREE BOOKS!
2 FREE NOVELS PLUS 2 FREE GIFTS!

HARLEQUIN®

super romance®

More Story...More Romance

She's as voluptuous as
Elizabeth Taylor, yet as
classy as Jackie Kennedy

Audrey Stone and her floral shop are thorns
in Gray Turner's side! All he wants to do is
wrap up his family's business holdings in
Accord, Colorado. But every move he makes,
she's there...in the way. Worse, now he can't
get her out of his mind!

Because of Audrey
by **Mary Sullivan**

AVAILABLE OCTOBER 2013

They say there's always a first time for everything

Mark Sharpe has been torn about JoJo Hatcher since he hired her. Yes, she's a great investigator. Yet she tempts him to cross the line between boss and employee—something he's never done. But when his teenage daughter is threatened, JoJo is the one he trusts to find the truth.

For The First Time
by Stephanie Doyle

AVAILABLE OCTOBER 2013

HARLEQUIN®

A *Romance* FOR EVERY MOOD™

Love the Harlequin book you just read?

Your opinion matters.

Review this book on your favorite book site, review site, blog or your own social media properties and share your opinion with other readers!